W9-DAJ-618

A
Woman
of
Consequence

A
WOMAN
OF
CONSEQUENCE

Sondra Gotlieb

ST. MARTIN'S PRESS
NEW YORK

Gotlieb, Sondra.
    A woman of consequence.

    I. Title.
PR9199.3.G645W6   1983   813'.54   83-2950
ISBN 0-312-88643-8

First U.S. Edition
10 9 8 7 6 5 4 3 2 1

First published in Canada under the title *First Lady, Last Lady*
by McClelland and Stewart

A
WOMAN
OF
CONSEQUENCE

1

Nini Pike, the prime minister's wife, did not want to get out of bed to inspect the new gardener's flower arrangements.

When Doreen, the housekeeper, brought up Nini's breakfast, Nini ignored the baccarat glass vase with a spray of mimosa, freesia and a blettila orchid that decorated the tray.

"You really ought to go down and see what that gardener's done with the dining-room bouquets, Mrs. P. He's got better ideas than any we've had in the last ten years. Mind you, I told him you like things different. Nutt doesn't like the arrangements, though. He says the mimosa sheds yellow puffs on the carpets."

"I am not interested in Nutt's opinion on shedding yellow puffs."

Nini was irritated at Doreen for repeating Nutt's observation. She had not spoken directly to Nutt for the past five years. Nutt had been butler in the residence for more than twenty. The wives of three previous prime ministers had been unable to get rid of him. Nini had been equally unsuccessful. Nutt was often drunk and always lazy, but he had a public-service classification that guaranteed him job security. His status was permanent until he reached a pensionable age.

"If Nutt is grumbling, the bouquets must be first-class," Nini continued without looking at Doreen. "Nutt is capable of walking through a compost heap in my dining room without noticing or caring."

"Mrs. P.—" Doreen protested.

"There is no need for me to go downstairs and inspect the bouquets, Doreen. Just make certain the gardener doesn't mix broccoli heads among the flowers, like that crazy Ikebana person who came last year."

Silently, Doreen reached over and pulled down Nini's bed covers, as she had done every day for the past six weeks. She was fast tiring of this addition to her duties.

"I'm staying in bed, Doreen," Nini snapped. "All day. I'm feeling dizzy."

Doreen disliked crossing Nini, but she had orders. "The prime minister says you're supposed to get up. It's been six weeks since your operation and Dr. Campbell said you could go to the dinner tonight. She says there's nothing wrong with you. The prime minister says you're dizzy because you lie around too much."

Doreen was using the prime minister's title as a protection. Usually she called Nini's husband "Mr. Pike," although she always addressed Nini as "Mrs. P." All women, except Eleanor Campbell, were reduced to initials by Doreen.

Doreen's face was expressionless, but her tone changed from apprehension to virtue as she continued her lecture. "I had a hysterectomy, too, you know, and I was cleaning windows in my sister's cottage three weeks later. And I was fifty-five; you're only forty-six."

Nini removed the linen napkin from the breakfast tray and spread it carefully across her lap.

"Of course, if you really feel sick, I'm supposed to call Dr. Campbell. That's what the prime minister told me to do."

It was Saturday and Nini knew that Eleanor would already be dressed in her knickers, scraping klister from her skis in preparation for a four-hour solitary lope along the trails. Eleanor had often told Nini, "Four hours of cross-country skiing is four hours added to your life span."

Nini gave some thought to Eleanor's philosophy and decided that, at this particular moment, the idea of knocking four hours off Eleanor's life didn't bother her at all. Today, she really needed Eleanor.

They had been friends since their childhood in Derby, a small timber town fifty miles west of the capital. Eleanor used to be a speed skater. Now her thrill was competing in running and cross-country-ski marathons. Every Thursday, at 7:00 A.M., she taught a mixed jogging class at the YMCA, urging on and streaking around gloomy men with paunches who padded their measured laps in the inner circle.

Nini spread part of her brioche with sweet butter that had been pressed into a clover-leaf design – she had bought the two-hundred-year-old butter press in Geneva. Eleanor had not touched butter since her fortieth birthday, six years ago, and had urged Nini to do the same. She'll live till one hundred and ten even if she misses her four hours' skiing today, Nini said to herself.

"I wish you would call Dr. Campbell, Doreen. Tell her my scar is festering from lack of margarine."

Doreen revered all doctors, even female ones. Nini's joke genuinely shocked her.

"Me? Say that to Dr. Campbell? Not if I live to be a hundred." Doreen picked up the phone and dialled Eleanor's private number.

"Doreen, at Sussex, Dr. Campbell. The prime minister is worried about Mrs. P. She won't get out of bed, even for the party tonight. I don't think there's much wrong with her myself, and you know I have practical-nurse training." Doreen listened briefly, then continued with enthusiasm. "Some years ago, yes. And I think you'd better come over and double check."

Doreen hung up the phone, announced that Eleanor was driving over immediately, and went out of the room in triumph before Nini had a chance to flash out at her.

It's because the polls show Barry losing, Nini thought. She was certain that, if it weren't for those polls, Doreen would never have said, "I don't think there's much wrong with her."

For a moment Nini imagined that she was the young Tsarevitch and that Doreen was Derevenko, his sailor attendant, who had massaged the young boy's hemophiliac bruises for ten years, then beat him after the revolution.

Nini rearranged her goose-down pillows and the eiderdown—something Doreen should have looked to—and began to think more rationally. "There will be a revolution at 24 Sussex," she thought, "although it's hardly Tsarskoye Selo. When Beatrice Keeley's husband wins the election, she'll put my Shirvans and Aubussons in cold storage and cover the floors with industrial carpeting. She already told me that if she had her way she'd turn the conservatory into a mud room for her kids. When those glue sniffers take over this place, Doreen will be sorry she's not bringing Nini Pike her breakfast in bed."

Nini had given much time and even some of her own money to the task of renovating the prime minister's residence. She had shunned the advice of the government interior decorators who fluttered from the banality of mock Versailles to lunatic trendiness. The last "art work" they had suggested for her walls was a framed piece of oblong plaster covered with protuberances resembling ovarian cysts. Perhaps it had been in honour of her hysterectomy.

Nini liked to say that she was a materialist in the best sense of the word. "I admire beauty and order. Is it a crime to find ugliness offensive? What if I do have seventy pairs of shoes covered in plastic baggies?"

The shoe collection had been revealed in a gossip column, and some of her husband's advisers warned that she was damaging his image. "I don't see what they're complaining about," she said. "I paid for the shoes out of my own money. There is no one who wears shoes longer than I do.

That's because I know how to protect the leather."

Nini's bedroom, as well, had been a source of distress to her husband's colleagues. She had imported two seventeenth-century beds from Alsace. The Egyptian cotton coverlet that protected her eiderdown was a Porthaults design, all butterflies – purple emperors and Duke of Burgundy fritillaries. Her curtains were made from Italian silk taffeta, their cut echoing the shape of the nymphalid butterflies.

The press had accused her of unpatriotic waste. "What is patriotic waste?" Nini replied – unfortunately, into a microphone.

Nini's admirers considered her elegance a minor art form. Others said she was narcissistic and snobbish. Nini admitted that she was fastidious – her favourite fairy story had been "The Princess and the Pea." But all she had tried to do was make the prime minister's residence as fine as the house where she had been born.

From her bed, Nini stared out at the heavy whiteness of falling snow. The snow had been falling steadily all morning and now it was increasing into a probable April storm, severe enough to delay arriving planes. But the possibility of a shut-down airport and a ruined party didn't bother her at all. Six weeks ago Nini would have been anxious because two of her most important guests were flying in for dinner. Today, all she cared about was finding a way out of a trap that had been set to destroy her husband and herself.

Six weeks ago, Nini had considered this evening as one of the most important in her life. In fact, she had wanted to put off her operation until the party was over. But Eleanor had insisted, promising that Nini would be fit in time.

The party had been Nini's idea. Barry had had his doubts. She had chosen the guests herself. All the rebels who had been whispering to the press about the need for a new prime minister, the ones who wanted to chuck Barry out and put Keeley in his place. She had personally invited the kingmakers, Jack Fowler, and Senator Gross, who lived two thousand miles away on the west side of the country.

"You'll see," she had told Barry. "This dinner will swing them around. They need to be shown that you love them. And you'll have their loyalty again." Nini's greatest desire in life was to soften Fowler's hostility and charm Gross's malice away – at least until it would be too late for them to dump Barry.

At a party as important as tonight's, every detail counted. The party had to be informal enough so guests would feel free to drink more than they intended, yet elegant enough to make them feel complimented. Nini had decided to foster spontaneity by serving Moët & Chandon '69, four jereboams – placed on silver trays in view of her guests, so they wouldn't be shy about taking seconds. And as each glass was poured, Nini would suggest a little reinforcement: *eau de vie de framboise* – "a kind of champagne cocktail served to Barry and me by the president of France." Even Mrs. Gross, who hid the whisky bottles from the senator when he spent a few days with her on the ranch, would accept. After two glasses, the guests would be flattered, not intimidated, by Nini's style.

Fowler and Gross would sit on her left and right respectively, their wives placed similarly around Barry. On the other side of each wife, however, Nini would put a young, heterosexual official, unmarried or between marriages, who would take the women downstairs and dance them slowly around the birchbark room while Barry, in the library, wooed their husbands.

Three days before her hysterectomy, Nini had spent four hours with Doreen in the third-floor office, checking the old dinner files, making sure the menu had not been served before, either to Gross or to Fowler. She had filled twenty-five pages of a loose-leaf binder with lists, suggestions and reminders.

BLACK TIE DINNER at 24 SUSSEX The third day of April

1. Make sure rye and Pepsi-Cola are available to Senator Gross before, during and after dinner. (Mrs. Pike knows there will be champagne for aperitifs, but the senator is from the west.)
2. Check price of Moët & Chandon against purchase made last year.
3. Place *small* bouquets of fresh flowers (no mums), white Delsey toilet paper and a box of Tampax in every bathroom. Mrs. Fowler is not yet forty. Pears soap only.
4. Mrs. Gross is allergic to eggplant. *For God's sake, NO moussaka.*
5. Tell Chang to clean his teeth, in his *own bathroom,* before he pours the wine at the table.
6. Mrs. Pike will polish the silver place-card holders herself. They are two hundred years old and belonged to her great-grandmother.
7. Mrs. Pike's dresses must be ironed forty-eight hours before the party. If ironed later, they crease too rapidly. A dress must be hung twenty-four hours after ironing before being worn. Iron the long red silk, the short black chiffon with sleeves and any of the new ones she may buy after her operation.
8. Mr. Fowler drinks only Sanka because of his hiatus hernia. Blue Mountain coffee in individual glass filters for everyone else.
9. Nutt must be out of Sussex by noon, April 3. He is not to return until the following day.

The list continued. Other directives had to do with the *placement*, the amount of time between each course, sufficient elbow room for guests (twelve inches each side), the choice of *gros point de Venise* napkins and her mother's glazed Spode pearlware for service plates. Nini was particularly anxious that the smell of stale food be removed. "I don't want it to stink like an English hotel dining room. And I include the Savoy in that category," she had told Doreen.

Two days before her hysterectomy, Nini had sat down to plan the menu with her chef, Yves Marius, in his kitchen. She had set her heart on *tournedos quatre étages*, the first layer a rare filet, the second soft veal marrow, the third a lightly poached egg and the fourth a rich wine sauce with truffles, covering the lower three layers. As the guests cut into the beef, the egg and marrow would ooze into the wine sauce and they would be as pleased and astonished as if Old Faithful, in Yellowstone Park, had squirted right on their plates.

Yves Marius was not sure he would be able to manage *quatre étages* and *calvados sorbet* at the same meal. The sherbet had to be stuffed into apples and surrounded by caramelized fresh strawberries, with an aureole of spun sugar.

But Nini thought of King Henry on the feast of St. Crispin. She summoned up the little chef's blood and stiffened his sinews. Yves Marius was a darkish, nervous Algerian but, after Nini's eloquence, he became as steadfast as an English longbow man.

At such preparations Nini had always been a master. But now it was April third, the morning of the party, and the idea of aureoles of spun sugar sickened her. She hadn't polished the place-card holders; she hadn't bought any new dresses. Nor had she checked the seating plan or asked Doreen if anyone had cancelled at the last minute. When Doreen asked questions about changes and additions to the black binder, Nini turned her face to the wall.

But Nini Pike was not ill. Her operation had been successful to the point of being a memory – and yet she could not bring herself to get out of bed. If her friends and servants were baffled by her behaviour, Nini herself had no doubts as to its origin. She was afraid. And she hated herself for being afraid. What, she kept asking herself, would happen to her husband when the truth came out?

Distractedly, Nini looked at the various glossies that lay scattered at the foot of her sickbed: *Vogue, Harper's Bazaar, Cosmopolitan* and the magazine that upset Nini the most, *Ms*. As soon as Doreen left, she picked one up, opened it at random and looked at the girl in the advertisement. She had high cheekbones, no breasts and long legs; she was Sue Houle, "photographer and concerned woman," and her Scotch was Dewar's White Label. Nini wondered if Dewar's Scotch would consider *her* a concerned woman. She flicked to another picture of a tall, slim girl with long legs and high cheekbones – this one was standing on her tip-toes, ready to jack-knife into a swimming pool from the highest diving board. She was the Stayfree Mini-Pad woman being active and independent. Repelled, Nini turned to the table of contents. The articles listed included "My Man Learned to Love My Job" and "How to Become Independent of the Man in Your Life."

They didn't say "husband" anymore, she noticed. She picked up another magazine and read another article called "Self-Fulfilment: Are You Willing to Take the Risk?" It told the story of Wendy Lorimer, senior vice-president of the Stanhope Insurance Company. "Wendy knows when to be controlled (at work) and spontaneous (in bed)." Wendy's goals were career mobility, personal freedom and to become president of the Stanhope Insurance Company. Wendy didn't seem to care about having children as long as she had a lover who would stimulate her erogenous zones.

Nini knew exactly how Wendy, the Stayfree Mini-Pad girl and Sue Houle would assess her life. She hastily turned to her horoscope. It read, "Your instincts tell you to abandon the past you have always honoured. Be reassured that you will not be alone when you've left your husband, because an old love will return to your life."

Nini was disgusted that tears were welling up in her eyes again. Self-pity, she thought, as they rolled down her cheeks. She was wallowing in it. But it did seem to her as if the articles, advertisements and especially the horoscope were directed at her personally, written precisely to mock everything she believed in.

Nini didn't understand the new rules laid down by these magazines. Her story would have been blue-pencilled, rejected by the editors. Gloria Steinem could use Nini as an example of what not to become. Nini was an anachronism; she would never fit into Sue Houle's or Wendy Lorimer's conception of the new woman.

In fact, Nini hated the notion of "the new woman." She had no patience with feminists, who had always seemed to her to use their political beliefs to mask simple, old-fashioned selfishness. Why did they have the power to bring tears to her eyes today? Because they seemed to be laughing right out of the magazine pages at the only thing that was holding her together – her devotion to her husband.

"Abandon the past you have always honoured," her horoscope said. "Leave your husband." Indeed. If it had not been for Barry, for her determination to protect him, she would never have been able to endure the terror of the past six weeks.

That old lover mentioned in the horoscope had returned to her life – but only because he wanted to destroy Nini and Barry Pike.

2

At Nini's insistence, and much to Doreen's chagrin, Doreen would wear a frilly cap and a white apron over a black dress for the party. However, upon seeing Doreen's varicose veins, Nini had permitted support hose as well as heavy wedgies, to which Doreen gave a thick application of old-fashioned chalky white polish. Her hair was cut short and curled tightly. Every Christmas, Doreen's sister, a beauty-parlour operator, made her a present of a strong permanent wave.

After her swift exit from Nini's bedroom, Doreen walked slowly along the upstairs hall, checking the triple layers of ebony and gilt frames for dust. The fine leaded window at the south end of the hall was kept permanently covered with a hunter-green velvet curtain. Nini insisted that the hall remain dim (gloomy, Doreen thought) because she was afraid that the sun would fade her etchings and lithographs, the Corots, the Manets, the Tissots, the Redons and the Renoirs that she had collected in Geneva. Every six months Nini would rotate her collection, bringing down more pictures from a dark room on the third floor, removing those already hanging and displaying the formerly hidden prints on her upstairs wall. Nini and Doreen set aside two days for this task; nothing was allowed to disturb them and no one else was permitted to carry or hang the pictures.

Doreen walked down the wide stairway and through the reception hall to get to the kitchen, which was off the dining room on the main floor. The black and white tile floor was covered with silk Persian rugs, none longer than five feet. Doreen never tripped on the carpets, but each new maid fell on her face a couple of times before she learned to walk around them. The staff and many of Nini's guests cursed these carpets as land mines, but Nini thought they provided an effective contrast with the great diamond-patterned floor.

Canadian paintings, mostly on loan from the National Gallery, were displayed downstairs – a Tom Thomson and some Milnes in the library, a Dallaire and a few untitled early primitives that appealed to Nini in the living room. The prominent oil in the front hall was a Lemieux, convent girls in blue uniforms eating their soup under the eye of a sinister nun. Two huge eighteenth-century Québec pine cupboards, Nini's own purchase, flanked the picture, and underneath stood a Louis XV *bureau plat* with ormolu mounts that she had bought in Paris. The two most striking objects in the hall, however, were identical five-foot-tall art-deco cobra lamps made in France by Edgar Brandt, the ironmonger, and Daum Frères, the glassmakers. The snakes stood on their coiled tails and each forked tongue flicked around the rose-coloured glass lampshades. Every visitor was struck by the two great *serpents lampadaires*. The more unkind wondered if the snakes were Nini's private emblem, poised and ready to strike.

Doreen, who had been with the Pikes for ten years, was proud of the fact that she did not gossip about them with the rest of the staff. But Nini's attitude was so peculiar that Doreen thought she should try to get some information out of the chef. Yves Marius had been with the Pikes since their time in Geneva, long before Barry was elected prime minister. Yves Marius, although a foreigner, might have some insight. Besides, Doreen had to see him about the bills for the dinner – they were outrageous.

The kitchen was filled with rows and rows of copper bowls, stew pots, omelette pans and saucepans, all hanging from tracks in the ceiling. Yves Marius had already lit the commercial-grade gas range and was browning the vegetables for the evening sauces in a huge copper *sautoir* Doreen could not even lift. The kitchen was redolent of garlic and onion. Doreen disliked the smell. She looked in disgust at the furthest counter in the kitchen. Shiny new Robot Coupe, Cuisinart, pasta- and raclette-makers, trout smokers, and ice-cream churns all stood together, unused. Nini could deny Yves Marius nothing for his *batterie de cuisine*, and he fiendishly insisted that she buy every new gadget that came on the market. Yves Marius would try each gadget once, announce that it would never replace his copper bowls, Sabatier knives or even his whisks and leave the latest purchase untouched with the rest of the machines on the counter. Bunches of dried mushrooms, garlic and shallots filled wire baskets hung over the stove. One huge counter was made of marble for rolling pastry and for candy-making; there were also wooden counters for carving and cutting, and stainless-steel counters for putting down hot pots and pans.

Doreen found Yves Marius near the south window clipping fresh basil from his hydroponic garden. He disliked having Doreen question him about matters of cuisine and had felt deserted by Nini since she had retreated to her bedroom.

"*Très bizarre*," he replied immediately when Doreen asked him what he thought of Mrs. P.'s behaviour. "Not one time is she down to spy. Always she tells me, 'Yves Marius, don't throw out celery tops. These, put in soup.' You know how she makes me crazy when I go shop. And I never cheat her one time in so many years. But since her sickness, *rien*."

It was clear that Yves Marius missed Nini's meddling.

Doreen opened the chef's black binder and looked warily at the accounts. Nini had always supervised Yves Marius. Doreen did not want the responsibility for the cost of the dinner to fall on her shoulders.

"I can't believe what you paid for those little fishes. Mrs. P. will have something to say—if she ever gets her motor going."

Yves Marius, who had been a sweeper in Marseilles, a bus-boy in Lugano, and a *sous-chef* in Priay, considered Doreen insular.

"A good chef never let a dead trout walk into his kitchen. I buy living fish and kill them *moi-même. Comme ça.*"

He grabbed by the tail one of the trout swimming in the nearby tank and slammed its head hard against the marble counter. For a moment there was a residual wriggling and then the little fish lay still.

"I do it perfect. Not a bruise on the skin. She will be beautiful *au bleu*," he said, looking fondly at the dead trout.

Doreen believed that Yves Marius puffed himself up with this gastronomic pedantry. She ignored the fish and changed the subject.

"I think she's sulking in bed because Mr. Pike's going to be a loser. And then where will she be? I guess she thinks it's hardly worth keeping the residence shipshape for someone else." Doreen paused, then continued with a hint of maliciousness. "Not that *I* have anything to worry about. I wasn't hired by Mrs. P. The government is my boss and I stay on even if she does go. If Mrs. Keeley is nice to me, I'll be nice to her," Doreen finished primly.

Doreen's talk was making Yves Marius nervous, and he could not afford to be nervous on the day of a critical dinner. He did not like the idea of working for Beatrice Keeley. She had already made public comments about the rich, expensive food being served at Sussex. He sought to reassure himself.

"I have no worries. I am now twenty years with Mrs. Pike. I stay with her always. Pikes have a nice place in Eleuthera. Small kitchen, but–" The chef shrugged his shoulders in an unsuccessful attempt to show his lack of concern. "First good weather for me since Tanezrouft."

Doreen had Yves Marius where she wanted him. He was clearly nervous, even defensive. Though she cared very much whether she worked for Nini Pike or Beatrice Keeley, she was not interested in letting an underling know it. Now she felt free to question the chef about what was really on her mind, without worrying about giving him the impression that she considered him an equal.

"You were in Switzerland, weren't you?" she asked casually. "That's where she found you–first you worked for that ambassador who died, Hilary-Moulds, and then Mrs. P. took you on."

Yves Marius felt threatened when anyone mentioned his brief tenure with Hilary-Moulds. "Mrs. Pike told me to be chef to ambassador Moulds. Only two weeks I was with him, before he dies. After, I went to Mrs. Pike."

"Do you remember a Mr. Roland Neville?" Doreen asked as she absently flipped the pages of the kitchen accounts book. "She knew him from Geneva. He's a big reporter now, makes a fortune writing terrible things about Mr. Pike in the magazines. But he used to be an ambassador." Doreen glanced briefly at the chef, then continued. "I was really surprised when Mrs. P. had him for lunch the day before her operation–when Mr. Pike was away giving a speech in New York. Of all the newspaper writers, I'd say that he's the meanest about Mr. Pike. You made the perch they had for lunch and he stayed till five. He's short, blond and blinks his eyes a lot. What do you know about him?"

Yves Marius was confused.

"I see Mr. Neville maybe two times at the residence in Geneva, because he was an old friend of Mr. Moulds. What should I know?"

"You don't notice much, do you, Yves Marius?" Doreen was exasperated. "Really clueless, aren't you. I think Mr. Neville has something to do with Mrs. P. acting so funny. When he left that afternoon, she looked as if someone slapped her face with that trout of yours. And she's had that look ever since."

Doreen marched out of the kitchen, leaving Yves Marius speechless. She was furious with herself for thinking the chef would be any help. And she should never have shared her suspicions with him. Now she was in the mood to track down Nutt and do him bodily harm.

3

Ten years ago, when Nini had first taken over the residence, she had quickly understood how the former chatelaines, as the women's magazines called the prime ministers' wives, had been victimized by Nutt, the butler. Any pride of position her predecessors had felt was first destroyed in the dining room. During formal dinners, conversation would cease as hostess and guests listened compulsively for Nutt's frequent, slurred-out stentorian orders to the frightened waitresses.

"To the left with the sauce boat. Follow the sole. Follow the sole. Left, left."

Nutt would clang two silver tureen lids together as a warning if he thought a waitress was dangerously tipping a tray of food over a foreign head of state. Everyone would look to Nutt, veinous and watery-eyed, standing back by the sideboard with the decanters, in tail coat and slippers that had been slit at the gouty big toes.

Powerful, misanthropic, indifferent, he'd blow his nose into a napkin, stuff it into his pocket, slowly pick up a decanter and pour a thimbleful of wine into the cracked glasses that he had deliberately selected for the guests. Wives of new prime ministers were broken in by Nutt before the last guest finished the bouillon.

Nini was different. When it was her turn to be chatelaine,

she refused to be wrecked and scuttled by Nutt. She determined to remove him from responsibility.

Even Nini's worst enemies acknowledged that she was an administrator to the manor born. She understood the secret of good organization. More importantly, she knew how the system worked – something her predecessors had failed to grasp. She knew it was impossible to remove Nutt because of his tenured position, so she scrutinized the public-service classifications and discovered an unfilled position at the residence called "head housekeeper," which outranked that of butler. After frank, yet discreet, discussion with wives at foreign embassies – the only establishments in the capital, other than nursing homes, which might employ a head housekeeper – Nini stole Doreen away from the American ambassador.

As Nini had intended, Doreen did not hesitate to pull rank with Nutt. Further, Doreen had cleverly strengthened her position by getting rid of intimidated maids on short-term contracts, replacing them with her female relations. The new waitresses and maids took their cues from Doreen. Soon Nutt was demoted to the status of bad-tempered old spaniel, waiting to be put away – if and when one of the women found time.

Even so, there were minor, restricted areas where he could still annoy. For instance, Nutt loved to supervise the vacuuming. As usual, this morning he wandered from room to room, waving his finger at the maid behind the machine, pointing to puffs and leaves on the carpets. The gardener was pulling flowers about in a huge arrangement for the hall when Nutt jabbed him hard in the spine. "Mrs. Pike won't like that bouquet. She likes simple flowers. What's wrong with roses? You're too fancy for her. You're a fancy man in every way, aren't you?"

The thin man was a little worried. He wasn't really a flower arranger: he had been hired by the head horticulturist in charge of the prime minister's residence and Government House to do a little part-time work in the greenhouse off the dining room. Doreen had happened to overhear his criticism of the bouquets he saw through the dining-room window at Sussex and, knowing Nini's fussiness about the flower arrangements, asked the part-time gardener to try his hand. Now he thought he might be fired for his sexual proclivities and wondered whether he could appeal to the Human Rights Commission. Nutt had been mumbling "Fancy man, pansy man" all morning.

The door bell rang. Nutt's only real job now was to answer the door, but he ignored the bell and continued.

"You spilled water on the table in the dining room. If the vase leaves a ring, Mrs. Pike will make you pay to have it rubbed out. She may be rich, but she doesn't like to spend it herself. That's what keeps her rich."

Eleanor Campbell stood outside 24 Sussex in her Norwegian cross-country boots, argyle knee socks and corduroy knickers, holding her medical bag. She had been on this doorstep many times before and she knew what it was to wait for Nutt's reluctant shuffle. The security at Sussex was monitored by a Mountie at the gate with a walkie-talkie. He attempted to communicate with the house, but Nutt never responded to the intercom system.

Nutt stared at Eleanor through the magnifying peephole. She generally wore a skirt if she came in her professional capacity, or a long shirtwaist dress when she was invited for dinner, which wasn't too often. Her unorthodox outfit this morning gave Nutt some hope that he could pretend not to recognize her. He returned, without opening the door, to hectoring the gardener.

Eleanor leaned on the door bell and the maids began to yell. Reluctantly, Nutt let her in.

"Didn't recognize you, Dr. Campbell, in those pedal pushers. Thought you could be a lady terrorist. They're worse than the men. Let me tell you, I can't be too careful, working for an important statesman. A lot of butlers have

25

been killed just by opening a door."

Eleanor did not want to waste time arguing.

"Take me upstairs, Nutt. Mrs. Pike is waiting."

But Nutt wanted a chat. "Now tell me, doctor. What's the matter with Mrs. Pike? Stays in bed day after day. It's bad luck having a sick person lying upstairs in this house. And you know how fussy she is. Trays going up, the maids sweeping with the broom upstairs instead of using the machine. She don't want the noise. Mind you, it's not all that different from when she's well. Always had her afternoon nap, you know. Only you women have the time for afternoon naps. So what's she got? Cancer?"

Eleanor thought she had better squelch his cancer inspiration.

"Mrs. Pike doesn't have cancer, and don't you dare start telling people that she does." She gave Nutt a stern look and proceeded upstairs by herself.

Eleanor had examined Nini many times since the operation and knew there was nothing physically wrong with her. Wordlessly she entered "the boudoir," as she called it, sat down on a gilt chair beside the bed and took out her stethoscope.

"Don't bother. There's nothing wrong with me." Nini was staring up at the butterflies on the inside of the canopy over the bed. Eleanor put her stethoscope back in the bag, crossed her legs, folded her arms and stared at her cross-country boots.

"Sorry about making you miss your skiing."

Eleanor didn't answer.

"I guess you think I should be more like you. Unspoiled. Remember when you visited me, years ago, in Geneva? You told me how spoiled I was. You said you didn't know anyone else who had a seamstress to make special passementerie buttons for her dresses, a husband who insisted his wife sleep late – even during the week – and a different party to go to every night."

Eleanor was suddenly angry. She disliked having her words distorted.

"I never said you were spoiled. You're trying to provoke me."

Nini turned her face to the sheet and pulled one of the pillows on top of her head. Eleanor hadn't seen Nini cry in more than forty years, and she was astonished.

"Nini, I wish you would tell me what's wrong. Barry's worried sick. I'm going to call a psychiatrist."

Nini threw the pillow at Eleanor and sat up.

"I'll kill you if you call in one of those boobies. I know exactly what's the matter with me. It's just that I don't know what to do."

Eleanor was not sure she wanted to be Nini's confessor, which she now suspected had been the reason for her summons. Like Doreen, she thought Nini's behaviour had something to do with the fear of not being the prime minister's wife; Nini was collapsing from the slow anticipation of her husband's defeat. It would be trite to tell her to tough it out, to think of happy retirement days in Eleuthera, or to tell her to be glad she didn't have a fatal disease. Eleanor and Nini had never discussed Barry's career in all the years Nini had been married. When he ran for prime minister, Eleanor had kept out of the campaign. She sent a note of congratulations when he won, and she and Nini resumed their friendship.

Apart from skiing and keeping fit, Eleanor was interested in only a few things – the practice of medicine, the company of other doctors, old friends from Derby and her own, very private, life. She didn't see how she could help Nini through a political nervous breakdown.

It would be stupid and dangerous to use the women's lib rhetoric: "You're living vicariously through your husband; don't be such an appendage; go out and study anthropology." Nini was forty-six and, until now, had seemed content with life.

Nini turned her face toward her friend. "Eleanor," she said, "I have to tell you about Geneva."

Eleanor was puzzled. She wondered if Nini had had an affair. But it was not like Nini to feel guilty about some peccadillo that had happened almost twenty years before.

"And you can't listen and sit on that little chair, too," Nini said, taking Eleanor's silence as a willingness to hear more. "What I'm going to tell you will take a long time. Lie down over there on the chaise longue."

Eleanor always sat in the Louis XVI ballroom chair when she wanted to examine Nini. The bigger the person, the smaller the chair, Nini thought.

"I don't feel like sprawling over that chesterfield like Mme. Récamier. I'm fine here."

Eleanor had acted as consultant to Nini's surgeon; she was an internist, not a gynecologist. Eleanor considered internal medicine to be the most intellectual of the medical specialties because of the engrossing detective work, the analysis of fact required to form a correct diagnosis. Each symptom or lack of symptom was a clue. She had been dubbed "Sherlock Holmes" by her fellow doctors because of her remarkable intuitive faculties and imaginative guesswork. Other doctors would send patients with strange and unusual diseases to Eleanor and ask for elucidation. Although she admitted that intuition and guesswork played some part in her diagnosis, she insisted that her "lucky guesses" were always based on a thorough knowledge of disease and the physiological processes. "My leaps of knowledge," she would say to an admiring colleague, "are always based on specific facts." Eleanor did not consider psychiatry to be based on any scientific fact and remained uneasy about being a pinch-hit psychiatrist to Nini. It would be unprofessional to stray beyond her specialty. But then, she did value Nini's friendship. . . . Anyway, how could Nini be having a nervous breakdown and still worry about chairs?

Eleanor shifted in the delicate chair and decided to stay. She hoped Nini's confession would be a short one.

The sound of the chair creaking was too much for Nini. "Eleanor, that chair cost me $2,500. It's cracking under your weight."

Eleanor had never paid more than $250 for a chair. That was her Naugahyde lean-back for the office – tax deductible. The mention of large sums of money made her nervous.

"Stay for lunch," Nini begged, already sorry for her harshness about the chair. "I'll have Doreen bring up a little cold lobster and Yves Marius's cucumber mousse. And wine."

Nini could be exasperating, but there was one thing in her favour this morning. Her words might be deliberately irritating but her voice was unsteady. Eleanor thought Nini had really lost hold, that she was dangling. And Eleanor was becoming distressed. Distressed enough, in fact, to let herself be drawn back into a rôle she had left more than ten years ago, that of "oldest friend and confidante" to Nini Pike. She walked over to the chaise longue, removed her cross-country boots and stretched out.

"I'm here for the day, Nini. What's bothering you? Is it the usual middle-aged *angst* most of my female patients complain about? Or something more specific?"

"Would you diagnose blackmail as a general or specific *angst*?"

"Specific," Eleanor said, immediately regretting her flippancy. "Are *you* being blackmailed?"

"Yes. By Roland Neville. About something that happened twenty years ago when Barry and I lived in Geneva, during the early sixties. Barry was first secretary at our UN Mission and Hugh Hilary-Moulds was ambassador – the one who died. I can't get out of bed, Eleanor. I'm paralyzed by Neville – and by the memory of Hugh Hilary-Moulds."

4

The *Tribune de Genève* was not a newspaper that catered to sensation. Most of the photographs, dated images of past presidents of the Swiss Federation, appeared above the obituary notices on the fourth or fifth page.

On April 17, 1962, the paper carried the following front-page headline:

PARKING IN GENEVA WHAT IS HAPPENING TO OUR CITY?
A DAILY PROBLEM

Beneath the headline, the only photograph on the front page revealed several Peugeots illegally parked on a cobblestone square. The photographer was even sufficiently inspired to show the FORBIDDEN TO PARK notice in plain view of the criminal motorists.

In the same edition, toward the lower left-hand corner of the front page, just under the parking scoop, a smaller headline read:

DIPLOMAT DIES IN HIS SLEEP

Every Genevois knew that there were thousands of diplomats in Geneva and that many of them died in their sleep. A reader of the *Tribune de Genève* would wonder why this particular diplomat merited front-page notice, second only to illegally parked cars on Place Molard. He would expect to discover the answer not in the headlines or the photographs, but in that special kind of insinuation that was always to be found in the sober texts of the Swiss press.

His Excellency Hugh Hilary-Moulds, Canadian ambassador to the Permanent Mission at the United Nations in Geneva, was found dead in his bed today, at 8:00 A.M. at his residence, by the butler, Julio Manolo Gomez. Although there was no obvious evidence of foul play such as knife wounds, contusions or bullet holes, a certain ambiguity surrounds the ambassador's demise. According to a reliable source, the state of his undress was unusual. No explanation has yet been given as to cause of death. What is especially remarkable is that the Canadian Mission has informed the cantonal police and waives its diplomatic immunity by requesting that an autopsy be performed. We are puzzled that a foreign government would allow Swiss authorities to penetrate its legal immunity from Swiss and Genevois cantonal law.

M. Barry Pike, first secretary at the Canadian Permanent Mission to the United Nations and now chargé d'affaires, was questioned by this reporter about these unusual events but refused to comment.

His Excellency Hugh Hilary-Moulds lived alone at the Canadian residence, Parc des Cèdres, in Chambesy. He was married to Lady Beatrice North, an Englishwoman. It is believed the couple is separated. Hugh Hilary-Moulds was considered one of the most able diplomats at the United Nations, and his name had been mentioned in the highest circles as a possible candidate for the position of secretary general of NATO.

He was formerly Canadian ambassador to Hungary, counsellor to the Canadian Permanent Delegation to NATO in Paris and first secretary in London during and before the Second World War.

5

Roland Neville had just completed his first year as the Canadian ambassador to Hungary. Geneva, and the Hotel de la Paix, were his government's rewards for enduring the tensions of living there. Though the uprising of 1956 had happened more than five years before, an atmosphere of repression and reprisals still prevailed.

Neville thoroughly approved of the practice of Western foreign offices allowing diplomats living in "hardship," meaning Eastern European posts, to return to the capitalist west once a year at government expense. But he despised the American term "R and R," for rest and recuperation. "Assisted leave," he thought, was much more civilized. Un-American phrases, as well as habits, were usually more civilized. Nothing irritated Neville more than being taken for an American, whether in Eastern or Western Europe.

The lobby of the Hotel de la Paix looked like an overstuffed drawing room. The furniture was vaguely French Directoire and distinctly Swiss Bourgeois. The softer cushions, the larger chairs, the carpets overlaying each other, may have been a perversion of style, but Swiss hotel-keepers knew that their clients preferred living in comfort to living in a museum.

The Paix was the best hotel of its class in Geneva; only a bit of carpet wearing thin and a few shabby armrests separated it in quality from the deluxe establishments. It was patronized by visiting delegations, ambassadors and men and women on the payrolls of a hundred countries. The oil sheiks stayed at the newly opened Le Président, and the old money from France and Germany went to the Bergues and the Richmond. The only person from the fashionable world who stayed at the Hotel de la Paix was Princess Grace of Monaco. Perhaps this was an old tradition of the Grimaldi family, which she did not wish to break.

During the day, Giorgio, the concierge, was always at his place at the small desk by the entrance. Three old men in green striped aprons took luggage up in the creaking elevator. If they were busy and the luggage stood too long in the drawing room, Giorgio would, in snappish Italian, enlist one of the young waiters who had mistakenly come out of the dining room for air. Giorgio and the employees were all Italian but the owner was a real Genevois, who watched from his office across from Giorgio's desk, like the manager of a bank.

At 4:00 A.M., however, the lobby of the Hotel de la Paix had lost its bustle and the night concierge, one of the old men, was sleeping by the telephones at the concierge's desk. No one noticed Roland Neville weave in, almost uncontrollably drunk; no one offered to help him into the little elevator. He thought he would die of suffocation in the small chamber but the door opened before he passed out. His room was close by. Luckily, he had not locked the door. His shaking hands could never have managed a key.

Although he was dangerously overloaded with Armagnac from Hilary-Moulds's party, Neville was not too drunk to remember that he would go into a coma if he slept through breakfast and his shot. Neville was alive because he had never been too drunk to forget the needle. He phoned the night concierge, placed an order for eight o'clock breakfast and fell asleep on the bed fully dressed.

The young waiter who entered Neville's room at eight

had been on room service only a week and kept his eyes averted from Neville as he woke him with doughy Swiss croissants and grapefruit. As soon as he left, Neville, still in his evening clothes, forced the food down his throat. He lay back, almost enjoying the sensation of his head detaching itself from his body and floating about the room, knowing the head would disappear completely if he lay one more moment in bed.

Suddenly, Neville felt a shortness of breath. The beginning of a coma, he thought desperately. He was seized by a sense of unbearable thirst. He had to act quickly. In moments, he knew, he would be paralyzed by panic.

With great effort he rose, removed his clothes and prayed that he would be able to manage the needle with enough accuracy to stay alive.

Neville, a diabetic, lifted the syringe out of the metal container of alcohol on the night table and carefully wiped the top of the bottle of CZI, crystalline-zinc insulin. He up-ended the syringe and inverted the insulin bottle, keeping the needle in a vertical position, then drew the plunger back to the forty-unit mark. Then he injected forty units of air into the bottle of insulin.

Neville looked at the syringe with the forty units of potent liquid. The CZI would act fast but, as he well knew, it vanished from the body quickly. He needed the sudden action of the CZI but he also had to have the slower-acting PZI, protamine-zinc insulin, which would remain in his system for as long as he slept.

A cocktail was necessary.

He up-ended the needle again, drew the plunger back twenty further units and put twenty units of air in the syringe. Then he picked up the bottle containing the PZI, put it on the needle, squirted air in the bottle and withdrew twenty units of insulin. He swabbed his thigh with alcohol, pinched his skin and plunged in the needle.

The CZI would go to work within an hour; the PZI would

take over afterward. His head rejoined the rest of him. The shortness of breath vanished. The floating sensation stopped. He felt in control. Twenty years of this routine had taught him exactly what to expect.

Neville had bought a six-month supply of PZI from the Pharmacie de Genève. Most of it was in the hotel kitchen's refrigerator. He was taking the insulin to Budapest because he didn't trust Hungarian pharmacies.

He looked at his watch. It was 8:45 A.M., April 17, 1962. "Not the first time I've been drunk on my birthday," he mumbled.

He lay back in bed, thought about eating at the Creux de Genthod and nearly retched, but he did not let himself close his eyes. He had observed that diabetics were comparable to incubator babies: both needed a rigid routine of feeding and medication to survive. He placed a call for his noon feeding. Then he closed his eyes.

At noon, the waiter dared to look at Neville when he came in with the cold chicken and sliced dampened cucumbers ("sweat *concombres*," as the hotel's English menu translated them). Less nervous, the waiter started to open the shutters to let in the sun.

Neville squelched the initiative immediately, sent the waiter from the room, ate and fell asleep again.

When he woke, he knew at once his body had rid itself of the poisonous Armagnac. He began to feel he would be able to enjoy the last day of his vacation before he went back to Budapest.

Neville was disgusted with himself for losing control and drinking so much at Hugh's dinner last night. But he felt calm now, and decided to celebrate his last evening in Geneva by dining alone at the Creux de Genthod.

Yesterday evening, everyone had said the Creux de Genthod was only good for lunch. Nini had described the long trestle tables under the plane trees along the shores of Lake Geneva, and the waitresses staggering out of the kitchen with huge platters of delicately fried perch. Hugh, in his rôle of dogmatic epicure, had pronounced: "You must sit in the sun and start with the garlic pâté and the Russian salad submerged in mayonnaise. Serious eaters never go to the Creux de Genthod in the evening. You won't see the lake, you can't feel the sun, and the perch will be more than three hours old."

When Neville arrived it was twilight, still warm enough to sit outside and still light enough to discern the white sails of the boats returning to the small harbour beside the restaurant. A few children were playing languidly on the wooden swings beyond the tables in the darkening park, and the waitresses moved slowly, lighting candles in the plastic *chauffes-plats*. He assumed they only hurried at lunch. He was in no mood to rush or worry and looked forward to a long evening by himself. One of the girls brought him a carafe of *fendant* and spoke.

"*C'est à vous, monsieur? Non? Je vous en débarrasse?*"

She had found a newspaper someone had left behind on the bench opposite him at his table. He told her yes, to throw it away, and then realized it was today's and that he could look to see if there were any news about the current trade negotiations. The minister might ask him about them tomorrow in Budapest. He accepted the paper and glanced over the picture of the illegally parked cars. His eyes settled on the headline, DIPLOMAT DIES IN BED.

He read the column three times and pushed the paper away. His eyes blinked incessantly.

He rose and went to telephone.

6

The next afternoon, Roland Neville was back in Budapest beginning his busy week.

Two days later, April 20, 1962, another piece concerning the diplomat who died in his sleep appeared in the *Tribune de Genève*, this time in the lower corner of page two:

THE AFFAIR OF HUGH HILARY-MOULDS

Dr. Emile Lagier, official coroner for the Canton of Geneva, has declared, after a thorough autopsy, including a toxicological screen, that His Excellency Hugh Hilary-Moulds died from natural causes. According to a reliable source, the Canadian authorities were alarmed because a small pin-prick had been noticed on the ambassador's left buttock. He had been found lying face down on the bed in formal dress excepting the portion of the body between hips and ankles. His trousers and underclothes had been pushed down to his ankles. He was still wearing his tasselled patent-leather evening shoes.

Dr. Lagier believes that the ambassador suffered from an infarction and says the prick mark on the buttock was of no significance. The doctor commented that perhaps the laundry left a small pin in his shorts.

The body is being sent back to his family in Canada.

7

Spring came early in Geneva in 1960, arriving a few weeks before Barry Pike reported for his first diplomatic assignment. The Pikes were newly married, and Nini was looking forward to diplomatic life – and to meeting their ambassador, Hugh Hilary-Moulds.

The offices of the Canadian Permanent Mission at the United Nations in Geneva were on the eighth floor at Chateau Banquet, a group of solid but commonplace buildings built around a well-kept garden. It was Barry's first day at work and he was impatient with the leisurely elevator that hesitated at each floor, exposing the names of the occupants. Strange names: Abulaphia, Khouri, Smouha, then the more familiar Swiss names, Pictet and Guisan. Later Barry discovered that Abulaphia was an Iraqi Jew and Khouri a Christian Arab and that both of them owned banks in Geneva. He never found out the occupations of the Swiss. The only commercial floor belonged to the Canadians; the rest were private apartments.

Barry rang the buzzer beside the heavy door of the Mission. It swung open automatically and Chantal, the Swiss receptionist who sat at her switchboard at the end of the large rectangular room, asked him his business in French. When he told her who he was, she switched immediately to accentless English, displaying, with some smugness, her linguistic ability and a knowledge of office procedure.

"Mr. Otis will show you around because he is our security officer," she said, pressing one of her telephone buttons. Her English was definitely better than Barry's French. At the same time, a call came in, to which she replied in fluent German, keeping her eye on Barry as if waiting for congratulations.

Barry had been given a security briefing at headquarters in Ottawa but each chancery had a different routine, depending on its layout. A short, balding man with a beer belly appeared almost instantly. Otis was only twenty-six. Too much rich food and drink, Barry thought; his next post ought to be Delhi. Barry knew the ages of all the officers because he kept a personal card index in which he marked the names, ages, promotions and assignments of every foreign-service officer for as far back as twenty years. Nini had laughed when he showed the cards to her, but Barry explained that it was the most efficient way to chart the careers of his competition.

As they shook hands, Otis said, "I'm afraid we must start with the menial aspects of our work. Let's straighten the carpet." Barry looked down and saw that the small green carpet he was standing on had slipped awry.

"All of us have received a memorandum from the ambassador about the damned thing. It drives him crazy if it isn't precisely centred. Every time we come in we're obliged to bend down and put it right."

Chantal giggled and Otis gave her a wink. She was in her mid-thirties, a pretty, dark woman with a little cellulite surfacing under her chin. Otis spoke flippantly, but his tone was deferential. As he was only an FSO 1, just recently off probation, Barry was his senior officer. Otis bent down and straightened the carpet himself, then led Barry out of the reception room into the corridor behind Chantal's switchboard.

"All the offices," he explained, "are outside the secure

area. Belknap's is right beside yours. He's not in yet, naturally, or I would introduce you. See the red light over that door? That's Hilary-Moulds's office. When you see the light go on it means that he's on the phone and is not to be disturbed. Chantal presses it for him when a call comes through. He's been on the phone since he's arrived."

Barry had hoped that he would meet the ambassador before Otis's security drill.

"Do all ambassadors have red lights?"

Otis shrugged. "Our former counsellor, Georges Dugay, has been on four postings and says he's never encountered one. Neither has Belknap. But I don't know anything about the telephone habits of ambassadors. Being an enfeebled FSO 1, I can barely lift my own telephone. Perhaps if they promote me to FSO 2, I'll have more strength."

Otis took a few steps farther down the hall and gestured to another door. "This office, next to the ambassador's, has a connecting door. It belongs to his personal secretary – Iris, the Snow Queen, who rules over us all. It's important to pay attention to Iris and abide by her judgments. At least for me. Your senior rank might give you more authority."

Otis didn't sound optimistic.

"I'm afraid you must remember not to leave your office even for a moment without locking your door," Otis continued. "It's a terrible nuisance. The offices are not in the secure area and anyone can walk in from the reception room or library and peer at your papers. We get a fair number of nationals who drop in to read old copies of the *Winnipeg Tribune* and stuff like that."

Otis shook his head, as if he were suddenly perplexed by something, and Barry wondered if the man were making a comment on the *Winnipeg Tribune* or if he were simply the distracted type. After a moment of awkward silence, the tour proceeded.

"Before you settle in, I'd better show you the comcentre and registry," Otis said over his shoulder as Barry followed.

"Remember – you can never take your key out of the Mission. There's a board in the registry and you have to hang it on the hook by your name when you leave the office."

At the end of the corridor were two doors heavily reinforced with iron grilles, marking what Barry knew to be the secure area. Otis pressed a buzzer, and an older man with an asthmatic wheeze wearing a cheaper suit than Otis's or Barry's opened the door with two separate sets of keys.

"Mr. Sloan is our senior security guard and he or his colleagues will always be here to open the door for you. We have four security guards."

He introduced Barry and continued.

"You realize, I'm sure, that the local staff, Chantal, the chauffeurs and René, who helps me with the consular stuff, are not allowed beyond the first door. They are not cleared for security and can't see the classified stuff. Just the officers, the communicators and the Canadian secretaries are allowed in."

Barry looked around and saw the communications clerk, Radcliffe, sitting at the clacking deciphering machines, which automatically decoded and encoded in- and outgoing telegrams. The clerk was in a sealed room with no windows off the registry. He waved to Barry through a locked iron grille.

"Every officer," Otis went on, "has his own pigeon-hole in the registry here. When you leave for the day, take your papers out of the pigeon-hole and from your in-box on your desk and then put them in the security shell here."

Barry noticed four green filing safes, one for each officer and one for the ambassador, lined up in a row against the wall of the registry.

"I see that Mr. Sloan has already marked your name on a pigeon-hole. And he's also got your name up on the board for the keys. Very efficient."

Mr. Sloan was a dour man who pointed wordlessly to Barry's box, without acknowledging Otis's compliment. Barry saw, through the grilled door, that the walls of the communications centre were thickly padded. He asked Sloan about it.

"It's the machines, sir. With the right equipment, people living on the other floors can pick up radio signals and decipher the telegrams, just from the sound. The padding reduces the chances of pick-ups."

Otis smiled. "Imagine old Abulaphia with a decoding machine. He's over eighty and lives with his ninety-year-old sister."

"It's regulation," Sloan said curtly. "The comcentres in all our embassies all over the world have padded walls."

Otis ignored him and pointed to one of the large green iron filing safes. "There's your security shell. You'll need the combination. Mr. Sloan marks the combination in a log and then gives it to me. You have to know how to work the combination. It's complicated, but Sloan or one of the other security guards will show you how. At least two people must have the combination to the shell."

Sloan looked even sourer. "Except for Mr. Hilary-Moulds. He's got an extra shell in his office. I've never heard of that happening at any other post."

"We make exceptions for our ambassador, Mr. Sloan," said Otis, mollifying. "I don't see anything wrong in him having an extra shell in his own office. Mr. Hilary-Moulds told me that Iris has the combination. She has security clearance. In fact, she's cleared to top secret. Since she organizes everything else, why not her boss's shell?"

Sloan was not to be convinced. "It's not regulation. We're supposed to have the combination. And I'm the senior guard. It's my job to make sure all the documents are secure right here in the registry."

When they left the secure area, Otis told Barry that Sloan was a difficult man. "He thinks we're questioning his authority. Hasn't enough to do. Just goes around looking for security breaches and answers the phone in the quiet hours.

Nothing to do except grumble, grumble, grumble. Whatever happens, don't leave any classified papers out overnight. He'll seize the documents, put a pink slip on your desk stating you have committed a security infraction and place a copy of the slip on Hilary-Moulds's desk. When you come into the office in the morning, you see the thing on your desk and – can you believe it? – you have to go and beg Hilary-Moulds to countersign your pink slip to get your damn file back. And Hilary-Moulds really over-reacts. I had a half-hour of lecturing on the importance of security. And that's the longest he's ever spoken to me at one time."

Otis escorted Barry to his new office. "I'll call the ambassador as soon as he's free and tell him you've arrived," he said. "He'll certainly want to see you right away. But the little red light is still on. You might have to wait a while." Then, just as he was leaving, he added, "You have, however, arrived on an auspicious day. Look." He pointed out Barry's window. "You can see Mont Blanc clear as I've ever seen it. It's usually covered in cloud. You're getting a special performance. Very symbolic."

Barry's window overlooked the Alps and the sudden clarity of Mont Blanc on this day gave him an oceanic sensation. Perhaps Otis was right: perhaps this was an omen. He knew he was going to do great things, something as remarkable as climbing that mountain. After all, he had already been promoted, while he was in Ottawa, from a probationary FSO 1 to an FSO 3 in less time than any of his peers.

Barry sat down, swung his chair to face the view of the Alps and pulled his leather-bound container of index cards out of his briefcase. He made a few notes under Otis's name, then looked at several cards he had particularly flagged, those listing the careers of the most successful diplomats, including Hilary-Moulds. He wondered if Hilary-Moulds had risen as quickly from FSO 1 to FSO 3. Not quite so fast, Barry noted with satisfaction.

He flipped to the present prime minister's card, and to those of the two most powerful officials in government, men who had once been foreign-service officers. Their patterns of positions and postings were significantly similar: important headquarters positions that became conduits to power and ambassadorial posts in large countries, which made them well known to the right people. Reviewing the career charts he had made for them, Barry calculated that he would have to be promoted from FSO 3 to FSO 4 within two years so that he would be ready to be an FSO 5 by the time he left. That would enable him to be made head of a small but important division when he returned to Ottawa after this Geneva posting was completed. His goal was to become head of the personnel division. From there he would be able to choose his own embassy or, if he liked, a position in a department where he would be given important policy responsibilities. Then he would have access to real power. He wanted to change things, to promote his own ideas, to do something worthwhile. It was, he thought, only the very powerful who could change anything at all. He had told Nini that, because it was so competitive, if he did not become the head of a division within four years, his diplomatic career would probably be a failure.

Barry needed Nini to overcome his sense of guilt. It was only after he had married her that he was sure of the righteousness of his own intense ambition. Nini wanted him to be as different from her father as possible. "My father wasted his life," Nini had told him back in Derby. "He calls himself a gentleman and a scholar, but all he knows is malt whiskies and vintage burgundies. He's jealous of anyone who's energetic. People say that I'm just like my mother, but that's not true. I have the inborn Sullivan lassitude and I need your energy to overcome it."

Only two things mattered to Nini and Barry: their marriage and his success. Within days of their wedding, Nini had begun to promote her husband with an aplomb that had almost gone out of fashion. And Barry, possessing all the essential ingredients for success, never failed to prove himself worthy of Nini's devotion. While at Oxford, he had studied languages for his own intellectual satisfaction, without neglecting the required reading in economics for his degree. His Russian and German became fluent. His French comprehension was total and he wrote well in the language. In the days to come, whenever a memorandum had to be written in French at the Mission, it would automatically go to Pike, who was quickly and good-naturedly crowned the resident polyglot by his grateful colleagues.

8

The Pikes' early weeks in Geneva were as unheralded as Barry's first day in his new position. Barry and Nini both found it difficult to make friends with the rest of the people connected with the Mission. The ambassador, Hugh Hilary-Moulds, was polite to Barry but never asked him to his residence. Moulds was of the school that believed ambassadors did not have to mix with their junior staff even to the extent of inviting new officers and their wives for a ceremonial drink.

Nini often questioned Barry about the ambassador and the others at the Mission, and Barry tried to satisfy her eagerness for news. He told her he assumed the ambassador's coldness had something to do with his personal problems. Hugh Hilary-Moulds was married to one of Lord North's daughters. North was a Labour Lord who owned real estate from Caracas to Houston and, according to Stephen Belknap, the other first secretary at the Mission, "one square mile around Buckingham Palace."

Soon after Barry's arrival, Stephen briefed him about the ambassador's wife.

"The Permanent Mission," Stephen began, "received a telex saying that the newly appointed ambassador and, presumably, his wife, were arriving from Paris at a specific time. Naturally, there had to be a reception committee.

Georges Dugay, the counsellor, was the senior man at the Mission then. He brought his wife, Suzette. When I heard Dugay was bringing his wife, I managed to convince my wife, Moira, to find a babysitter for our kids and come shake hands as well. Even Otis came. And he does the security and consulate stuff and bloody little else.

"Well, His Excellency came down the first-class exit all by himself. Georges naturally asked him about Mrs. Hilary-Moulds. He replied tersely that she was unwell and would come to Geneva 'by and by.'

"A few days later, we learned by accident that Mrs. Hilary-Moulds (or 'Lady Beatrice') had been in Geneva for quite some time. Julio, the ambassador's chauffeur, told Otis—who for some reason seems to be Julio's confidant—that he had received a personal call from Hilary-Moulds in Paris a month before the official arrival.

"No one could figure out how the hell Hilary-Moulds knew Julio's home number. He told Julio to pick him up at the airport and not say a word about it to anyone at the Mission. Hilary-Moulds was accompanied by this speechless lady, *'habillée comme une princesse, mais comme elle avait le cafard,'* according to Julio. Julio was instructed to drive the depressed princess, who was covered in alligator—the pumps, bag and spectacle case (Julio used to be a driver for Hermés and knows about alligator)—to the Clinique Beau Rivage, one of Geneva's many 'safe houses' for the rich and demented. Very posh. The best for Lord North's daughter. Hilary-Moulds stayed there about half an hour, returned to the car alone and went straight back to the airport. A month later, he made his nice clean entrance. Three months after his arrival, I asked the ambassador if Mrs. Hilary-Moulds was joining him. The bastard replied, 'My wife does not enjoy diplomatic life, and she has decided to stay in Paris.'

"The significance of this whole story," Stephen finished, "is not that Moulds's wife was crazy and that he didn't want anyone to know. It's that he had to have a chauffeur pick him up at the airport to take him to the clinic. Always '*le grand luxe.*' If His Holiness had taken a taxi no one would have been the wiser."

Nini used to tell visitors that the dirt in Geneva was hidden under the huge clock of flowers in the Jardin Anglais, just beside the lake. "Just think," she would say, "its face is made of pink begonias and the numerals blue alyssum, and yet the clock is always accurate." Nini liked to watch the gardeners snip and control the green cover, making sure the face of the dial did not creep out of its circle.

Both Nini and Barry wondered how Geneva could be so cosmopolitan and yet so bland. Barry said it was like a clean Tangiers, but Nini called it a giant Montessori kindergarten. "The Genevois are the teachers," she would explain, "making sure the children, we foreigners, behave nicely on the streets. Every Genevois carries a piece of chalk in his pocket in case he witnesses an accident. Then he can play policeman and draw a diagram on the road to show where the fenders clashed."

To Nini, everyone in the city was suspect. She thought the old ladies who walked dachshunds on the Route de Malagnou had poisoned their rich husbands in Arizona or Rumania and then come to Geneva because the taxes were low and the streets safe.

Nini had a favourite story to illustrate the Swiss character. The Canadian Permanent Mission to the United Nations, situated, as it was, in a group of apartment buildings, was owned by a large European conglomerate. The parking spaces beside the buildings were divided by iron poles with chains, instead of civilized white lines. One evening when Barry backed out, he veered too far to the left and knocked one of the poles slightly awry. He wondered on his return home, whether to call Lustig Regie, the manager of the building, to report himself. Nini pointed out that the Mission, like all the tenants, paid an exorbitant rent and that there had even been talk of signing petitions against the awkwardly placed poles.

"Every rent-payer," she told Barry, "will be delighted that you banged into one of the conglomerate poles." But Barry, more prudent than Nini, decided to call the Regie. He was informed that the accident had already been reported by all four Swiss tenants who had watched as he bent the pole.

"I knew Geneva would suit me," Nini wrote Eleanor not long after her arrival, "as soon as I saw the lake in the middle of the city with that artificial geyser spraying straight up. It's paradoxical to look at Mont Blanc from a café on the quay, sipping a fresh young *fendant* right beside those vulgar gold and diamond shops – Vacherin Constantin, Gubelin, Patek Philippe. They sell such bulbous jewellery. During my four weeks in Geneva I haven't once seen anything beautiful in their windows."

Nini discovered that there were more rich people in Geneva per square metre than anywhere else in the world, except Monte Carlo. She liked the fact that Kuwaiti sheiks and exiled Alexandrian Jews shared the same apartment block in which she lived, and that across the street from her apartment on the Route de Florissante she could watch tax refugees from Hollywood and Hampstead being driven by their Spanish and Yugoslavian chauffeurs. She liked the idea of diplomats meeting at conferences, forever discussing nuclear war, and of delegations of Bulgarians and Peruvians comparing the management techniques of the Turkish and Canadian post offices.

People told her that Geneva was full of spies and that they had been there since the time of Elizabeth, Empress of Austria-Hungary, who was stabbed to death on the quay in front of the Hotel de la Paix. They assured her that some contemporary spies were famous enough to be pointed out as tourist attractions. Others had better cover working for the United Nations.

As first secretary at the Permanent Mission, which Nini often pointed out to her husband was much better than being second or third, Barry's salary and allowances were more than adequate. And Nini had money of her own. Further, the Canadian dollar was worth four and a half Swiss francs, and a good meal cost ten francs. The newlyweds chose a big, sunny furnished apartment on the Route de Florissante with three bathrooms, a dining room big enough to seat twenty-four and a living room stuffed with Swiss *moderne* furry chairs and amoeba-shaped coffee tables. They also had a live-in maid and a laundress who came once a week. Nini judged themselves to be rich, and when she was unexpectedly bequeathed a large sum of money from her Aunt Delia's estate, the assessment became unchallengeable. The legacy that came to her was a considerable one, owing to the fact that while Aunt Delia had been living at the Ritz in Paris for forty years, she ventured outside in all those years only to buy a few cold-cuts from the *charcuterie* around the corner. Unlike Nini's other relatives, Delia didn't even drink.

There were so many reasons for Nini to be happy that she felt she had no right to complain about Geneva, but she was terribly lonely. It would have been nice to have a friend to sit with during the long afternoons at the cafés. There was no question of Nini working: she knew only English in a country where even the butchers spoke at least three languages. Also, the rôle of the diplomatic wife was to help her husband entertain, not to steal jobs from less fortunate women. In any case, the idea of working never occurred to her. It was difficult enough to negotiate purchases at the Grand Passage or to attract anyone's attention at parties with a French vocabulary of fifty words.

The result was that Nini had the odd sensation of having too much time on her hands while feeling exhausted at the thought of any kind of activity. Barry suggested that she take a few courses at the University of Geneva, but Nini had never been a scholar. Failure, she believed, would be inevitable. Being newly married and living in a foreign city took all the energy she could muster.

Every day Barry would return from the office and ask her what she had done with her day.

"Nothing," she would answer. "Walked and watched. What should I do?"

"It doesn't matter what you do, as long as you enjoy yourself."

She was taking French lessons from an elderly Russian emigré lady but was unable to grasp the fine points of grammar.

"How am I to enjoy myself when I can't speak? Have you ever listened to me ask for a kilo of string beans, let alone gossip about the Aswan Dam at dinner parties? You pick up languages easily, and I don't. Do you know it takes me half an hour to enter a *tabac* to buy a newspaper? I'm so afraid of sounding foolish."

Nini paused while Barry went over to the bar and mixed himself a Scotch and soda.

"You're too much of a perfectionist," Barry observed. "In Geneva, everyone speaks English. You just don't like being the object of condescension. Lots of the American and English wives don't even bother to learn fifty words of French. They seem happy enough playing bridge among themselves. Perhaps you should try to make friends with them." He drank his whisky quickly, got up and poured himself another, which was unusual. "You're lonely, that's the trouble. We have too many acquaintances, not enough friends."

But Nini didn't want to be like the women Barry was referring to. They were tourists, outsiders, although many had lived in Geneva for years. During the first weeks, Nini had found exploring the city and chatting to migratory cocktail acquaintances flying in and out for diplomatic conferences, sufficient for her needs. But now the novelty of sightseeing had disappeared and Nini was discontent, not so much with supercilious merchants and indifferent diplomats as with herself. She didn't want to be a tourist anymore; she had to be recognized and admired, not talked down to at parties. She was boring people with her narrowness and ignorance and felt she would never be an asset to her husband. What good was she doing wandering aimlessly through mushroom markets and lingering anonymously in cafés?

She was aware that bridge-playing provincial wives never became part of the golden city, that occidental Casbah of sophisticated international technocrats, displaced Alexandrians and bizarre aristocrats who ran refugee movements and gambled in casinos. These were the people Barry should meet and from whom Nini wanted approval. This was the milieu in which she had to excel, or she would be no better than those "English-only" wives whose trademarks were vacuity and complaint.

Nini had been an only child, and the slightest alteration in her humour had been a compelling subject of conversation for her parents. She would eavesdrop on their whisperings, their intense analyses of Nini's sulks or high spirits, her clever talk or new dress. If she was dejected because she hadn't been chosen as the star in the school play, her father chided her for always wanting centre stage. But her mother would say, "There's nothing wrong with being ambitious, but moping won't get you anywhere." Nothing she ever did at home passed without comment and attention. How could she sustain being ignored and forgotten now? She had never looked forward to a life of calm oblivion, nor did her husband.

"I don't think you will benefit," she said to Barry, "from having a little brown hen for a wife. And that's what people in Geneva think I am. It's all very well for me to stare at the diamond watches in Patek Philippe, but what am I accomplishing for either of us?"

"You're over-anxious," Barry consoled her. "People will

pay more attention to you once you learn French."

Barry tended to believe there usually was a specific remedy to a general problem. It was a great comfort to Nini. "Why don't you go to the movies in the afternoon? It will accustom your ear to the speech. You'll learn more from Fernandel and Arletty than you will from that old Russian woman. I think she takes your confidence away by making you concentrate on subjunctives. And never be afraid of shopkeepers. You have the money, Nini, use it."

Nini sighed, thinking of future humiliations.

"This is Switzerland. In a capitalist country, be a capitalist," Barry insisted. "If you spend enough, the shopkeepers will speak slowly and listen to you without smirking. And don't worry about sounding childish or foolish when you're the one who's paying. I can tell you one thing: no one will be unkind to you in this country if you're free with Aunt Delia's money. They'll embrace you when you return. And buy yourself some good clothes. You have parties to go to, parties to give." He drained the last of his second drink, thought of a third, rejected the idea and went on with his lecture.

"Europeans like smart-looking women. Each time you visit a *couturier* or a seamstress, you'll learn something. Ask them to correct your speech. What you need is more exposure to local customs."

It wasn't as if Nini didn't like going to movies and visiting *couturiers*, but she was beginning to feel too unworthy to follow her natural tendencies. "Indulge yourself," Barry said, "and you will excel." So she did.

Nini began to attend matinée showings compulsively. Every day she would leave the bright sun on the streets and sit in the smoky, gloomy cinemas on the rue de Rhone, desperately trying to catch the argot of Jean Gabin or the ripe Provençal accent of Fernandel. There would only be a certain number of new films playing in the city, but Nini would visit each one over and over until some of the language became understandable. Her grammar was poor but her ear was good and, after a month of daily movies, she began to comprehend the story. Every evening Barry insisted she tell him the plot in French. If she thought she had missed the point of a single character she would return the next day and concentrate harder.

After six weeks she had the courage to pass her mornings in an equally compulsive manner, visiting antique shops and private galleries, forcing herself to draw the owners into conversation. Wisely, she always bought something the first time she entered and, as Barry predicted, this made the dealers happy and welcoming even when she returned the following morning. She bought lavishly and stayed long in each shop, practising her French with the now-tolerant attendants until it was time for the afternoon movie. Nini's knowledge of modern prints, Old Masters and eighteenth-century cabinet making increased greatly.

After two months, she felt sure enough of herself to enter a *maison de couture*, begging the remote *vendeuses* to correct her French as she chose the *peau de soie* or the *crêpe de Chine* for her Nina Ricci suits and Patou dresses. It took six months of relentless cinema-going and almost all of Aunt Delia's money before Nini felt that some of her ambition might be realized.

As her confidence grew at parties, she would thrust in a *"vraiment moche"* or a *"Je me débrouille en français"* with an excellent accent, making sure her tone sounded blasé or meek depending on the expression of the listener. Nini soon spoke sufficiently well to deceive the listener about her real comprehension.

While Nini braved the challenges laid out for the wife of any diplomat in a new posting, Barry, contrary to his expectations, found challenges at the Mission disappointing. Within weeks of his arrival, he was bored. The work at the chancery was simply not sufficiently stimulating for his intellect or taxing of his energy. He soon began to look around for special projects to keep him busy, much as he had found himself doing at Oxford. One project in particular proved to be a success.

Although nothing in Barry's formal responsibilities called for it, he was eager to polish his Russian. Using a portion of the many slow hours in his day to read Russian, he discovered he was genuinely interested in demographic trends in the Soviet Union. As far as he could tell from his reading, the learned journals and the foreign office had ignored the subject entirely. During his free evenings and the slow hours at the office, he gathered and collated as much scholarly material in Russian, French, German and English as he could get his hands on. He carefully presented and analyzed the growth and movements of the huge and varied ethnic groups within the Soviet Union. He came to some unusual conclusions, and his work resulted in a thirty-page dispatch. Hilary-Moulds said only that it was good but when the dispatch reached headquarters, it was circulated as far up as the prime minister. Word came back urging him to publish because of its originality. "Penetrating. Profound," the PM had written on the margins. Barry's brilliance and energy became a matter of public record.

By the end of the Pikes' first six months in Geneva, Barry felt buoyed up by the recognition he had received for his own initiative, and Nini was justifiably proud of the results of her determination to be more than a "little brown hen of a wife." So much so that this new sense of "belonging," which Nini and Barry had come to enjoy, underwent only a minor setback on the occasion of Nini's first real experience with "la vie diplomatique" – unexpectedly, a Rhodes scholars dinner.

The dinner was held at a restaurant in Evian-les-Bains, in France, a favourite resort of the English at the beginning of the century. It was a small but high-toned group, with the Duke of Devonshire and Lord Cutting invited as special guests. The former Rhodes scholars were Senator Peel, a

Southern gentleman whose ancestors fought in the American Revolution, and a stuffy young American who had lived in England for many years and had taken on protective colouring. "T.S. Eliot without the talent," Barry said. The others were the Maharajah of the Sacred Thread, who was an old Etonian, and the Giffords, a young South African couple. Gifford was a diplomat, somewhat junior to Barry, but his wife was the daughter of an English earl.

Nini had the place of honour between Senator Peel and the duke. For the first part of the evening she barely spoke but, encouraged by the wine, she finally began to relax and when the port and nuts were set on the table, Nini felt at ease. Although they were in France, the dinner was specifically designed to evoke memories of Oxford. Nini had tasted the port, and she found it pleasant to sip the strong, sweet wine while cracking nuts. She kept forgetting to pass the decanter to her neighbour on the left and the duke would kindly remove it, pour some for himself and pass the decanter on.

None too quickly, Nini noticed that she was the only person speaking. Everyone was staring at her, yet she knew she wasn't drunk. She looked across at Barry, who kept lifting his eyebrows and turning his head in a peculiar jerking motion. Nini looked at the earl's daughter, who had a superior, almost mocking expression. She seemed to be waiting for something. Everyone was watching Nini and waiting. Nini shut up and hoped for a clue. Senator Peel looked troubled; the duke was fidgeting on her other side. With obvious exasperation, the senator nodded at the earl's daughter — who rose, stared hard at Nini and then walked out of the room. The gentlemen rose but Nini still sat with a walnut in her hand. She saw no reason to leave, since she did not have to go to the bathroom. But it was quite terrifying. The men remained on their feet looking down at her. The senator spoke gently.

"Mrs. Pike, I think it's time for the ladies to leave. Why

don't you join Mrs. Gifford outside and keep her company."
Horrified, Nini rose and rushed out of the room. Mrs.
Gifford was sitting in a small ante-room reading a French
newspaper. She looked up when Nini entered.

"Terribly sorry about walking out first. You are the senior
lady. But poor Senator Peel didn't know what to do. He
waited for you to signal me but you just sat there eating
nuts. We should have left when they brought out the port.
Port is only for the gentlemen. You must know that."

Mrs. Gifford then ignored Nini completely and returned
to her newspaper. There was nothing else to read in the
room. After ten minutes of absolute silence, except for the
sound of Mrs. Gifford turning the pages, Nini asked for
directions to the bathroom. The haughty woman indicated
an unmarked door. There was one booth and only a tiny
mirror. But the sinks were rather quaint. As she washed her
hands, Lord Cutting and Barry entered.

Lord Cutting said gamely, "The French don't believe in
separating the sexes. Same one for men and women, I'm
afraid."

Barry said, "My God, Nini, you're washing your hands in
the urinal."

9

Nini's parents, the Sullivans, were small-town rich folk. Her great-grandfather, a Protestant innkeeper, had come to Canada from Belfast and built a timber mill near a stand of white pine outside the garrison settlement of Derby.

Her grandfather hired an architect to design a clapboard mansion set on thirty-five acres of land sloping down to the Gatineau River, from which he could watch the logs floating downstream to his mill. The house was built in the "picturesque" style, with Swiss, Moorish and Greek accents in the bargeboard trim and with two belvederes that rose almost as high as the steeple on the Catholic church. Nini was born to her own tennis court, to formal Italian and perennial English gardens, to a greenhouse and even a bandshell folly covered with clematis vines. Nini's grandmother kept peacocks, not chickens like the rest of the wives in Derby.

The people Nini loved best were from the town where she was born. Her husband was from Derby, and although his family could not count financial success among its achievements, the Pikes were considered by the Sullivans, with reservations, as a family of standing.

Barry Pike's grandfather, the Presbyterian minister, lived in a plain seven-room brick manse attached to the church on Main Street. The old reverend's living expenses, aside from the free use of the manse, were paid by voluntary donations from the congregation. No precise annual sum was stipulated. He received a meagre cheque every Christmas, and the cheque never went beyond the sum he received in his first year – even if the oat crop "might have been worse," as Derby farmers described a favourable year. The major donor to the congregation was Mr. Sullivan, who didn't mind wet or dry years, not being a farmer. Mr. Sullivan slept easily through Reverend Pike's sermons, knowing he had done more than anyone else for the old minister.

The Pikes and the Sullivans lived within four blocks of each other and the women exchanged invitations for tea. Although the two families were considered social equals by the other Derby people, there were contrasts in the way each family lived.

Barry bathed once a week in the wash-tub set out in the kitchen, using the same water his grandparents had used. Nini bathed whenever she wanted to, in her own bathroom. Her Scottish nanny filled, emptied, and scrubbed the large porcelain tub after Nini got out. Mr. Sullivan was amused by the Pikes' stinginess and called Barry's grandfather "Holy Cod" because the minister saved on food by eating dried codfish, the cheapest form of protein available in Derby during the winter months. "It's for him and the old wife," Mr. Sullivan used to assert. "Not just for the hired girl." He was unwilling to make the connection between the minister's frugality and the source and amount of his income.

Barry Pike was nevertheless a glamorous figure to Nini because he was five years older than she and the smartest boy in the high school. He had been born and raised in China, where his father had been head of a large mission in the Hunan district. It was known in Derby that Barry had his own amah until he was eight and that his parents had been carried around in sedan chairs by coolies. The Chinese nurse, and especially the sedan chairs, had raised the standing of the youngest Pike in the eyes of the Sullivans. Barry's parents had died of virulent amoebic dysentry in Kaifeng within a few months of each other. Barry returned to Derby, and his grandparents, when he was ten.

Mrs. Sullivan, a true colonial, revered everything British and when Barry Pike won a Rhodes scholarship to Oxford, she decided that he was just the man for her daughter. Mrs. Sullivan, Queen of Derby and three counties, had mixed views about her own subjects. She approved of friends and neighbours, because they were reliable and loyal, but had yet to find one person she considered to be her peer. Barry Pike, she thought, might be different. He would do great things far from Derby.

Society in Derby, by the time Nini was born, consisted of descendants of a few lawyers and merchants who lived on Quality Hill, a section of town near the river that had a rise of twenty-five feet. Nini's family had been the only one to stay rich in the twentieth century; a plague of alcoholism had decimated the remnants of Derby's old families.

Mrs. Sullivan had little use for the few young men who returned home to take over their fathers' dry-goods stores or law practices, and she secretly felt her husband lacked gumption because he refused to leave the village.

Barry Pike had shown no particular interest in Nini, but this was partly due to circumstance: he had not returned home during his Oxford years. Meaningful, if elliptical, conversations were nevertheless carried out between Mrs. Sullivan and Mrs. Pike. The former once observed that Barry would probably marry abroad.

But Mrs. Pike was reassuring.

"I hardly think it. He'd lose the Rhodes money and, of course, *we* have nothing to give him except our love."

Subsequent to this conversation, Mr. Sullivan, after encouragement from his wife, and several rum toddies, took the old reverend aside and said, "If your grandson has his head screwed on, he'll know where to look so he won't have to worry about his pennies."

Nini was aware of her mother's wishes and every time she heard Barry Pike's name mentioned in a complimentary way, she over-reacted.

"I'd rather marry the honey man," she would say, or "Marriage is out of the question: I'm going to be an art historian."

Nini was taking an M.A. in Art History at the University of Toronto, but her studies were not going well. She thought the professor was more interested in the study of iconography than the beauty of the paintings, and could not get excited about the metamorphosis of the lamb and its symbolic meaning during eight centuries of pagan and Christian art. Her professor returned her M.A. thesis marked D, and said she would be happier taking an art-appreciation course at night school.

Barry Pike had earned a Ph.D. in Economics and was entering the diplomatic service when he finally came back to Derby to spend a few weeks with his grandparents. Nini returned the same summer and told her parents that all the men she met were boring or taken, and that she was going to abandon her M.A. thesis. It had been easy to tell her parents these things because she knew of something worse, which had to be kept secret.

During the past winter, Nini's menstrual cramps had become so prolonged and agonizing that she missed weeks of school. After many examinations, including one under a general anaesthetic, Nini was told that she had endometriosis.

"Endometriosis," the gynecologist explained, "means, in your case, that the lining of the uterus is scattered throughout the pelvis. I'm sorry to say that the probability of your ever becoming pregnant is remote. I've never seen or heard, in my own personal experience, of a patient with endometriosis who was not, to all intents and purposes, barren. We do not know what causes the disease, but we may be able to do something about the pain. There is no doubt that you will have to have a hysterectomy sometime in the future. If we can reduce the pain to the minimal discomfort level, we'd prefer to put off the operation until you are much older."

And he said nothing more. Because she was an only child, Nini didn't have the courage to tell her parents. Possibly they would never have to know, she thought, as it was unlikely she would marry.

No man would guess from her appearance that she lacked the basic element of womanhood. She looked into the mirror. "My pink and gold butterfly," her father called her when she was little. Even now her father would hum "The Lass with the Delicate Air" in her honour – and to her disgust. She wore no make-up. Unlike most blondes, she had high colour. Nothing wrong with her figure, either, Nini thought, scrutinizing narrow waist and satisfactory roundness above and below. Her legs could be longer – she was only five-foot two – but her ankles were slim, her calves didn't turn out and, so far, there was no flab around her thighs. She was pretty enough to make men turn around when she walked by. The essence of her beauty was the contrast between her delicate features and the seductiveness of her body. There was nothing boyish about her. "It's quite ironic," Nini thought, "I look as if I could birth a litter of eight."

The only person Nini confided in was her best friend, Eleanor Campbell.

Eleanor Campbell was the doctor's daughter. Her grandfather, a stonemason from Perth, came to Derby to build greystone houses for those who did not want clapboard. The stonemason managed to raise enough capital to establish a patent-medicine factory on the main street in Derby. Dr. Campbell's Apple Linctus became famous during the

1880s for curing dysentry, bronchitis and ladies' fatigues. Although it had the unpleasant odour of rotting fruit, its thirty-per-cent alcohol base gave a revivifying jolt to many girls with green sickness.

Eleanor's grandfather built his brick house opposite the factory in a gesture of bravado, saying his family would benefit from its recuperative fumes as they sat on the spool-work verandah that circled the entire house. One of his six children survived – a son, who inherited the factory. This Campbell lost faith in apple water, and went to medical school instead. He returned to Derby, sold the factory and became the town's only doctor. He sired Eleanor, the first girl born to three generations of therapeutic Campbells.

Nini's and Eleanor's friendship was enhanced, as well, by Nini being small and pretty and Eleanor being big and awkward. Eleanor, the athlete, lumbered and never left Nini's home without causing inadvertent destruction. It was Eleanor's foot squashing the seedlings and Eleanor's thumb snapping the handles off the Worcester teacups. Nini's mother referred to Eleanor, when she was out of hearing, as "the Derby bull."

Despite her clumsiness with the teacups, Eleanor had a precise manner of thinking. From the age of twelve she knew she wanted to be a doctor and thereafter never let her emotions splutter about and distract her from her goal.

Nini's desires always appeared nebulous compared to Eleanor's. Nini wanted to marry, travel in Europe and become well-known, but not vulgarly famous like a movie actress. She had never really been serious about becoming an art historian; she had thought it was a good thing to be in case she didn't marry until very late. Nini really believed that Eleanor's decision to become a doctor was a way to take her mind off important events in life, like marriage. Eleanor had never once been asked out on New Year's Eve during her high-school or undergraduate years. Medical studies would take so much of her time that she wouldn't have to worry about dating.

"Do you ever have any fun?" Nini asked Eleanor.

"Some, this year. It's not so bad being the only girl in my class. One morning I came in to the dissection room a little late. The boys were very quiet when I pulled the sheet away from my cadaver. It was a woman in her sixties. There was a penis stuck in her vagina."

Nini was shocked.

"They hate women who take medicine," Eleanor explained.

"What did you do?" Nini looked ill. "I would have run out of the room."

"Don't be silly. I pulled out the penis, held it as high as I could and asked all the men to check between their legs. I said, 'One of you guys must be missing something.' Even the anatomy professor laughed."

Nini thought she would never have had the courage to respond that way. Although they were the same age, Nini felt much younger than Eleanor and for the first time, she felt like the weaker one. She told Eleanor about her uterus.

"It's hardly the end of your life." Eleanor shrugged. "Lots of women don't have children and are perfectly happy. I certainly wouldn't be upset if it happened to me. Why do you want to marry, anyhow? You'll tie yourself to some prig less intelligent than yourself, and spend all your energy massaging his ego. That's why medical students marry nurses. A nurse will always look up to them. I ought to marry a nurse."

"I can't believe you wouldn't be upset if you had what I have," Nini replied. "You *must* want to marry and have children."

"I wouldn't mind having a child – but not if I had to live with a man."

Nini barely heard Eleanor, absorbed as she was in her own misery.

"Why don't we buy a nice big old house," Eleanor continued, "and live together? We could have fun. Later, when I finish medical school, we might adopt a refugee baby. You don't have to be married to get one of those children from the camps."

Nini was momentarily flattered, as well as astonished.

"You mean you'd be content, living with me and some Korean baby, the rest of your life?"

"Why not? We get along very well. Everyone needs stability in life."

Eleanor's words were casual, but her voice had a warmth that disconcerted Nini and made her want to draw away. Still, she didn't want to hurt Eleanor's feelings.

"No matter what you think now, I'm sure you'll want to marry and have your own children. You're just angry with men because the medical students have been mean to you. I know that when we're both eighty we'll want to be in the same old-folks' home. Of course, you're the only person I can really talk to, but I think it's early to start living together now. Listen, Eleanor, after three weeks with me and my fussy, neurotic ways, you'll be certain to change your mind."

"Nonsense," Eleanor said. "I never change my mind. You always do."

Nini wasn't sure about anything in her life, except that she didn't want to spend it with Eleanor.

Barry Pike came for dinner the second day after his arrival from Oxford. The meal was difficult. Neither Nini nor Barry spoke, and Nini found her mother irritatingly loquacious, almost coquettish. After dinner, Mr. Sullivan insisted that the young people take a walk by themselves to inspect the freshly painted blue and white roof on the folly near the river. He practically shoved them off the terrace. Barry, almost six and a half feet tall with enormous hands and feet, wore (for the first time in his life) a suit that did not belong to his father or grandfather.

The shock effect of Barry's gigantic height and long extremities was offset by the regularity of his features and by the thoughtful, almost scholarly, attention he paid to what was being said and what there was to see. The blue eyes behind the horn-rimmed glasses looked intently at whoever was speaking – and at every object in the house. Then the eyes would withdraw their gaze, as if they had come to their own conclusions. Were Nini in a better mood, she would have said that he had an intelligent face.

Nini looked very fair that evening, with her grey eyes and long white lashes; it was too early in the summer for her to have a tan. To Nini's shame, Mrs. Sullivan had informed Barry that Nini had a "complexion that both princesses would be proud of." Mrs. Sullivan assumed that Barry's Oxford connection would make him receptive to her references to British royalty.

Nini deliberately wore an old dress that her mother wanted her to throw away. She felt humiliated at being put in such a ludicrous position, and could barely look at Barry.

The pair stared at the bandshell folly for ten minutes in absolute silence. Then Barry, who could stand it no longer, spoke.

"I know what you're thinking. 'The pious Pikes are after the Sullivan money.' And I don't blame you. There's nothing to equal the hypocrisy of religious people. They inevitably turn into fortune hunters."

The Sullivan style of life had always been a staple of conversation in the Pike household. Barry's grandmother loved to speak of the latest Sullivan extravagance, from sable coats to jam recipes. She would tell Barry, "I couldn't and I wouldn't wear the fur of trapped animals against my skin. I'd shiver even more thinking about the cries of the poor wee things." Or, "Sugar and berries, only sugar and berries, that's what she puts in the jam. Never pectin. Pectin's for penny-pinchers. She says it takes away the flavour."

Barry was only too aware that his grandparents wanted him to marry into a family where sable coats and jam without pectin were everyday occurrences, and he felt contempt for his grandparents and for himself. His self-hatred increased when he found himself impressed with the proportions of the Sullivan dining room, and it increased even further when he realized he envied Mr. Sullivan because he was the only person Barry knew in Canada who kept a wine cellar.

Barry was captivated when Nini and her mother played with their crystal goblets, sipping and remarking on the wine (the only remark Nini made during the dinner). He marvelled at the way they carelessly threw their linen napkins in front of them when they left the table. To him, they were stylish and unlike any other women he had known.

Impressed, and guilty because he was impressed, Barry tried to cleanse himself by pointing out his grasping nature to Nini.

It had never occurred to Nini that she was richer than Barry. That summer she could only think of her own defects, and she was surprised and amused by Barry's frankness.

"There are worse deceptions than marrying for money. What if you married a girl and then found out she couldn't have any children? *And* that she knew it before she married you? What could you do? She'd have you where she wanted you. You couldn't even reproach her parents. They probably wouldn't have known."

Barry had been seeing an English girl, who received a first in English Literature, for three years. They had usually talked about Milton and Donne between a few cold kisses. She was a serious scholar who never spoke about personal matters.

Nini's vulnerability made him hate himself less. "It's not your fault you can't have children," Barry said shyly.

Nini was silent for a moment, then decided to let Barry's perception go unremarked, unchallenged. "How do you know? Maybe I played around at university and got syphilis. Maybe venereal disease has ruined my insides."

Barry smiled. "If you're trying to shock the missionary's son, you're not being successful. For some reason – unjustified – you want to think as badly of yourself as possible. So let's just make a pact. I'm here for three weeks and the only interesting person in Derby is you. I don't want to marry you for your money, and you won't marry me because you say you can't have children. Let's forget about marriage and enjoy ourselves."

For the first time since the doctor's diagnosis, Nini felt relaxed. She wanted to tell Barry about the rest of her defects. Until now, Barry had not been a real person, just someone made up by her mother. That situation had changed dramatically in the awkward few minutes beside the newly painted folly, their first moments alone together.

"You know, I'm going to be an alcoholic when I'm forty," Nini said seriously. "My father is borderline and his two sisters take a cup of gin in a tablespoon of coffee every morning. At lunch, it's a cup of gin in a tablespoon of milk. No one can tell what they have in their glasses. You must have noticed them staggering to church on Sunday. I have the Sullivan alcoholic genes."

Barry laughed out loud. "Your mother's not an alcoholic and you are exactly like her. But more intelligent. All the women I've ever known have been insipid. No one could say that of you."

When Nini and Barry decided to marry, three weeks later, Barry refused Mr. Sullivan's offer of money.

"That's dowry money," Barry told him. "No man who respects himself accepts dowries. Give the money to Nini; put it in her name. She knows about painting and antiques. Perhaps she'll do a bit of collecting if we go abroad."

Barry convinced Nini to say nothing to them about her

endometriosis. "There's no point upsetting your parents. I don't want children. Looking after you is happiness enough for me."

They had a traditional wedding in early September. Nini had dearly wanted Eleanor to be her maid of honour, but Eleanor had returned to medical school and said she couldn't take the time off.

Mrs. Sullivan adored Barry but did not understand why he didn't want some control over Nini's money. "That boy's ambitious, energetic and intelligent," she told her phlegmatic husband, "and he certainly knows what he wants. He'd do very well in business, or anything else he set his mind to. Why, he's so energetic he can hardly sit through a family dinner. It's as if a pause to eat the sherry trifle would distract him from his future."

10

Nini hoped she had chosen a reasonable compromise between her own and Roland Neville's idea of a place to lunch. She was not at a loss for good restaurants. After six months in the city, Nini felt she knew her way at least around the restaurants. But as this was a one-day, first-time visit to Geneva for Neville, Nini feared that he might expect something "authentically" Swiss – perhaps a working man's café serving cheese fondue in the presence of Swiss yodellers. Aside from a personal aversion to "le folklore" and its stepchild, "artisant," Nini didn't want to be distracted by knee-thumpings and sing-songs. She had been astonished when Neville had called her from Budapest to ask her to lunch with him. It was unfathomable that he should want to see her after what had happened between them. She resolved that her curiosity would not be diverted by a floor show.

Nini stood in front of her bedroom mirror, wondering how she had looked during the time she and Roland had been so close. "I must look better now," she thought. "I'm happier." She hadn't seen Roland for more than two years, long before her marriage to Barry. She had met him in Toronto while he was spending a sabbatical away from external affairs as a lecturer in political science at the University of Toronto. He used to ask the brighter students to his room in the evenings, to listen to records and discuss how their political and economic ideas could change the world. Nini was not one of his brighter students. But she had a larger apartment in the same building and Roland would meet her on the stairs, tease her about her stylish clothes and compare his bleak room to her more comfortable suite stuffed with furniture from her mother's attic in Derby. He hated "things," as he called her wicker chairs and slop basins filled with plants. He told her that all a person needed was what he carried in his head and stored in his heart.

Roland Neville was the first man Nini had ever met who believed that ideas were more important than bottom lines on ledger sheets. The men in Derby never talked about anything except real-estate deals and hockey and, until she met Neville, the boys she went out with were stockbrokers' sons whose ambitions matched their fathers'. Roland must have seen her as an unusual convert to his monkish, Marxist vision of life. For her part, Nini fell quickly in love with him because he was the first intellectual she had ever met. It was through Neville that Nini discovered she had a weakness for men who talked well. She would attend his parties and keep her mouth shut while he and his coterie would figure out how to share the wealth with India and the Negroes in Alabama. She became a butt of their jokes: they made fun of her upbringing in Derby, her parents and her pleasure in shopping. Once, when talking about New York, she mentioned Saks Fifth Avenue, and everyone laughed. But despite her humiliations, Nini would always wait until the bright students left and would stay on to help Roland clear away the beer bottles. He was a tidy man who hated seeing the remains of what he called "the orgy" in the morning. He seemed to like Nini and gave her flattering, if mocking, attention, even if she was "an ignorant girl with materialistic compulsions."

Roland Neville was not a handsome man. He was fourteen years older than Nini, short, with a barrel chest; his hands and face were covered with freckles and his eyes blinked constantly behind his rimless glasses. Nini had always been physically shy and was never the one to make the first move with her accounting- and business-school boyfriends. Roland's age and indifferent looks gave her a kind of sexual confidence. One night when they were alone in his room cleaning up, she kissed him on the cheek and asked him if they might see more of each other. He smiled and told her that she was far too inexperienced for him, but added that it might enlarge her perspective of the world if they went out together.

Nini and Roland began to date. They would spend their time together sitting in taverns, in the railway station, or, occasionally, in a small park in a seedy area of town, so that Nini would find out how the real people, the "authentic" ones, lived. Neville told Nini that she had been stunted intellectually by her sheltered childhood in Derby, and that his purpose in seeing her was to develop her humanity and understanding. Fancy restaurants, even concert halls, re-pelled him because they were the gathering places of the bourgeoisie.

Nini was fascinated by Roland and felt miserable because she knew her instincts would never be as pure or as worthy as his. She used to imagine herself working beside him at some mission in Calcutta, although she was not quite sure if there was such a thing as a Marxist mission. Nini, hardly a conceptual thinker, could not generalize about Marcuse and Veblen as the other students did but, after a couple of months spent in Roland's company, she believed that she had succeeded in becoming the senior acolyte in his reli-gious order. One night when the others had gone, she surprised herself by trying to sit in Roland's lap while he was correcting essay papers. He got up so suddenly that she slid to the floor. He warned her never to approach him in such a way again.

"You have a terrible sense of timing," he said.

About fifteen minutes later, he set his papers down and put his arms around her. They kissed.

"Don't kiss with your mouth open," he said. "You're too eager. Not an appealing quality in a woman."

Then he opened the day-bed and told her to take off her clothes. She was sorry she had started on this course and wanted only to return to her suite, but she hadn't the courage to disobey Roland. She got under the covers without her clothes and he climbed in beside her, wearing his boxer shorts, black socks and undershirt. He jiggled her breasts, and rubbed his body against hers. They rubbed, puffed and sweated for about half an hour. Roland, despite Nini's best efforts, was obviously not attracted by her nakedness. He rose abruptly and said, "You really don't know what to do with a man. I always suspected you must be totally inexperienced. Now I see that I was right. You're rather an awkward love-maker." Roland did not look at Nini when he concluded coldly, "Get dressed and go back to your place."

Nini cried all night and missed her classes for two days. The third day she waited in the stairwell when she knew Neville was about to return from university, but she ran back to her apartment as soon as she heard his steps. On Friday night she heard his students arrive and the sounds of the party, but she didn't go downstairs. All night long, listening to the party, she imagined that she would kill herself and wondered how Roland would react when he saw her corpse. She decided it would be best to die peacefully in bed from an overdose of pills, but all she had in her medicine cabinet was aspirin. Cutting her wrists like the Romans while lying in the bathtub was another possibility: it was supposed to be a lengthy but painless way to die, though for her purposes it had its drawbacks. On the one hand, she would certainly look ludicrous sprawled dead in a bathtub wearing a flannel nightgown; on the other, the last thing she wanted was to reveal her naked body to Roland again. She couldn't believe, however, that Roland would never call her again and, with that thought, she finally slept.

Late in the morning Neville phoned, asked her why she hadn't come to his party and invited her for tea. Nini, terribly excited, immediately went shopping, bought a present of chocolates and then, after some contemplation, and remembering Roland's admiration of Prescott, bought an early edition, in two leather-bound volumes, of Prescott's *Conquest of Peru*. She wrapped the gifts in a piece of old Chinese silk her mother had given her and tied them with fine leather straps, one of her impulse buys before she had met Roland.

He said very little when she walked in and merely handed her a cup of tea. She imitated him, wordlessly putting the presents in his lap. He unwrapped the gifts, stared at the chocolates and the books and sighed despairingly.

"You've learned nothing and never will. What's been going on in your silly head during all our discussions? You daydream, simply daydream. I don't like presents and I don't like people who think presents are important. To top everything, you've bought me chocolates. Don't you know I'm a diabetic? And you wasted your money on these books. Paperback editions are good enough for anyone."

He rose and paced about his room, frustrated with Nini's lack of understanding.

"What do you think I am, some sort of whore?" His voice was high. "People like you think buying a present will put everything right. You're a child of your background and I can do nothing to change you. God knows I've tried. And you've spoiled it."

Nini shook her head, remembering the rage that had distorted Neville's face when he said "wasted your money." She remembered, too, how defeated and ashamed she had felt. How different she was now, she reflected, seeing her reflection in the mirror and behind her the bedroom—

hers and Barry's room. She turned from the mirror, collected her bag and ran down to the car. As she drove to the restaurant, she kept thinking about Toronto.

She had run out of Neville's room and upstairs to her own apartment. A few moments later she heard his footsteps at her door, the rustle of the silk wrappings and the sound of him walking downstairs. The chocolates, the books in their wrappings and the leather ties lay on her mat.

After that, Nini had seen Neville only by chance at the university library or in her building. He continued his usual gatherings Friday nights but she never resumed her friendship with his students because she couldn't bear to hear his name mentioned. In the spring, he left Toronto.

On her honeymoon in Italy, Barry mentioned that Roland Neville had been appointed ambassador to Hungary. Barry knew she had met Neville in Toronto, but was unaware of how painful their relationship had been. Had she described it to him, Barry would have become angry and hostile toward Roland; Nini thought it might hurt Barry's career if he was deliberately rude to an ambassador. She was naive and eager for Barry to succeed. How could she tell him that her depression about her sterility was inextricably mixed up with an aborted affair with Roland Neville? Her belief in her femininity had been so damaged that she had been unable to attract anyone (except Eleanor, she thought wryly) until Barry came along. Barry was just as intellectual as Roland, yet he restored her confidence in herself. He was amused and he even approved of her "thing-obsession" and told her that she made him happier than he ever had been in his life.

When Nini heard Roland's voice on the telephone, she knew her bitterness had vanished. All she felt was amazement and curiosity. She was certain Roland had lost the power to make her feel vulnerable. She readily agreed to meet him for lunch, but, for a reason she could not explain, she didn't mention her date to Barry.

11

As Nini and Roland were shown to their table near the road in the little garden at the Auberge de Nyon, Nini again worried that Roland would be disappointed by the lack of typically Swiss clientele. The restaurant was filled with groups of black, pink and amber people, all foreigners, United Nations delegates, Africans, Swedes, Indonesians. True, there was a real Swiss farmhouse across the road and terraced vineyards on the mountainside, but the vineyards were being dug by imported labouring men. Turks, Nini guessed.

"This is perfect," Roland Neville said. "Just what I was looking forward to. And it's so warm for November. Imagine still being able to eat outside." He picked up his glass of white wine and drank it down like vodka.

"I'm being impossible," he continued. "You must be surprised I called you. I won't give you any more of this inane foreplay. I hate chit-chat. I've asked you to see me for a specific reason. And I will not enjoy lunching with you unless I can explain why I'm here. I behaved badly in Toronto and I want you to soothe my conscience. I find that I need your forgiveness."

Nini had been hoping he wouldn't mention Toronto and the unpleasant memories she'd been brooding about during the past hour. But before she could respond, he said, "I should have written you a note when you married. But I was annoyed that you didn't invite me to your wedding. No," he corrected himself, "annoyed is not the proper word. I have nothing to be annoyed about where you are concerned. Unhappy, I should say. Unhappy more with myself than you. I've bought you a wedding present."

Just as Neville was reaching for his briefcase, the waiter set down two plates of escargots. Nini had ordered the meal in advance. She hoped Roland liked snails.

Neville ignored the food and proceeded to take two volumes of Prescott's *Conquest of Peru* from his briefcase. He handed them to Nini. "They're first editions. I bought them in London. Hardly a recompense for my behaviour. Once I told you that I didn't approve of gifts. Forgive me. It was an arrogant and harsh thing to say. This is my way of apologizing and you must allow me that luxury."

Neville left Nini no time to offer her thanks for the belated gifts. "You were the most beautiful and intelligent woman I had ever met," he said. "That's why I kept seeing you. I haven't met any woman since who appealed to me as much as you do. It was your misfortune to be my laboratory experiment. At the time you had no reality for me other than just that."

Neville sped through his confession in a self-possessed way, glancing only occasionally at Nini, who said nothing.

"When I realized my experiment wasn't working, I loathed myself, and childishly I blamed you. If Nini Sullivan couldn't turn me around, what woman could? In one sense – the most important as far as I'm concerned – our affair released me. I finally learned to accept myself as I was. You taught me to bend to my instincts.

"I'm a homosexual. I knew that even while I was seeing you. You were the victim of my deception. I should have told you, but I was weak; it was impossible for me to cope with the idea that I would never be able to love a woman erotically. You must understand that I was desperate to love you as another man would have. But I'm just not made that way. It has nothing to do with your beauty or sexuality. This is not an easy confession for me to make, Nini. I've come all the way from Budapest to tell you this. Does that mean anything to you? Are you shocked?"

"Not shocked," Nini said, staring at her untouched escargots, "but surprised. You seemed so masculine. I guess I don't know many homosexuals. I would have thought you would have to have limp wrists, like the hairdressers. Is that a crude thing to say? It's just that my knowledge is limited."

For diversion she attempted to pry an escargot from its shell, sneaking at the same time a look at Neville's wrists. They were wide and hairy.

"I must have behaved very badly," Neville rejoined, not answering Nini's question.

"Yes. Well, in a way you did," Nini said slowly. "For a while I even did think there was something wrong with me. You hurt my self-esteem. But it didn't last long," she lied, and the snail came free of its shell.

"There was–is–nothing wrong with you. The fault was always mine."

"Let's not talk about me forgiving you," she said suddenly. "As soon as you called me you were forgiven. And I've never received such a wedding present. The books touch me, of course, but your honesty, your coming here specifically to say this to me is the most generous gift I have ever received. What I feel now goes far beyond appreciation or gratefulness. Please don't apologize any more."

Nini thought she could almost fall in love with him again but in a better, safer way. She was relieved because an absurd sense of guilt, of being unfaithful to her husband, vanished as soon as Roland confided in her.

Now Neville sipped his wine instead of gulping it.

"Delicious. Absolutely delicious. The wine, the surroundings–and, especially, being with you. I feel strong enough to ask you another favour." Roland paused. When he resumed, there was a different quality in his voice. "I'm proud to be a member of this privileged group—men of history, I should say. You must admit I'm in good company. Think of Leonardo, Oscar Wilde, Proust. We have enriched civilization. But for some reason, most people are afraid of us. I don't know why. We're a bit like the Jews, I suppose. Not an original observation on my part, actually. Proust made the point. Can you keep this conversation to yourself, Nini? I have been very frank. Or do you feel compelled to tell your husband?"

Nini was intending to repeat everything to Barry but, as soon as Neville spoke, she changed her mind. He had honoured her with his confidence. She had no right to share it with anyone.

"It's your secret, Roland. There is no reason for anyone else to know."

Neville looked slightly uneasy, as if she hadn't quite understood him. "I really don't care if people do know. I'm not ashamed of the way I am. But few people want to understand."

"You're quite right," she assured him. "Most people have ill-thought-out prejudices. Why should you suffer from that? I won't tell anyone, not even Barry, although he's not like most people," she added quickly.

The waiter set a large salmon trout in a foaming butter sauce in front of them.

"I've never seen such a fish," Roland exclaimed. "What a change from Budapest. Next time I'm going to stay in Geneva for more than a day. I'm beginning to think it's normal to be followed in the streets, spied on by the maid and to have my bathroom wired for sound by the KGB. I had hardly realized how starved I am for good food and gossip."

Nini laughed and Neville continued, serious yet relaxed.

"I can't talk to anyone like this in Hungary, Nini, really. The listeners use positively anything that can be twisted into scandal. I've seen people turned into basket cases because the security police found out they were sleeping with their third secretary's wife. But that's enough about that. For twenty-four hours, Hungary doesn't exist for me. Now tell me about what's going on in the Permanent Mission here. Did Hugh tell you that I'm one of his oldest friends?''

"Yes, he mentioned you," she lied. "But no one in the Mission would dare call him by his first name. Tell me about him," she asked eagerly.

"I've known him since Oxford. We even vacationed in Greece before he married Beatrice. I was his junior in Paris and it was Hugh who recommended me for the Budapest post. I followed him as ambassador. It's important to be on good terms with him, Nini. When Hugh Hilary-Moulds recommends, headquarters listens. Your husband will profit by having Hugh as his mentor. And if Barry wants to get ahead in this game, he ought to hang onto Hugh's coat-tails. I'll never rise as high as Hugh, of course. Haven't got the same connections or ambition. But I consider him one of my best friends. You know, he teases me about my clothes. Hates my suits."

Neville was wearing a jacket with loud red checks.

"He once said I look like an eager sports announcer instead of a brooding, diabetic diplomat. The remark flattered me. I'll never buy a pin-striped suit. That's just one of the differences between us. Now, who else is at the Mission? I want to know everything. How do you like it here?''

"I like Geneva," Nini said carefully, "but I am a bit lonely. Except for Barry, I have no one to talk to – among the women, I mean. I need someone to gossip with. There's no one except Moira Belknap and Iris Beamer, and they think I'm a dose of strychnine."

"Come on, Nini, you're being too guarded. What's the matter? If I can trust you with my confidences, you can tell me yours. Maybe I can put in a good word with Hugh."

Nini knew that once she started she'd never stop. But she

didn't care. Roland was her friend and she was eager for a sympathetic ear.

"Well, the first few months we had no friends at the Mission. Stephen Belknap was perfectly decent to Barry at the office but I never heard from his wife at all. I'm sure it has something to do with Stephen and Barry having the same rank. Stephen must look upon Barry as a troublesome rival. Barry is so energetic, you see. He gets up every morning at five, puts animal skins under his skis and climbs up Mount Salève – instead of skiing down, like everyone else. He'll then arrive at the office at nine, with, say, a perfect draft of the speech the ambassador is due to make to the ILO. Stephen, on the other hand, is a likeable, intelligent person who has a tendency to catch cold when things get hectic."

The waiter appeared again, carrying a bowl of little yellow plums, *mirabelles*, with *crème fraîche*. He urged them to eat; these were the last fruit of the season. Nini's appetite was stimulated by the excitement of at last having a confidant. She took a large portion, dousing the plums with the rest of her wine.

"It's the Palais des Nations scandal that will get the Pikes and Belknaps together," Nini said cryptically. "Until now, all I've had to go on is what Barry tells me. No one has been gracious enough to ask me over. So I pump Barry mercilessly for gossip as soon as he comes home from the office."

The plums were delicious but the sun had disappeared and Nini felt chilled. She started to put on her sweater and Roland leaned over to help her.

"You see, Roland, there's been a kind of a tension at the office – Hilary-Moulds seems to favour Stephen one day and Barry the next. Barry's more interested in policy than in administration and spends hours interpreting and analyzing speeches for the ambassador. Stephen does other things for Hilary-Moulds – like measuring the space in his residence to make sure the government refrigerator will fit in.

"Hugh Hilary-Moulds doesn't see the Mission staff outside of working hours—except for Iris Beamer, his personal secretary. I've spoken to Iris a few times on the telephone and asked her to leave messages for Barry. But she has a hoity-toity manner and would never pass on any message of mine. Is it customary for ambassadors to be so aloof with their juniors, Roland?" Nini didn't wait for an answer.

"Iris really runs the Mission, you know. I don't mean to be so critical of your friend, but Hilary-Moulds speaks as little as possible to any of the officers. You're not that way in Budapest, are you? His instructions are all in memorandum form—even if Stephen and Barry are sitting in the next office. With the door open! The instructions are dictated to Iris and she deals them out capriciously. Don't you think that's an odd way to conduct business in such a small office?"

Nini stared penetratingly at Neville for several seconds and it was clear that this time she wanted an answer.

"People bother Hugh," Neville said carefully. "He really doesn't like being too close to anyone. It's just his style."

"What about Iris, then?" Nini demanded a bit sharply. "Have you ever met her?"

Neville shook his head and gestured to the waiter for another bottle of wine.

"She's attractive, late thirties, small, dark, with her hair pulled back in a chignon. Barry says she looks like a Bolshoi dancer a wee bit past her prime."

Nini paused. "It took me three weeks to piece that description out of what Barry told me," she said almost to herself. "She dresses well—rather à haut chic, I understand. The secretaries call her "Windsor," after the Duchess. Everyone at the Mission hates her. Don't you think it's bad form for an ambassador to have an affair with his assistant?"

Nini knew she was being indiscreet but it was so good to have someone to gossip with besides Barry. The sun had returned and warmed her neck.

"Not because it's sexually immoral, but you do agree it causes messy office politics?"

Neville shrugged non-committally.

"Perhaps," she said, "you're more broadminded than I am, but I think it's unhealthy to know exactly what's going on with your one and only during work *and* having the last word in bed, too."

Neville was smiling in a way that Nini remembered from Toronto. She realized she was sounding provincial, a bit priggish. "Of course," she said, modifying her position slightly, "no one knows for sure if Iris is really Hilary-Moulds's mistress. They haven't been caught in any compromising positions. No stroking or kissing during office hours."

At this Neville burst out laughing and said, "Go on, you're amusing me."

Nini understood that he wasn't mocking her. He was genuinely enjoying himself.

"And although Julio drives them home – both sitting like royalty in the back seat of the Oldsmobile – Iris is always dropped off and picked up at her own apartment. Otis – he's the security officer – checked that out."

Nini paused, hoping Neville might have something to add, but when he remained silent, she continued.

"You've heard that Hilary-Moulds has the reputation of liking intellectual ladies, haven't you? It's even rumoured that, when he was first secretary in London during the war, he had an affair with Virginia Woolf, or whatever she did with men. I suppose you'd know all about that. He's a very cultivated man, quite obsessed with *objets d'art*."

Nini gave Roland an uneasy glance, knowing his objections to materialism.

"He collects chess sets, original prints, carpets and art-nouveau jewellery. Did he always have those tastes? Not that anyone in the Mission besides me cares about such things. Barry sometimes says that Hilary-Moulds is too much of a dilettante to be really serious. Is it possible that he's become something of a myth in the diplomatic world?"

"Absolutely, Nini," Neville replied, pouring her more wine. "Apart from his literary connections, he is, after all, the son-in-law of Lord North and knows every banker in the world – Jardines in Hong Kong, the Rothschilds, and the stuffy Swiss ones, too. Beaverbrook used to ask him to dinner during the war. And he has the most remarkable connections with the third world. Some of their leaders knew him at Oxford, where he studied constitutional law. At least two of his African school pals asked him to draft the constitutions of their countries when the British left."

Neville finished his plums with gusto, even sucking on the pits a bit noisily.

"And what a career," he went on. "First secretary in London before and during the war, then Paris as embassy counsellor, then in 1950 to NATO when the Cold War was at its coldest – NATO attracts the ablest young men, you know, the technocrats who are such an influence in Europe now. Moulds met most of the future European prime ministers; he dined with them at the Paris bistros when they were just junior officials having fun together. He spoke French and German perfectly and was the youngest officer in the Canadian foreign service to become an ambassador."

The waiter came round with a second bowl of plums and Nini and Neville both helped themselves. Many of the tables had emptied and no new clients had entered the restaurant. The luncheon hour was almost over. Nini had been to this place before and she knew no one would rush them.

Neville continued enthusiastically. "Hugh's reports from Budapest on the Communist-bloc countries were read avidly all the way up to the prime minister – who was so impressed he sent them to Eisenhower. The prime minister never reads ambassadors' reports. They say if Hugh does well here, he might become a serious candidate for the

NATO secretary-general job in Paris, although I gather some people say it will be hard for anyone who hasn't been in politics and been a minister. I'm a bit jealous, I suppose. But he deserves the job. He's a professional. That's my highest compliment."

Neville looked away from Nini and stared at his surroundings, his eyes blinking. He seemed as satisfied with the restaurant as he did with himself.

Nini decided to tell Neville about the Palais des Nations affair, if there was time. She looked at her watch. They had just over an hour before Roland's plane.

"I guess he is the perfect diplomat," she said. "But you might think that an ambitious man like that would be a little more careful. I would have thought he'd be humiliated. I even think humiliated is too feeble a word. If it had been Barry, I think he would have slit his throat. Or resigned. But Barry would never allow himself to get in such a position. Anyway, what I know about correct diplomatic behaviour wouldn't buy you a *café au lait*. Perhaps Moulds's reaction was that of a professional."

"Nini, I suspect you know a lot about correct diplomatic behaviour."

She was grateful for his compliment.

"But what are you talking about?" he asked.

The soft November sun now shone directly on Nini's face. She felt relaxed and happy and was dying to tell Roland everything. "Well, Hilary-Moulds was supposed to chair a meeting about fishing rights with the American, Soviet, Japanese and Norwegian ambassadors and a few others. It was to take place in one of those green rooms in the Palais des Nations, facing Lake Geneva. The old League of Nations building is rather what Albert Speer might have designed for Hitler's new Berlin. It's overblown beaux-arts, Greek temple – or Roman amphitheatre – fitted with green marble from top to toe. Nothing but wasted space for wasted talks. Vast and pretentious enough for mediocrities to feel at home. You can see I haven't much time for those UN people."

"You're harsh, Nini, very harsh. I still have hope." He spoke with a smile.

"Did you know there was an international architecture contest for the construction of the League of Nations building? Le Corbusier sent in the most visionary blueprint but it was rejected because it had been drawn in pencil instead of ink. Typical."

Neville shook his head as if he, too, regretted the loss of Le Corbusier's genius. She prattled on, pleased with her story.

"Stephen, Barry and Iris accompanied Hilary-Moulds to the meeting. It was an awkward group, but Barry and Stephen went along because Hilary-Moulds likes to walk around in front of the other ambassadors with a trail of assistants.

"Despite his reputation as a ladies' man, I don't think Hilary-Moulds is very handsome. I saw him once at a large reception at the UN, but he didn't talk to me. We weren't introduced. Anyway, you know what he looks like – pudgy hands, pudgy face with a grey cathedral moustache that points up to an insignificant nose. Did he always have that moustache? I think he's about thirty pounds overweight. When he climbed the front stairs of the League of Nations building, he breathed heavily, Barry says. His cheeks were pink, not healthily so, but high-blood-pressure pink. Barry thinks that in addition to chessmen, prints and jewellery, the ambassador collects rare old cognac."

Nini hoped she didn't sound too catty.

"They settled in the marble room, Iris beside the ambassador and Barry and Stephen well behind. All Barry saw was the folds of skin between the ambassador's white collar and grey head, and Iris's chignon held fast with her silver art-nouveau comb.

"Barry and Stephen were there for ceremonial reasons

only, because the ambassador had not asked or told them about his negotiating position." Nini expected Roland to comment on this aspect of Hilary-Moulds's professional behaviour. But he sat quietly, saying nothing. She continued.

"The first speaker, Kamizuki, began a long speech in Japanese. There was no simultaneous translation, and Barry and Stephen, out of boredom, began to exchange notes like the boys in the back rows at grade school. Stephen wrote that Hilary-Moulds had given Iris the comb. Apparently, he had presented it to her in the Oldsmobile while Julio was driving. Julio immediately passed this information on to Otis."

Neville sipped his wine slowly as Nini spoke, listening carefully but never interrupting.

"Time passed and the voice of the Japanese ambassador went on. Stephen, by this time, was making a list of the cheapest fondue restaurants in Geneva, for Barry's information, and Barry was looking at a paper with the recent promotions of junior officers that had just come in on the telex from Ottawa."

Nini paused, hoping Roland would make a little joke about boring UN meetings, but again he was silent.

"The Japanese stopped talking but the English translation did not begin. When Barry looked up the Japanese was still standing, as if he had not finished his speech. Hilary-Moulds, who had been sitting at the head of the table, had disappeared. Iris was rushing out the door. Everyone, except for the standing Japanese, sat in silence. After several minutes, the Norwegian, who had been sitting next to Hilary-Moulds, announced, 'I don't think the chairman felt too well.' No procedure had been set down for such an event. The ambassadors began to mull over something other than fishing rights, with Kamizuki still on his feet. They voted unanimously to find out if their chairman was alive or dead. The American, Soviet, Norwegian and Japanese ambassadors trouped through the door, with Barry and Stephen following.

"Hilary-Moulds was just outside the ante-room, lying face down on the floor. His trousers and shorts were tangled in a bunch around his ankles and shiny black oxfords. Iris was kneeling, her face hidden, only her silver comb showing to its best advantage. She was inserting a suppository between Hilary-Moulds's buttocks."

Nini stopped talking and stared at Neville, waiting for his reaction. He shook his head as if he felt some mild distress for his friend. Nini decided that Roland was being rather close-mouthed about Hilary-Moulds, given the peculiarity of the scene. She tried to be as fair as possible.

"It's difficult, I know, in Switzerland, to buy even aspirin in other than suppository form. I suppose we can't pre-judge their relationship absolutely," she interjected before proceeding with her narrative.

"Certain signs, according to Barry—an eyelid flickering, a tremor through the body—made it obvious that Moulds was not only alive but aware of his audience. However, every-body thought it best to pretend he had lost consciousness. Iris kept her position when the ambassadors walked in. They were paralyzed at first sight of the prone figure, then simultaneously turned their eyes from the exposed flesh. Barry said Hilary-Moulds might have been a mutilated corpse and the ambassadors squeamish mourners by the open coffin."

At this, Neville chuckled.

"Iris, apparently satisfied with the successful disap-pearance of the suppository, began to pull Hilary-Moulds's shorts up his fat, hairless legs. Barry stooped to help. The shorts were embroidered at the hem with fancy lettering, "N of L" entwined through a coat of arms that included a leek rampant. North of Llandudno, Barry thinks. Hilary-Moulds must have inherited his father-in-law's underwear.

"It was difficult rolling the body side to side to pull up the clothes – the ambassador still lay defiantly doggo. Iris couldn't have dressed him without Barry's help. They finally pulled the trousers on, leaving the buttons undone and the braces trailing on the floor, and heaved him over on his back so they could loosen his tie and collar. Barry said later he was wondering if Hilary-Moulds, lying face-up in view of the frozen ambassadors, could maintain the illusion of being unconscious. Barry took off his jacket and placed it under Hilary-Moulds's head, but Hilary-Moulds's eyes remained firmly closed. Iris finally spoke, cool as a head nurse: 'He needs a blanket.'

"The ambassadors woke from the trance, removed their jackets and covered their colleague. The American went first, then the Russian, followed by the Japanese and the Norwegian. It was, Stephen described later, as if they were laying wreaths, especially since an order of protocol prevailed in the dropping of the coats."

The waiter came to their table and placed the bill beside Neville. Without stopping her narrative, Nini leaned over, took the bill and continued.

"The ambassadors stood about for a bit, wanting to leave Hilary-Moulds alone so he could open his eyes. But where could they go without their jackets? The American consulted with the Russian and they decided to go back to the conference room to resume their meeting, leaving Barry and Stephen to watch over their boss – and the coats. The ambassadors left without argument; the last, the Norwegian, closed the door," Nini concluded.

"And that was that?" Neville asked.

"That was that," she replied, "except for the party. A week later, the Pikes and the Belknaps received a formal invitation to dine with the ambassador at his residence. It's tomorrow night and I can hardly wait. You have to agree, Roland, that Hilary-Moulds is cooler than most. In fact, looking back on the whole affair, I'd say that he was a man trying to turn a misfortune into an advantage."

"A lesser man," Neville agreed, now laughing, "would certainly have taken a long vacation far from the witnesses of his humiliation. The story, however, proves again that I must congratulate Hugh for his professionalism. I don't think I would have been able to behave with such equanimity. And we have to remember that Hugh's health isn't all that it should be. I know that he suffers from high blood pressure. He drinks more cognac than is good for him. Did he mention his high-blood-pressure difficulties to anyone afterward?"

"He said nothing," answered Nini.

"Hugh follows the gentleman's credo: 'Never apologize, never explain.'"

"Except to Iris," Nini replied.

"You shouldn't worry too much about Iris. Hugh's a very complex man and I've never known anyone to get the better of him. She may seem like the queen bee – but Hugh knows how to keep queen bees in their places. Look at Lady Beatrice."

Before Nini had a chance to ask, "What about Lady Beatrice?" Roland put a restraining hand on hers and took back the bill.

"This is my lunch. You've provided the entertainment."

He left a wad of Swiss francs on the table without counting and looked at his watch. Nini realized that it was time to leave the sun, the vineyards and a few amber delegates who were still sitting over matching-colour brandies. The two of them rose and left together for the airport. As she drove Roland through the countryside, she wondered why he hadn't said more to her about Hilary-Moulds. He seemed content, however, and kissed her on both cheeks when she dropped him at the entrance to the airport in Cointrin.

12

The same evening Barry was sitting on the fake-fur sofa
Nini so disliked, correcting a draft of Hilary-Moulds's next
speech. Nini sat by him sipping Cointreau, wanting to talk.
"Homosexuals, Barry. Tell me what you think."

He looked up.

"Why should I think anything? What's put them in your
head?"

"Well," she said, "there seem to be more than I realized."

"So what?" he replied, still half engrossed in his work.

"It always surprises me. I'm usually the last to know."

"This sounds ominous." He laughed. "Are you hinting
that I might be keeping a dreadful secret from you for the
sake of my career?" Carefully he put down his papers.
"Let's play this game. Sit on my lap and test my hetero-
reaction instincts. How soon will you ring the bell?"

Nini knew it would be too soon and stopped him from
unbuttoning her blouse. She did not want to be distracted
from her thoughts just then.

"I was just wondering about homosexuals because I think
I'm a bit of an innocent."

"Innocent!" Barry exclaimed. "What about Eleanor? First
pass made by best friend, right in your home in Derby."

"Eleanor's different."

"Different from what?"

"Different from the men."

"So you're saying lesbianism is okay and male homosexuality is not?"

"I'm confused." Nini didn't want to betray Roland.

"Then what are you talking about?"

"Oh, I bumped into a diplomat from the Swedish embassy. Somebody said he was queer."

"What's his name?" Barry asked.

Nini thought quickly. She knew she would break any confidence if she judged it critical to Barry's career. But, she reasoned, as Roland Neville had no relevance to Barry's life, his secret could not be of any use to Barry, either. She decided it wasn't necessary to mention Roland.

"You don't know him. But he didn't look or act queer."

"Most of them don't," Barry said. 'There's nothing wrong with homosexuality. I just can't understand it myself, that's all. Look at the writers and the painters who were homosexuals. On the other hand, it does become a problem in a foreign ministry."

"What do you mean?"

"Lots of countries, especially the Muslim ones, disapprove of homosexuality. Not that it isn't rampant there. But it's against the Koran. Some Islamic countries have been known to put diplomats to death or cut off their arms if they're caught with a boy. And, of course, a single male, especially a homosexual, posted in an Eastern European country presents a problem. He becomes lonely and picks up boyfriends who are certain to be controlled by the KGB. Imagine how easily you can have a nasty case of blackmail on your hands."

"Do you disapprove of homosexuals?" Nini asked.

"I don't approve or disapprove. They're a fact of life. I believe they should be free to accept their natures, but without too much *sturm und drang* for the rest of us. Is that enough about homosexuals, Nini?"

He pulled her on his lap and began to undo her buttons, this time with more success.

13

It was the evening of Hilary-Moulds's party and Nini was excited to be meeting the enigmatic ambassador at last. To get to Hilary-Moulds's residence, the Pikes drove along narrow Swiss roads lined with tall hedges; there seemed to be a blind curve at every turn. There were large round traffic mirrors at each point where the hedges and driveways met.

"The mirrors are necessary," Barry explained, "because the hedges block the view of the approaching cars."

"And the hedges are necessary," Nini replied, "because they block the view of the curious from the estates of the rich."

Hilary-Moulds's residence was called Parc des Cèdres. It was landscaped in the Italian style, with gravel walks that could have been used as measures in a geometry class and cedars trimmed to perfect triangles. Each cedar was separated from the other by a small, smooth ball of yew. The distance between the yews and cedars was arithmetically precise. Hilary-Moulds's gardener was obviously an expert in topiary.

The Pikes' invitation said "7:30 for 8:00" and they had sufficient time to sight-see as they walked up the path edged with the regulated, perfectly clipped bushes. Three cement benches – the kind, Nini thought, that give you piles – were placed in a semi-circle on the largest rectangle of gravel at the high part of the garden where the mountain view was best. The house itself was enclosed by another wall of cedars, each at least twelve feet high. Everything was white gravel and evergreens, with a patch of finely mowed grass just at the entrance – not a flower in sight.

"Very austere, very masculine," Nini said to Barry. "An urn of red geraniums would belittle the landscaping. Mother would loathe it."

Barry and Nini were the last to arrive. Julio greeted them and showed them into "le petit salon." "Le grand salon" was for larger dinners and more important people, as Nini learned later. Hugh Hilary-Moulds, wearing a *sang de boeuf* velvet smoking jacket, rose and kissed her on the cheek.

"Who's this?" he asked. "Fresh and pink as an Ursuline novice. It must be Nini Pike. Exactly how I imagined you. I hate formal introductions, don't you? Barry, sit down beside Mrs. Belknap. Nini will stay near me. What a becoming dress. Most of our Canadian diplomatic wives save dinner dresses for wearing in their coffins. You are about a hundred years from that. But I'm old. Do you think I should save this jacket for my coffin?"

"I like your jacket," Nini replied.

"Let me tell you a secret," Moulds went on. "I met your mother eons ago. She invited me for tea in that sumptuous house in Derby. Did she ever mention my name? I was probably too insignificant for her to remember, but *she* was a memorable woman. I think you will take after your mother. Very definitely. Except that you are prettier. Please don't tell her I said so."

Nini's mother had mentioned Hilary-Moulds coming for tea a thousand times, but Nini was too proud to admit it to him.

There was a young woman sitting in a black leather armchair, wrapped, sari fashion, in a Madeira lace table-cloth. She looked as if she hated everyone in the room. A young blond man was standing beside her; he smiled at Nini. This was the first time Nini had set eyes on Stephen and Moira Belknap.

Another woman rose at the sound of Hilary-Moulds's voice. He gestured vaguely at her.

"You do know Iris."

"Mrs. Pike and I have spoken on the telephone," Iris said. Iris was wearing a long navy silk hostess gown, with a cream lace collar. Expensive but not actressy, Nini thought. She had imagined Iris dressing rather theatrically. Her hair was pulled back with the help of the silver filigree comb.

Barry went over to Moira, and Hilary-Moulds sat down beside Nini on a large black sofa. Stephen went to another part of the room and carried back two occasional chairs for Iris and himself. The ambassador was ebullient. Nini found it impossible to imagine him without his trousers and shorts, lying on the floor inhaling a suppository. Could an anus inhale, she wondered.

Except for a few eighteenth-century harp chairs, the furniture was made of black leather. The room would have been sombre if it were not for about a dozen silken prayer mats hanging, like tapestries, on three walls. The fourth wall was almost all mirror and the delicate colouring of the Orientals, blues, reds and mauves – glowed in double and even triple image because of the glass. Hilary-Moulds had brought the furniture and the rugs from London. They were his personal belongings. The mirror had been paid for by the government, at Hilary-Moulds's insistence. When he left Geneva, everything in the room would go except the mirror.

"Julio makes excellent Manhattans, not too sweet," Hilary-Moulds said. "I hope you don't think cocktails are vulgar. I must say I adore them. Naturally, we have wine and everything else if you prefer."

Nini had the impression that Hilary-Moulds was speaking exclusively to her. The earlier arrivals had no drinks at all. She said she would try a Manhattan.

"Good girl. And what will you have, Mrs. Belknap?"
Stephen interrupted.

"Call her Moira. She hates the sound of Belknap."

Moira ignored her husband.

"Apple juice, please."

Moira was staring in mid-distance, not focussing on anyone. Barry leaned over and tried to catch her attention. Stephen said something to Iris about skiing. Hilary-Moulds and Nini had Manhattans, Barry and Stephen whisky, and Moira seemed satisfied with her juice. Iris was drinking champagne from a tulip-shaped glass. Nini would have preferred champagne, but it had not been suggested as a possibility.

Nini tried to concentrate on the ambassador. Build up his ego a bit.

"I really do like the colour of your jacket," she said. "It's the same *sang de boeuf* shade you find in those old Chinese vases."

"My girl," he said, "that's a compliment coming from you. After all, I know the house where you were born. Not to be sneezed at. The bargeboard, the Chippendale and especially the Spode. Your mother hasn't sold it, broken it or traded it for a Mercedes?"

Nini told him that her mother had given her the service plates as a wedding present.

"Use them. Use them," he said. "Don't keep them packed away in the cellar. But wash the plates yourself. Never trust the help. My wife's father gave us eighteenth-century Venetian glass when we married. But Bea let the servants do everything. And of course, the glass is gone, smashed to atoms. Barry is lucky to have married you. And I don't say this because of your mother's Spode plates."

Moira was speaking to Barry. He sat there, nodding seriously, patiently, his six-foot-six frame in a tense crouch. Moira's voice carried across the room.

"Geneva is a fleshpot. I can only feel clean at the top of

the Salève, where the air is clear and I can see all the way down the mountain. If I don't climb to the top at least twice a week, I feel corruption in my soul."

Barry said, "Well, I go up there to hack around on my skis. I work better after exercise."

Hilary-Moulds winked at Nini.

"Mrs. Belknap must be reading *Heidi*. I'm delighted she's taking an interest in the regional literature. Do you have this need to escape from the fleshpots around us?"

"If I climb to the top of the Grande Rue shopping for antiques, I get vertigo," Nini replied. "I drink a glass of wine at the Café des Artistes at the end of the street, which usually restores me to health."

"But Nini," Moulds exclaimed, "that is my secret place. It's a student's café, but they do serve a good, crisp pizza. I sneak away and stuff myself when I'm supposed to go to one of those boring Swedish parties. Next time we'll go together to the café. Would you like that?"

Nini wondered if Barry was included in the invitation.

"Bring your Manhattan to the table. Julio is giving us the high sign. Soup's on. I hope there is something delicious to eat."

Hilary-Moulds took Nini by the arm and led her into the dining room. The rest followed at a distance. Hilary-Moulds whispered, "What is Mrs. Belknap wearing? I spoke of coffins earlier. Perhaps that's why I think of a shroud."

Nini decided to be truthful.

"I believe she must have made a table-cloth into a sari."

"You're absolutely right! No wonder there is something familiar about the material. All those tiny shops in Madeira, with mats and cloths pinned up on the walls for the tourists. I vacationed there last year. See, there are gravy stains on the skirt. I now understand why she doesn't feel clean in the lower regions."

The table was laid with standard government china and silver. Someone had placed a couple of zinnias in the centre

97

of the table. Nini had expected something more from Hugh Hilary-Moulds. The first course was already on the plate – hard-boiled egg in aspic, with shredded green pepper. Nini was put on Hilary-Moulds's right. As he sawed through the egg in silence, the ambassador looked distressed.

"I thought the egg was supposed to be runny. I told Juanita *oeuf mollet.* That means soft, doesn't it? Not cemented. Juanita is Julio's wife. He's a first-class chauffeur and butler, but Juanita is definitely not a first-class cook."

"When you employ a married couple as your servants, one compensates for the other," Nini said. "I've never seen a husband and wife in service with equal capabilities. It's practically a scientific law."

Hilary-Moulds looked at her as if this were the most profound statement he had heard in all of his diplomatic career. His voice was serious.

"You are going to be a very successful wife. I can't say how jealous I am of Barry."

Barry, hearing his name, looked away from his empty plate. He had already gobbled up his egg, and decided to talk to Hilary-Moulds.

"Sir, did you have a chance to look at my analysis of the negotiations taking place at the GATT meeting? I wonder if we should say something to the British. They seem to be taking too much for granted. I was speaking to Peach from Trade and Commerce and he says his minister is unhappy with their attitude. We are, after all, in the driver's seat with the copper."

Hilary-Moulds looked annoyed.

"I thought Stephen was to do the analysis."

Stephen reddened.

"I hope you don't mind, sir. We traded assignments. Barry's just had six months with the Trade and Commerce people back home. He really is more familiar with the subject than I am. I'm doing the labour relations next month for the ILO meeting." Stephen paused, considering his next sentence. He decided to risk honesty. "Actually, I was planning to take Moira and the children away for a few days up to Villars. For some hiking. The trade paper was to be finished next week." He paused again, but received no reply. "I told Iris about our switch."

Hilary-Moulds didn't look at Iris.

"Of course, I don't mind you going on holiday, Stephen. But I do like to know who's doing what. I'm an *amateur* of your drafting style. You have a succinct way of putting things. I shall miss it."

Barry stared at his plate. His drafting style was just as good as Stephen's, probably better.

"I'll be looking forward to what you have to say about Vaskov, the Bulgarian lout who is running the show at the ILO. Keep an eye on him. He's trouble," Moulds said, asserting his authority.

During the exchange, Nini had kept her eyes on Iris, who was as rigid as a beagle sniffing partridge. She kept one hand raised, like a paw, holding her wine glass.

"I didn't think you'd mind, Hugh," she said. "Stephen has been working very hard. And Barry wanted to give him a hand. Mrs. Belknap is pregnant and the doctor thought she should get away for a few days."

Hilary-Moulds touched Moira on the arm.

"Not to fuss. Not to fuss. I'm delighted with the news. Iris was right not to bother to tell me. Iris, you made the right decision, as always. How many children do you have now, Mrs. Belknap?"

"Three."

"Ambitious lady."

Hilary-Moulds seemed to have forgotten or deliberately ignored Barry's question.

The next course arrived: mixed-up rice and peas and dry chicken dampened with canned morel mushrooms, which to Nini retained the taste of metal. After a mouthful of this food, Hilary-Moulds put on his glasses, speared a mushroom with his fork and held it at eye level.

"I think it's poisonous," he said. "When I dined with Hubert Humphrey at La Perle du Lac, I ate the same sort of crinkly mushroom—perfectly edible. These are not. Juanita is angry with me because I told her the coffee this morning had been re-heated from the night before. Her mother is a gypsy and these mushrooms are Juanita's revenge because I was rude at breakfast."

"The mushrooms are not poisonous, Mr. Hilary-Moulds, just canned," Nini interrupted. "I buy morels fresh at the Saturday-morning mushroom market on the quay."

The ambassador spoke as if to himself.

"Juanita doesn't go to the mushroom market on Saturday morning like normal people. Too busy practising her mother's curses, which will make me writhe in pain and have a loose stomach. Juanita said she was going to serve an Italian specialty this evening, copied from the personal recipe book of our Sardinian laundress. *Risi bisi,* she called it. *Risi bisi.* It sounded appetizing in Italian. But this damn mess is just rice and peas. I used to shove them off my plate at boarding school. There, at least, the cook didn't mix the rice with the peas."

Hilary-Moulds seemed upset and began to separate the grain from the vegetable with his fork.

"What super food."

Moira spoke.

"We never eat anything like this at home. We can't afford it," she explained. "The boys get Kraft Dinner from Denmark. Ostermann Petersen sends it in tax free. I give Stephen *boules de Bâle* in the evenings. He doesn't need anything else because of those rich lunches he's always getting asked to. Steak in garlic sauce, salmon trout in hollandaise, filet of perch *meunière.* Business lunches. Naturally, the wives are never invited."

Moira darted a glance at Nini as if she thought Nini might be the exception to the rule.

Iris asked, "What are *boules de Bâle*?"

"The poor Swiss in Carouge eat them for their supper," Moira replied, failing to answer Iris's question.

"Carouge is a working-class district in Geneva, mostly inhabited by transient Portuguese and Spanish workers. Not typically Swiss at all. There is no such thing as a poor Swiss," Hilary-Moulds said.

"All the *charcuteries* in the less fashionable districts – including the one where we live – sell *boules de Bâle*," Moira insisted.

Stephen explained. "They're enormous sausages that look like pale, giant slugs. Made from offal and the parts of animals no one likes."

Moira seemed pleased to have the centre of attention. "I splurge for Sunday lunch – if Stephen is home. I get a rump steak from the boucherie chevaline. It's excellent. Come for lunch." She invited the company. "I'll bet there's no one here at this table who'd dream they're eating horse meat."

There was silence for a moment.

"Ah, yes," Hilary-Moulds said, "I have passed those butcher shops with the little prancing pony signs."

Moira was genuinely enthusiastic for the first time that evening – except for the moment when she had spoken of mountain-tops.

"My boucherie chevaline is clean and pleasant and thoroughly supervised by the Swiss authorities. The butcher has a display of fresh flowers on the counter. His ponies are raised specifically for slaughtering. You don't eat the old nags ready for the glue factory. That's just an Anglo-Saxon prejudice."

"I'm so glad you are immersing yourself in Swiss customs and culture," the ambassador answered.

Moira looked at him suspiciously. Iris spoke placatingly. "With the three boys, Moira, you must have to watch your food budget. I'm sure they're worth the scrimping and saving. Have you any children, Mrs. Pike?"

Barry glared at Iris. He always answered this question for Nini.

"We don't have children." His voice was loud. Barry became annoyed when people mentioned the word "children." He knew it made Nini think of nursing mothers staining their blouses and dropping La Leche pamphlets wherever they went. The more aggressive manifestations of motherhood made her hostile and self-conscious because of her own inadequacy. When the subject was raised, Barry was always quick to protect Nini – from herself as well as from others.

Hilary-Moulds didn't seem to care for the subject either. "Do you shop at the boucherie chevaline, too, Nini?"

"I'm a provincial with country prejudices. We never ate horse meat in Derby – or pony meat, for that matter."

"Provincial? You have been here only a few months and yet you speak good French, go to the mushroom market, and know how to dress for dinner. Tell me in what way you are a provincial."

The Manhattan and the wine had gone to Nini's head and she felt at ease with Hilary-Moulds. She wanted to confess her secrets, her weaknesses.

"I still have a provincial habit," she said, "which I inherited from mother. Barry thinks we're silly. Mother orders pure-silk satin squares from a lady who lives in Antwerp. She sews Belgian lace around the edges."

"Very elegant. I see nothing silly about pure-silk satin squares."

"Well, you see, mother and I provide them for our house guests. The ladies. The squares are supposed to cover up undies that might be left on a bedroom chair when the guests are changing. Barry laughs at me when I hand a square to a guest. He says I'm prudish, which is another way of saying provincial. But it is our family tradition."

"Barry doesn't understand your kind of fastidiousness," he said. "He's a restless, zealous man. When I see Barry loop and coil his extraordinary body among diminutive Japanese, Koreans and Burmese, giving each a small but highly concentrated dose of his attention, I can only admire. Why, your husband mediates truces between third-world nations with the compunction and fairness of a Spock mother inspecting the finger-paintings of her triplets. I wish I were as single-minded as he. Barry will go far."

"Do you really think so?" Nini asked, trying to make her voice sound casual. "Barry's terribly conscientious. He really does drive himself. My father never worked as hard as Barry. I think I'm Barry's only vice."

"You are his greatest asset. He'd be an impossible man if he didn't have you to soften his edges. You make him human."

Nini was not sure whether Hilary-Moulds was complimenting her or insulting Barry. But the wine and the ambassador's attention made her happy and she didn't want to spoil the moment by clarifying the ambiguity in the ambassador's remark.

"If you were my wife," Hilary-Moulds went on, "I'm sure we wouldn't be eating glutinous rice pudding for dessert. This must be rice left over from the *risi bisi*. Juanita has mixed raisins with it instead of peas. I have a thrifty cook. Except I never see any of the money she saves on my meals. Though you'd never suspect it, I do give her a generous food budget. I'm not one of those ambassadors who lives off allowances and pockets his salary."

Moulds's voice rose higher and higher.

"When I was a first secretary," he continued, "there was one skinflint who used to have a display turkey at his Christmas party. He'd invite the world and everyone would stare at the buffet table, waiting for the carving. This was just after the war and people were hungrier then. Well, somehow the waiter never got around to cutting up the bird, being under strict instructions from Her Excellency to leave it untouched. The next day the ambassador and his

103

wife went to a ski hut in Gstaadt and were sustained for a week by the show-piece on their buffet table." Hilary-Moulds let out a disgusted snort and asserted, "Juanita does not spend my allowances at the market to buy good food for my guests. She deposits it in her private pension fund at the Banque Suisse."

Hilary-Moulds's voice suddenly disappeared and he sounded resentful and sorry for himself. "Here I am, Hugh Hilary-Moulds, ambassador of the sixth largest trading nation in the world, and I daren't invite anyone who matters to my house for dinner because of a crazed, mean cook. There are certain key people I must entertain, but they all live in the fleshpot, as Mrs. Belknap describes this town."

A distasteful look crossed his face as he glanced at Moira.

"Geneva has led them to expect too high a standard at dinner parties. Don't let any Puritan tell you otherwise, Nini. Jane Austen was right. Everything happens at parties."

"Who are the key people you must entertain?" Nini asked.

"Everyone from columnists with the *New York Times* to Jamal, the Indian Maharajah, who wears the Sacred Thread and is head of the refugee movement. Everyone from visiting American senators, like Hubert and Averell, to Moorehouse Dhroshky, president of the Thoreau Institute. Among other activities, he seems to be bankrolling third-world intellectuals who are certain to become top despots in their respective countries."

Nini felt rather smug because she had met a few of the key people.

"Mr. Hilary-Moulds," she said, "perhaps you don't know it, but we live in the same apartment building as the Moorehouse Dhroshkys. In fact, we are on the same floor and I chat with Nicole, his wife, over the balcony. Nicole and I share a pot of geraniums that sits on the dividing ledge. I water it on Mondays and Thursdays and she waters it Tuesdays and Fridays. We let it dry out over the weekend. That's Nicole's geranium theory. They have a much larger apartment than ours – she sleeps three servants. Barry saw Averell Harriman pass by our door on the way to the Dhroshkys' for dinner. I wouldn't have known who he was but Barry recognized him. Once, when Barry went to Milan to lecture on international something, Nicole asked me to fill in at the last minute. Isaiah Berlin and the Maharajah were my dinner partners." Nini cast a guilty eye at Barry but he was not paying attention. Moira and Iris seemed to have their eyes on her, though. Nini realized Moulds's attention was a great social coup. She decided to ignore the women's glances.

"The Maharajah took off his shirt and showed me the Sacred Thread. It's worn cross-ways over his heart and must touch his skin." Nini drew a line across her own chest to make the point. "We ate fresh *foie gras* and *mandarines givrées* for dessert. You know, they squish up the mandarin, mix it with ice cream, and stuff it all back into the empty shells and put the little caps back on so they look like real fresh oranges. *Tromp l'oeil* cooking. Nicole says she knows how to train servants. Their butler is not married to the cook. I didn't realize that Moorehouse Dhroshky was important to our country."

Nini was tipsy – but not too tipsy to think she sounded foolish.

Hilary-Moulds, however, did not seem put out by her prattling or by her vaguely gauche disclosure of high connections. He was thoughtful.

"Dhroshky has tremendous contacts. A very useful man. I have never been to the Dhroshkys' for dinner. But then I've never asked him to Parc des Cèdres. Impossible, with Juanita brewing such potions in the kitchen. The prime minister is coming to Geneva in a few months for the opening of the Eighteen-Nation Disarmament Conference and I must give him a grand dinner. Who is to cook it? The Sevillian shrew? If I want to have exploratory discussions with certain key people, including Dhroshky, I must find a chef between now and the time of his visit."

Even in her inebriated state, Nini was interested to notice that Moulds still felt he had to climb.

"Iris has interviewed several chefs," the ambassador continued. "But she is no judge. You seem to know far more about these things than Iris."

Nini, who had become a bit self-conscious about her revelations, wanted to compensate. She thought she had a brilliant idea.

"If you give me a month, perhaps I can find you a chef. Perhaps I can steal one from one of those superb country restaurants in the Haute Savoie. I don't think they're paid all that well."

"Nini, will you go to all that trouble for me?" Hilary-Moulds sounded genuinely grateful.

Nini smiled winningly. This was a master stroke for Barry.

"But let's make it a project for the two of us," Hilary-Moulds added. "You do the initial research and then we'll test the restaurants together. We can take my car and driver and thoroughly penetrate the French countryside. My girl, you have made me happy tonight."

14

When the Pikes drove from the Parc des Cèdres to the dark
main road with the high hedges, Nini thought it had been
the happiest evening in Geneva since their arrival. She had
expected to be snubbed and instead she had been made the
confidante of a man who had known the Duchess of Devonshire, Emerald Cunard, Lady Diana Cooper and Nancy Mit-
ford. Hilary-Moulds had said that he had had tea many
times with Rebecca West, but he refrained, discreetly, Nini
thought, from mentioning Virginia Woolf's name, or, for
that matter, Lady Beatrice, who had been a senior wrangler
in mathematics at Cambridge. At that moment Nini felt the
equal of Virginia Woolf and Lady Beatrice. More than
equal – she could be relied upon not to go insane. Nini tried
to restrain her excitement and to think constructively about
chefs.

They reached the corner of Florissante nearest their
apartment, but instead of turning into the parking lot, Barry
drove past it to Malagnou and to the centre of the city on the
rue du Rhone. Nini became aware of Barry for the first time
since they had left Parc des Cèdres and thought he looked
grouchy. It was understandable: he had had to sit next to
Moira Belknap all evening.

"If you tell me where we're going, I'll tell you about my

new project given to me by His Excellency, the Mould," she said happily.

Barry did not reply, and in an instant, Nini's good mood turned to irritation. She felt that every time she enjoyed herself, Barry deliberately chose to be glum.

"It's almost eleven thirty," she said. "Nothing is open except the Ba Ta Clan."

Again, silence from Barry.

Nini decided to try to coax Barry out of his ill humour by pretending not to notice it. "But I don't mind going to a night-club," she went on airily. "The Ba Ta Clan is certainly respectable. The waiters never force champagne on the customers. And the girls always wear a G-string. I'm sure the place is carefully regulated by the Geneva authorities, maybe the same ones who guard the probity of Moira Belknap's boucherie chevaline."

Nini pushed a little more. She knew Barry had never been to the Ba Ta Clan. "You must have heard about Mitzi from your United Nations colleagues. She's this year's favourite. Kamizuki goes all alone just to watch her French *écolière* routine. She appears on stage in long braids, wearing a blue *tablier*, and carrying a canvas sack of schoolbooks on her back. It's funny – all those old men in the front rows pretending they're looking at a school-girl undressing just for them. Her act is very well polished. I enjoyed it when the Dhroshkys took me. It's kind of a tomboy tease. And when she rubs pink chalk on her nipples even the waiters laugh."

At last Barry spoke.

"I'm hungry. I want a steak and *frites*. We're going to the Brasserie de Commerce. It's still open. You can't eat at the Ba Ta Clan."

Nini's gaiety, which had been sustained by the scaffolding of alcohol, disappeared – Barry's mood was powerful enough to pull her down.

The Brasserie de Commerce was a large café on the Place

Molard across from the Grand Passage, the busiest department store in Geneva. By day, it was frequented by clerks and shoppers eating sauerkraut and sausages. By night, the Brasserie de Commerce specialized in cheese fondue – the locals ate it with hunks of stale bread before retiring. Nini believed fondue was the most indigestible combination in the world – raw kirsch, sour wine and kilos of melted Gruyère. She wondered why people didn't have heart attacks right on the spot.

The café was still open and the fumes of cheese and wine from the fondue pots bubbling on the tables nauseated her. The paper table-cloths were covered with drippings of old cheese and the waiters, in long white aprons, gave them black looks as they entered. It was closing time. When Barry ordered a steak, their waiter appeared mollified – it would take less time to eat steak than fondue. The waiter, old and disdainful, gave them clean paper place-mats and set out the chafing dishes that were the hallmark of the cheaper Swiss restaurants. They did not speak until the waiter brought Barry's food on a huge platter and dumped it on the chafing dish, leaving Barry to help himself. Nini couldn't stand it any longer.

"Why are you so angry? What did I do wrong?"

"You didn't do anything wrong."

"Are you upset because I'm going to help Hilary-Moulds find a chef? This can only help you, Barry; it will create a tie between us and him. You complain that he never consults you. He's bound to pay more attention to you now, especially if I find a chef."

They were almost the only ones left in the café by this time and the waiters were ostentatiously turning up chairs.

Barry helped himself to the last of the *frites*, ate them and then spoke.

"Hilary-Moulds doesn't want me to come on the restaurant-testing jaunts. He wants you. But that's all right. You'll have fun if you go with him because you like that kind of thing. My first concern is your happiness always. . . . But I'm afraid you'll be hurt, Nini," he continued. "You're keen now but later you'll be disappointed."

"Why should I be disappointed? Don't be irritating and moralistic."

"He's using you."

"I can't see how he's using me! How can we be harmed if I do him a favour? After all, I am your wife. You're certain to benefit."

When Barry spoke, Nini realized that she had never before heard such a bitter tone in his voice. "Hilary-Moulds called me single-minded at the table this evening. What hypocrisy! He's the most single-minded, ambitious man I have ever met. All this fuss about chefs and entertaining," Barry said disdainfully. "It is for his selfish goal. He wants to become secretary general of NATO. He thinks he can oil the prime minister and impress him with his contacts. He needs the PM's recommendation. And he's flattering you now just so he can use you."

Barry overtipped when he paid the bill.

"What if he is using me? What harm can come to us if I help out? How can I lose? How can you lose?"

Barry did not answer and they drove home without speaking.

15

To Neville, the streets of Budapest appeared to be inhabited by a race of helots – hunchbacks with bandy legs, dwarfs with blackening teeth.

Where were all the handsome, the talented? Neville thought they must all have escaped to the west in '56. Only the Russians looked healthy to him. The young soldiers had straight bodies and good teeth. Power and health always go together, he thought. The Russians were the potent athletes, the Spartans who watched and listened and controlled the streets.

More than six years had passed since the Russians had come into Budapest; it was almost a year since Neville himself had arrived. Yet the shock of the Soviet presence was so powerful that it seemed to him the great act of intrusion had occurred only yesterday.

Occasionally, Neville would see a group of older Hungarian writers and artists sitting briefly in one of the cheaper coffee houses, fearful of gathering too long, fearful of being seen, fearful of each other.

There were, however, a few artistic people whose faces had not yet set into expressions of permanent anxiety. These were the younger artists, those on the state payroll who dined regularly with the richer party members at the Bor Pince restaurant. Neville ate there fairly regularly and the former owner, now the manager, had sufficient independence to ask him, along with selected officials and favoured actors and musicians, to private suppers at his restaurant. This was where Neville met Janos.

To Neville, Janos was an Austrian count among the Magyar peasants. Janos was slight, with aquiline features, blond hair and a delicate body. His father had, in fact, been a bourgeois doctor. But by recanting his background, Janos had managed to get a good job as back-up tenor in the state opera chorus. In the midst of the old, imperial décor of the Bor Pince restaurant, Neville and Janos discovered a common interest: Budapest's architecture.

They liked to walk on the Pest side of the city because Neville adored the fantastical art-nouveau villas peculiar to Budapest. The buildings all showed the effects of violation, their windows broken, their walls pitted with bullet holes from the uprising or perhaps from the war. No one seemed to live in them any more except the odd party official who used his influence to get the state to splash a bit of paint on the exterior. The villas, Janos explained, had been built by the bourgeoisie before the turn of the century. It did not surprise Neville that the Hungarians officially looked down on them as less aesthetically interesting than the classical houses of the nobility in the eighteenth-century old town. Even Janos disliked the ruined middle-class beauties and preferred the simpler lines of the aristocratic houses.

Neville and Janos were very careful. Janos never went to the Canadian residence and Neville had no idea where he lived. For a while, Neville worried that Janos might be a KGB plant. But, he reasoned, a spy would want gossipy tidbits about the foreign community, and would encourage him to repeat conversations between the Minister of Agriculture and Neville's unsatisfactory Number Two. To the contrary, however, Janos seemed to resent Neville's official activities and became sullen and jealous if a third person were mentioned.

"Don't talk about your fancy friends and your fancy servants. It depresses me to think that you care about them." This suited Neville very well. They discussed art, aesthetics and travel. Their favourite subject was planning their new life together if and when Janos could get out of Hungary. Sometimes Neville suggested Majorca and they spoke of buying citrus groves. Sometimes he would say that the Greek islands had fewer tourists and they would design villas built into the cliffs facing the sea. But usually Neville insisted that New York should be their goal. Majorca and the Greek islands were for *rentiers*, idlers, and they would become bored within six months. Neville was certain that Janos was talented enough to get a job with the chorus at the Met. Neville would be free to continue his diplomatic career at the United Nations.

They had two places of rendezvous.

The first was a sixth-floor walk-up flat in one of the bleak new workers' buildings far from the centre of Budapest. They met at one of the busiest intersections and rode three miles on the streetcar to the stop nearest their destination. The flat consisted of two rooms and was furnished with four mattresses, an enormous couch protected with antimacassars, a sink filled with onions, four cooking pots and some clothes hanging on pegs on the walls. An old German bicycle was chained to the couch. Seven people lived in the two rooms, and on Thursdays they all worked the day shift.

"We're lucky to have this place," Janos explained. "One of the men who lives here owes me a favour. But he asked us not to use the toilet."

The toilet was on the third floor and served half the occupants in the building.

The second rendezvous was in the centre of the city, in one of the turn-of-the-century villas so admired by Neville and despised by Janos. The villa had a rococo wrought-iron door and eight unfurnished, uninhabited rooms; there were intricately inlaid wooden floors and large tile heating stoves

113

in each room. The tiling on the stove in the room Janos and Neville used was exquisitely embossed with a coloured pattern that formed the shape of a woman's head, with the long tendrils of her hair winding about the stove like vines. Unfortunately, the stove was never lit, the windows were sealed off with cardboard, and the wall-paper was stained with water in summertime and frosted over in the winter. Janos always kept a couple of blankets stuffed in the old stove. Although no one lived in the main body of the house, a caretaker occupied a basement room and she opened and locked up after them when they left. Neville couldn't tell from her greasy, lined face and heavy body whether she was forty or sixty. She had the same red henna dye in her hair favoured by most of the women who lined up for cabbages in the mouldy, smelly food stores.

"Don't worry about her," Janos said. "She owes me a favour, too."

Neville once asked why the house wasn't filled with people, like the workers' flat.

"It's reserved for government big shots and they're haggling over what they should do with it."

Roland Neville was known in the diplomatic community, and by his own staff, as being very strict about security. His colleagues thought he was slightly absurd, however, over the shoe affair. During a routine security sweep of the American embassy, a listening device was found in the heel of a junior officer's shoe. Neville thought it ludicrous, as well as frightening, that some low-level clerk from the KGB listened in on other people's farts. He imagined the clerk transcribing the flatulence of foreigners in a log – along with whatever else he chanced to hear. Neville made every member of the Canadian staff send his shoes back to Canada for inspection. The whole embassy shuffled around in thick socks and spoke only about the weather; they all wore rubber boots outdoors. Two dozen new pairs of shoes were sent to Budapest from Vienna through the diplomatic bag, accompanied by a special courier.

"What are you complaining about?" Neville snapped at his Number Two. "The government has bought you all new shoes."

Neville used to give Janos presents of books and cigarettes and, occasionally, Scotch; and once, Janos presented him with a record he had made of some Schubert *lieder*. Neville ceased this exchange of gifts when he heard from a diplomatic colleague about the Norwegian first secretary.

The Norwegian was the only member of the diplomatic corps who had actually managed to be asked for an informal drink by a Hungarian family. All entertainment of foreign officials took place at restaurants – hardly anyone had met a real Hungarian family or had seen the interior of a Hungarian home. The Norwegian had developed a distant but amicable friendship with a sound engineer. The engineer was a neighbour and occasionally asked the young Norwegian and his wife to his flat for a glass of wine and some fruit. He lived in three rooms with his wife, his children and his mother-in-law, who carefully rubbed each fresh plum clean before she handed it to a guest. The two couples discussed music. The engineer worked for the Hungarian state recording studios and was fascinated by new sound techniques that were being developed in Germany. The diplomat loaned him the latest records being produced in the west. From time to time the Hungarian couple even came to the Norwegian's rooms and listened to recordings. It was, according to Neville's diplomatic colleague, a kind of post-Stalinist cultural exchange.

The last time the Norwegian saw the engineer was at his flat; the mother-in-law polished his brandy glass as well as the fruit before handing it to him. They had a desultory discussion about the attraction of the Beatles and the engineer's wife handed him a package.

"My husband is too shy to give this to you. But he was the sound man when our orchestra recorded the Bartok String Quartets in the studio. Play them on your machine and tell him whether you think the sound quality is good enough for export. Whatever you think, please keep the records in memory of our friendship."

When the Norwegian arrived home, there were two senior AVN men from the Hungarian Secret Service waiting for him outside the door. They were rough and knocked him about and accused him of being a spy. When he protested, they said he had stolen Hungarian documents and ordered him to open the package of records.

Hidden between the cardboard covers and the records were official-looking papers bearing the Hungarian foreign-office seal.

A few months earlier, Oslo had expelled several Hungarian diplomats for spying. Budapest had to be revenged. The Norwegian and his family were forced to pack up and leave within twenty-four hours.

After that episode, Neville refused to accept anything from Janos and gave him only Camel cigarettes.

Apart from the inflated *forint*, the most useful currency in Budapest, Neville discovered, was a package of Camel cigarettes. He was amused that Camels, not Pall Malls or Gauloises, had the most cachet in Hungary. He saw that Janos was miffed when he gave him a carton of Pall Malls as a birthday gift instead of Camels.

"You know I'll have to smoke these. They can't be used for trading. Hardly anyone actually smokes Camels, except the big shots."

Neville was aware that Camels were used by Hungarians as "key money" for apartments; five cartons, Janos had said. A few packs were sufficient to buy a good seat at a concert. When Neville first came to Budapest, he discovered that there were rats in the embassy kitchen and that his cook indifferently mashed their dung into the potato dumplings that seemed to be the daily special at the residence. Neville was kept awake all night by water dripping into a tin bucket from a leak in the ceiling. But it was impossible to fire the cook, to hire a rat catcher, to contract for a roofer. He could not look up a roofer's name in the telephone book because there was no telephone book. Plumbers, cooks, all workmen had to be procured through Attila Berendi, Neville's contact in the Hungarian foreign office.

When Neville complained, Berendi shrugged.

"Don't tell me. All the embassies have troubles. Everyone has to wait his turn. Do you know how long the British sinks have been plugged? Your rats are not our number-one priority, my friend. Why don't you keep a cat if you are afraid of rats?"

His first Christmas in Budapest, Neville sent Berendi four cartons of Camels along with the usual two bottles of Crown Royal. It did not take more than a week for a tiler, a rat catcher and a new, agreeable cook to arrive at the residence – all on the same day. The leak was instantly repaired, the rats disappeared, along with the old cook, and the new cook assured Neville that she would make him veal Esterhazy with fresh meat and cream. Periodically, there would be a return to potato dumplings; then Neville went downstairs to the kitchen and silently handed Eva, the cook, a carton of Camels. During the following weeks, his meals would be relatively sumptuous.

It was, of course, illegal to import any kind of foreign cigarettes, other than Russian or East German, to Hungary. And Neville had to admit that Janos was right: he hardly ever saw anyone actually smoking Camel cigarettes. Except once.

The foreign minister of Hungary, very high up in the party and very close to the Soviets, gave a large dinner party at the Citadel restaurant. The room was full of foreign diplomats and their wives, and Hungarian officials – Hungarian officials never brought wives to these functions.

Each table was decorated with flags and place-cards. A carton of Camels was placed at every third place setting. The foreign minister smoked two packages during the meal and confided to Neville that he would probably die at sixty from lung cancer.

"But what can I do? I can't give it up."

Neville was not displeased that his colleagues and staff thought he was a fusspot about security matters. He believed it was imperative to pay attention to such details in a police state. And he realized that some people might consider his relationship with Janos a security risk.

He explained his moral position to Janos one evening in the cold, mildewed upstairs room.

"The sin is in the shame, not the act. There is no way I can be blackmailed. I feel no guilt about our relationship – I know I have the strength to resist intimidation because I don't care who knows that I am a homosexual. I believe a person may do anything he wants sexually as long as there is no residual shame attached and no harm to anyone. It's not a good idea to flaunt one's behaviour, because that's asking for trouble. But if it comes to a crunch, they can't touch me. I simply don't think I'm doing anything wrong."

Janos said that he had no qualms. In this world, everyone had to look out for himself.

"It doesn't matter to me one way or the other. I'm just a gypsy. You're the one who has secrets to give away."

Neville had not told headquarters that he was a homosexual. It was not their business and it should not make any difference. Look at the difficulties he was having with heterosexuals on his own staff. Neville believed that the best protection against the AVN and the KGB was an embassy with good morale. When his rather homely secretary complained of loneliness, Neville worried that she might become susceptible to compromising suggestions. She would have no strength to resist harassment. So he sent her to London. He found out that his married guard was drinking on duty and had him removed, with some difficulty. Weepy secretaries and boozing guards were vulnerable in a police state.

But increasingly, Neville's main concern was to get Janos out of Hungary.

He wondered if his old and worldly, well-connected friend, Hilary-Moulds, might have a few ideas when he next visited him in Geneva. The ambassador might just have a special understanding of his position and a willingness to help.

16

Barry and Nini both slept badly the night of the ambassador's dinner and their argument. In the morning, they dressed in silence. Then Barry sat on a chair far from the bed, put his head in his hands and spoke remorsefully.

"Last night was my fault. Hilary-Moulds didn't pay any attention to me, so I took it out on you. My behaviour was childish. I sulked like a baby. I don't know why I can't control myself. Without self-control, I'll never get anywhere in life. It's detestable that I let my feelings show like that. And Moulds notices everything."

Nini was gratified that Barry spoke first and she forgave him immediately. Now Nini resented Hilary-Moulds for paying attention to her at the expense of her husband. She tried to reassure Barry, because it frightened her when he dwelt on his weaknesses. If Barry wasn't confident, what would happen to her?

She combed her hair, facing the mirror, and spoke to his reflection.

"You were fine at the party. It was afterward, when you were alone with me, that you showed your feelings. It doesn't matter what you say when we're alone."

"I just can't get through to the man," Barry continued, still immobile. "I don't even know what I'm doing wrong at the office, never mind the dinner. The fact is, Belknap knows how to handle him and I don't. Maybe we should leave Geneva."

"For heaven's sake, Barry, you are over-reacting," Nini said. "I don't think you should take seriously anything that Hilary-Moulds did or didn't do last night. He had too much to drink and so did I. He's a man of whims. And I'm sure he's jealous of you." She turned to face Barry and continued, gesturing off-handedly with the hair brush. "You have this tendency to give people the answers before they have thought of the questions. Your competence threatens Hilary-Moulds. Your job is to make him feel competent. Act meek and mild. If he thinks you can be used to his advantage, he'll change his attitude. He needs you. He can't really rely on Belknap. And that Moira gives him hives. I hate it when you criticize yourself. It's pessimistic, negative and unnatural to your character. You won't profit from scourging yourself."

Nini opened her drawer and picked out a new Givenchy scarf, which matched her tweed skirt.

"What a tough girl you are," Barry said, feeling better. "Maybe you should help old Moulds find a chef. We shouldn't worry about his motives. You're absolutely right. Other people's motives should not be our concern."

He rose and scooped some coins off his bureau and let them fall noisily in his trousers pocket.

"He's probably forgotten about the chef, which will be all to the good," Nini said.

But Barry wasn't so sure. "I think you should help him if he rings you up. He was serious and wants to make a splash. Why don't you consult Nicole Dhroshky? Just in case he does call you. She knows everything."

With order and happiness restored, Barry decided to walk the four miles to the office and Nini was already relishing the details of her talk with Nicole. She wondered how much she should tell and if it would go against Barry's interest if Nicole knew that he was having trouble with Moulds.

Moorehouse Dhroshky, an American, the son of a Russian count and a New England Moorehouse, was president of a heavily endowed cultural foundation named the Thoreau Institute. The benefactor of the institute was a recently deceased billionaire who had owned important abbatoirs from Chicago to Patagonia. When General Eisenhower had been elected president, pork bellies went through the roof of the commodities exchange and the Thoreau Institute was born. Dhroshky had a chauffeur, two secretaries and a suite of offices sectioned off from the living quarters in his apartment.

It was not unusual for Moorehouse to take a few minutes off from his duties at the Thoreau Institute and share perceptions with the women attending his wife's reading group on Wednesday afternoons. The first time Nini had been invited to a Wednesday, her hostess warned, "We will be concentrating on the unhappy sources of Henry James's genius," and Nini was afraid.

She remembered all too clearly the gatherings at Roland Neville's she had attended as a student in Toronto. Those parties had taken place in a single room decorated with a large poster, Picasso's *Guernica*. The entrails of the horses and mutilated children were illuminated by lamps made from the usual straw Chianti bottles. Nini used to wonder what happened to the contents, since the sole beverage drunk at the gatherings was beer. She decided that the wine must have been poured down the john, given Roland's Jacobin tendencies.

Nini remembered how much she disliked the parties, sitting on the floor, dumbly nodding agreement as the others condemned materialism, self-conscious because she was the only one wearing a cashmere sweater. She had tried to reform. She changed to lumberjack shirts and read bits of Marx. But in the end she had been reduced to laughing with the others, who continued to say that she was an unrepentant philistine, innately vulgar because of her "materialistic obsessions."

The first time Nini was invited to Nicole's intellectual afternoons, she was determined not to make the same mistake and wore a drab, khaki-coloured garment that had been lying in the bottom of a trunk. It was creased and ill-fitting. Nini crossed the hall to the Dhroshky apartment full of confidence. A maid answered the door and led her into a large room with many things – Louis XIV carved tables, smaller round tables with long taffeta skirts covered with ornaments, enamelled snuff-boxes, Fabergé jade and nephrite flower pots, other *objets de vertu* from France, Germany and England, and ivory netsuke carvings. Ancestral pictures in gilded frames hung in two rows on the walls. The hostess, in a red Japanese kimono, was lying on a canopied bed supported by four thick, spiralling Baroque posts and playing with a Siamese cat. Nini thought she looked like a Balinese temple dancer, with her dark, slanted eyes and her arms always in motion as she stroked and lifted the animal. Nicole had told Nini that her vitality was due to Negro blood, claiming a Voodoo priestess as her great-grand-aunt.

A number of extraordinarily well groomed women sat around the bed in gilt ballroom chairs chattering in French, Italian and English. They might have been fashion editors for *Vogue* or the private clientele of Balenciaga waiting to view the fall collection. Two white-gloved waiters were pouring champagne while the maid, in an organdy apron and cap, passed a giant hollowed-out brioche filled with fresh *foie gras*. The room smelled of Bellodgia perfume and Balkan Sobranies, and Nini, for the first time in her life, felt like a frump among the bluestockings.

The other women barely glanced at Nini as she joined the

group and continued with their intense conversations. But Nicole eyed Nini up and down with disapproval and gestured to her to sit beside her on the bed.

"Have you got your period today, or what? You look terrible."

Nini told the truth. "I didn't know I was supposed to dress up. I thought this was going to be a literary discussion group."

"Dress up? Dress up? What has one thing got to do with the other? I hardly see the connection. Sloppy dressers, sloppy thinkers. You don't have to go around looking like Trotsky's wife to prove you have a brain."

Nini simply did not know what to say.

Nicole pushed the cat away to give Nini more room on the bed.

"We were supposed to have a general discussion about Henry James, but Madalena over there is talking foolish nonsense about Tacitus. I never rely on Tacitus as an historian. A wonderful story-teller, yes, but he has no long view of history whatsoever."

Madalena was a plump, fair woman wearing a handsome knit suit and fine leather shoes. She was speaking Italian. Although Nini did not know Italian, she began to worry seriously about Tacitus. From the sound of the name she knew he must have written in Latin. Nini had spent the past three days reading *The Golden Bowl* and still hadn't a clue about the unhappy sources of Henry James's genius.

"Oh, do cheer up, Nini, and have some champagne while I tell you about everyone here."

Nicole sounded kinder.

"Madalena is a professor of philosophy at the University of Geneva and her husband controls all of Fiat's foreign holdings. Quite a lot, believe me, for an Italian company. That mousy looking woman with the white collar that only convent girls should wear is Edna Schwartz. But what do you expect from American women? They always dress like

124

adolescents. Nevertheless, Edna is brighter than she looks. Her husband is the *New York Times* correspondent and definitely will be managing editor in a couple of years."

Nini noticed a woman in a Peter Pan collar dressed without the same chic as the others, listening to an elegant blond woman speaking in French. Mrs. Schwartz's expression was eager but strained, as if she were having a hard time understanding the language. Nini decided she would talk to Edna Schwartz, but Nicole prevented her from leaving the bed.

"The gorgeous dark girl wearing the sari is Lila, the Maharajah's sister. Her looks are better than her brains. Look at the ruby on her finger – it's pigeon blood from Burma, two hundred years old. The rubies mined today are junk. The finest rubies always come from the surface of the mines, and they exhausted the top layers in Burma years ago. I wouldn't touch a Brazilian ruby myself, which is all they have these days."

The Maharajah was, Nini knew, the High Commissioner for Refugees, and very influential. She remembered having dined with him at the Dhroshkys' when Barry had been out for the evening. She wished, with chagrin, that she had remembered the elegant dinner when she dressed in her ridiculous khaki uniform today. Neville's gatherings were still fresh enough to have clouded her mind, she reflected unhappily.

"The rest are not so interesting," Nicole continued. At this point, she spread her well formed hands down in condemnation. "I invite the others as fillers. Don't bother with them, except perhaps Blanche. Blanche Foucault is *très vieille* France. A real pain in the ass. Because she's a Bourbon princess and her husband is Henri Foucault, she thinks she's Mme. de Staël and Marie Antoinette rolled into one. Mind you, I have to admit that Pompidou can't pee without Foucault's first pressing on the kidneys."

Nini realized that the tall blond woman dressed in Hermés suede, bending the ear of Mrs. Schwartz, was Princess Blanche. Or Princess de Foucault? Nini wasn't sure of the nomenclature. She classified herself mentally as a filler until Nicole spoke again.

"And you, darling, are going to add some nice young, fresh blood to my gatherings. I'm a vampire, you know; it's part of my heritage. I like new blood. Don't worry about Henry James or Tacitus. Just be yourself and talk about anything you like. You're as pretty as the Maharajah's sister but you must take the trouble to iron your clothes. And you are much smarter. Only you don't know that yet. Don't be intimidated by these people. Or by me."

There was a hush among the women when Moorehouse Dhroshky walked into the bedroom. Trim, fair and balding, he had features so precise they might have been drawn with an etcher's needle. Nini thought he looked like a descendant of a sixteenth-century northern ecclesiastic portrayed by Dürer or Cranach, kneeling at the Virgin's feet. She could not detect a trace of Slav in his bearing or face.

Moorehouse's manner was diffident as he shook hands with and smiled at each woman. Finally he sat beside Nini on the bed and said, in a pure Back-Bay Brahmin accent, "Nicole's friends are rather exotic. It's reassuring to see someone like you here, so close to home. I'm very glad we're neighbours, in every sense of the word. I met your husband at lunch the other day. He was most impressive. A genuine asset to your country. A sensible man. It's hard to find a sensible man these days."

Nini was always thrilled when someone praised Barry. She instantly thought that Moorehouse Dhroshky was a sensible man, too.

After attending Nicole's Wednesdays for several months, Nini thought she knew Nicole well enough to drop in for an informal tête-à-tête. Nicole said she preferred people to visit her because she liked to be close to Moorehouse in case he needed anything. Nini had never actually noticed Nicole doing anything for her husband, but Moorehouse always came in for his little chat when Nini was present. She wondered if Moorehouse were sufficiently challenged as president of the Thoreau Institute; he never seemed in a rush, like Barry. Occasionally, the telephone rang in his offices and one of the secretaries would call him. He'd wave her away saying, "Not important, I'll call back later," and continue telling Nini about sailing in Cape Cod with the Kennedys or how the peasants used to dress for feast days on his father's estate in Vitebsk.

Nini had asked Barry what the Thoreau Institute did. He could not give her a clear answer, nor could anyone else. And yet people were certain the Dhroshkys were important, although no one was precise about describing Moorehouse's activities. Nini was gratified that the Dhroshkys had taken such interest in an unimportant person like her. And she was also more than a little curious as to why.

This afternoon Nicole was on the balcony, knitting. She was extraordinarily adept with her hands and could make lace placemats or upholster sofas. Once she had promised to bead an evening bag for Nini, if she found the time.

"Nini, sit down and tell me something interesting while I finish this sweater for Moorehouse. He has fourteen already and thinks I'm crazy to make any more, but I can't help it. If I didn't do something with my hands I'd become psychotic and gun down officials on the Pont de Mont Blanc or take the wrong kind of lover. Be careful how you choose your lovers, Nini. Make sure they have your husband's interests at heart. I assume you care about your husband. You should. Moorehouse admires him so much."

Nini did not know how to handle this sort of talk. She had no lovers, but would never admit this to Nicole. Nini was fairly certain that Nicole hadn't any, either, since she hardly left the apartment except in the evening with Moorehouse. As far as Nini could tell, they always returned home together.

"Have a drink. What would you like, a dry martini?

Rinaldo will bring you a dry martini."

It was only three o'clock and Nicole was drinking coffee. Nini felt that Nicole was testing her for alcoholic tendencies. She wished she had the courage to accept the challenge.

"Coffee, please," Nini said a bit sharply. She was dying to ask Nicole exactly what sort of lover could help a husband, but she thought she had better avoid the subject of lovers. Her questions would surely seem naive to a Frenchwoman.

"Have you ever met our ambassador, Hugh Hilary-Moulds?" she began instead. "We were at his residence for dinner last night and he needs a good chef. He recruited me to find one. Can you help at all?"

"Of course, I have met him. But I don't know him. What is he like?" Nicole seemed uncharacteristically interested, and Nini was encouraged. So many people were of no importance to Nicole.

"He has a good sense of humour and collects Persian carpets." Then Nini decided to take a risk. "I could have him for dinner with you and Moorehouse if you like."

Nicole had already declined several of Nini's invitations because the guest list had not been tempting. She always asked Nini who was invited before she decided not to come. This time she let Nini's question hang.

"What does your husband think of Hilary-Moulds?"

Nini decided to hedge.

"He has a tremendous reputation, you know. They say he might become secretary general of NATO. He certainly has influence. Barry says all the evolving nations listen when he speaks."

"Don't tell me about evolving nations. Who knows what those people think? They change their alliances every week, like bedsheets. I want to know what your husband thinks. Moorehouse and I respect your husband's views."

"Barry hasn't formed any opinion yet," Nini said primly. "Hilary-Moulds is a bit hard to get to know."

"Barry must have an opinion. He's been working with

the man for months. Clearly, they don't get along."

"Of course, they get along. It's just that I don't feel it's right for me to give you Barry's opinion of his own ambassador. If you want to know what Barry thinks, ask him. What does Moorehouse think of him? He must have some sort of an opinion."

Nicole did not answer, but called Rinaldo and muttered something to him in Italian, then turned to Nini and pronounced, "Be quiet for a second. I must concentrate on this stitch. It's tricky and I need silence."

Nini felt rebuffed and wondered if she ought to leave. She was half out of her chair when Moorehouse ambled in.

Nicole looked up at him and said, "Nini here says Hugh Hilary-Moulds needs a chef and wants our help. Do you want to have dinner with him at the Pikes' apartment?"

Moorehouse appeared delighted and said it was a wonderful idea. Nini admired the way he feigned ignorance of the fact that three of her invitations had already been rejected by his wife.

"But as much as we would love to come to you, I think that we should all dine together in a restaurant at Priay. The chef is an old friend and might know someone who would suit the ambassador. Naturally, you will all be my guests."

He took out a small appointment book from his inner pocket and poised his gold pencil, a movement so quick and unexpected that Nini was startled.

"How about a week Sunday – lunch? If the ambassador isn't free we can make it any day he desires. Let me know and I'll call the chef in advance. Or better still, I will get my secretary to call the ambassador's secretary. That's the ticket."

Nini realized that Moorehouse's suggestions would solve some looming problems. Hilary-Moulds might have disliked meeting the Dhroshkys at the home of an underling. He was unpredictable about protocol, one day claiming to despise it, the next citing the most ancient rules if he believed they were to his advantage. Moreover, she didn't want to hire a cook who was better than Juanita and possibly annoy the ambassador. Barry would probably want her to do the cooking herself. He felt it was showy for a first secretary to serve catered dinners. Nini hated cooking. Until now she had always won the argument, saying that she could hire whom she liked because it was her own money. It would, however, be much more difficult convincing Barry to hire a chef if he had to entertain Hugh Hilary-Moulds. And the whole matter became all the more tangled in Nini's mind when she remembered that the whole purpose of the exercise was to find Moulds a chef.

Moorehouse had solved a great problem that Nini hadn't even anticipated until this moment. No one could blame the Pikes for anything if they were guests of the Dhroshkys.

Nicole put down her knitting and sealed the agreement.

"Let Moorehouse arrange everything, Nini. He knows how to do these things better than you."

17

Several days before the luncheon in Priay, Moira Belknap telephoned Nini to invite her to her house.

"You have never seen my work, have you? I thought you'd probably be alone tonight since our husbands will be pigging it at another one of those men's affairs. Come on over, unless you're going to some grand party on your own. I won't give you anything to eat, because you're not exactly the Kraft Dinner type." Moira giggled a bit. "Be here at seven sharp."

At first Nini didn't know what her "work" meant. Then she realized it was Moira's paintings.

The Belknaps lived in a large old Swiss-chalet type of house that appealed to Nini. Rambling blossoming roses covered the balconies circling the second floor and the house was surrounded by a substantial garden with a number of cherry trees. Although she came exactly at seven (Nini was always punctual), no one answered her ring except a toddler wearing an unpleasantly heavy diaper, slung low and exposing a nasty rash. The child bumped wordlessly into Nini's legs and then wandered into some dark passage. The kitchen was just off the entrance and the remains of breakfast were on the table. A large vat of jam, toast crusts and boiled-egg shells shared space with plastic bowls and spoons covered with congealed macaroni, flecked with orange: the children's supper.

A boy of about twelve stood at the smoking stove frying a dun-coloured thing in a pan.

"Mother's in her studio," he said and turned back to the frying and the smoke. Nini headed toward the sound of adult voices. The Belknaps did not seem to have any furniture save Turkish hassocks, a bookcase made with bricks and lumber slabs, and a large refectory table that felt sticky (jam? honey?) when her hand accidentally touched the surface. A welcome smell of turpentine suddenly overpowered the wet diaper fumes that had permeated the house and Nini found herself in a large room with stacks of paintings, easels, palettes and every kind of artist's paraphernalia. At the centre of the rubble, in burgundy tweed with matching accessories, stood Iris, watching Nini's face as she entered.

"How are you, Mrs. Pike. It really is my fault that you were invited here. I understand you are something of an art historian. I think you ought to see what Moira is up to."

There was a sound of crashing pictures and Moira, her pregnancy showing through her smock, heaved out a huge canvas that had been stuck under the others.

"Do you like it?" she said to Iris, ignoring Nini. "Is two hundred dollars too much? It took me a long time to paint."

The portrait was of Hugh Hilary-Moulds, sitting outdoors in a wicker chair wearing a wide straw hat. It was a vacation portrait; he had no jacket and the sky was very blue.

Nini was a little jealous—she thought of the hours Moira and Hilary-Moulds must have spent together. "When did he sit for you?" Both women were silent until Moira finally spoke in a resigned voice.

"He didn't sit for me. I used a colour photograph that Iris let me borrow. She wants to give it to him as a birthday present. It's supposed to be a surprise."

The portrait was an excellent likeness, showing Hilary-Moulds in a relaxed, happy mood. Moira, Nini thought grudgingly, had the technique of a professional.

"I haven't painted many portraits. I can't afford sitters and this is my first commission." She looked at Iris anxiously.

Iris's face was impassive as she stepped back to get a better look. Nini suddenly felt sorry for Moira and guessed that Iris wasn't going to let go of two hundred dollars. She was clutching her leather bag too tightly. Iris turned to Nini.

"And what do you think of it?"

"I'm sure it's worth the price," Nini replied at once.

Nini had been glancing around at the rest of the paintings: murky abstracts, reminiscent of every popular style of the past forty years. But the portrait was different – and better.

"The likeness is unmistakable. Your strength is definitely in portrait painting," she said to Moira.

"No one wants portraits these days. They are too old-fashioned. And it takes too much time, when you think how little money you get for them. This represents three months' work. Besides, the last thing I'm interested in is achieving a superficial likeness. I'm aiming for a true psychological portrait. I want to reveal the inner being, like Velásquez or Dégas. Not that I'm in their class yet."

"But," Nini insisted, "a good likeness is not that easy to get. I've seen too many portraits that are merely jack-o'-lantern faces on the canvases. You have good technique and a careful eye. Your draftsmanship is first-class. Capitalize on what you can do and you should be able to evoke something deeper."

Moira did not look displeased with Nini's comments.

"What was the amount you settled on before you commissioned the portrait?" Nini asked. She hoped that her question would not be considered meddling.

"We didn't speak of money," Iris interrupted. "Moira hadn't done any portraits before and she volunteered to paint it on spec."

"But you did ask her to paint it." Nini did not want to alienate Iris for the sake of Moira, but she was curious as to who first took the initiative.

"Oh, yes, I asked her if she was capable of doing it, and she said she would give it a try, just for the experience. Quite honestly, I don't know if I want to spend all that money on one painting. I do have my eye on a Beluchi tribal carpet that Hugh admired last week at Devonians. The carpet is more expensive than the portrait, but it's probably a better investment. I'm not cheap when I buy a present, you understand. I just want to spend my money wisely."

Nini wondered about the depth and nature of Iris's relationship with Hilary-Moulds. She didn't think Iris was that well entrenched. It might be risky to give him a surprise portrait. A carpet was definitely safer. She decided it was best to keep quiet. She had said what she believed and now Iris sounded cross. Moira was too self-absorbed to give Nini anything but the most ephemeral gratitude.

With some confusion, Nini guessed that Iris had been invited to come well before seven. She was standing there with her gloves on and Nini gathered she was ready to leave. But Iris gave Moira a sort of nod, as if they had something pre-arranged – apart from haggling over the price of the portrait. Moira suddenly took on the air of a hostess. Nini wondered if a negative jerk of Iris's head would have signalled Moira to tell Nini to leave.

"We may as well sit down." She pulled up a few kitchen chairs and produced a kettle and a jar of Nescafé. "I feel like coffee, how about you girls? I usually entertain in my studio and let the kids run loose through the rest of the house. They know they're not supposed to bother me in here."

Moira shut the studio door firmly and Iris took off her gloves, looked around for a clean surface to lay them on, decided her bag was the safest place and swiftly snapped it open and shut.

"Where was the photograph taken?" Nini asked.

"On the Riviera," Iris said. "I took it."

Neither Moira nor Nini asked any more questions about the picture.

"And how are you getting on in Geneva, Nini?" Moira asked. "Don't you get bored? No family, no work, and a full-time maid. What do you do with yourself all day?"

The kettle had not yet come to a boil but Moira poured the water into the three cups and then added the Nescafé, giving each cup one stir with the same spoon. She shoved cups in front of Iris and Nini.

"You could take some courses at the university," Iris commented, looking dubiously at her coffee. "Is your French adequate to follow the professors? Of course, you'd have to produce papers written in French. That's more difficult than just listening."

Nini had thought again about taking a few courses in art history at the University of Geneva, but her written French was still non-existent. Besides, she was not interested in receiving a show of pity from either Iris or Moira. Her life was far from empty—but if it had been empty, Iris and Moira would have been the last to know.

"I'm quite happy as I am now. The day really isn't long enough. And I have made quite a few friends."

"Yes," Moira interrupted. "The Dhroshkys. It's nice that they have taken such an interest in you. She's very picky about whom she sees. Have you ever been there for dinner?"

"Well, I went once. Barry wasn't able to go."

"I suppose she does things very well. Being French and having so much money," said Iris. She tasted her coffee and grimaced.

Nini thought it best not to dwell upon Nicole's entertainments. The subject aroused a kind of wolfish manner in both women. She followed Iris's lead and tasted the coffee. It was vile.

Moira smiled wickedly. "The Dhroshkys have been in

Geneva a long time. They know a lot of people. Even chefs."

"Oh, they know everything," Iris affirmed. "Mr. Dhroshky's secretary called me last week to ask whether the ambassador would join him and his wife and the Pikes at a restaurant in Priay. She said something about finding a chef for Hugh."

A child screamed and banged on the closed door but Moira pretended not to hear.

"I'm surprised you didn't mention Iris's name to the Dhroshkys," Moira said to Nini. "The ambassador would never make a decision about hiring—or firing—a chef without consulting Iris." Moira looked immensely pleased and drank down her coffee with relish. "Iris really should have been included in that invitation," she added. "You know how invaluable she is to the proper functioning of Mr. Hilary-Moulds's office and domestic staff."

Nini felt that if Hugh Hilary-Moulds had wanted Iris present, he could have mentioned it himself.

"Well, it doesn't matter to me, one way or another," Iris said. "I can do my job without being wined and dined by the Dhroshkys. As long as Hugh enjoys himself. It was thoughtful of you to suggest the idea to the Dhroshkys, Mrs. Pike. Hugh and I both appreciate their concern."

"It wasn't my idea, Iris," Nini lied. "I don't control the Dhroshkys. But would you like me to mention your name to them? I could do that."

Nini knew that Nicole would never agree to include Iris.

"Not in a million years. I said I don't care one way or the other, and I don't. Luncheon parties don't mean a whit to me. I will buy that portrait, Moira," she continued without pause. "Julio will pick it up in the morning. Make sure he takes it to my flat. I don't want Hugh to know a thing. We're going to spend the whole day together on his birthday. We haven't even planned what we'll be doing. But it will be something simple. Just the two of us. That's what he really likes best."

18

"I think we should walk to the *vernissage*," Barry said. "You need the exercise."

Ten days had passed since the disastrous luncheon with the Dhroshkys and Hilary-Moulds.

During that time it had rained relentlessly, a heavy, soaking rain with mists so thick that shop windows could not be seen from a few feet away. Nini had not left the apartment since the rain began.

"It's the *bise*," Barry explained, "the north wind from the mountains. It always comes to Geneva and settles for a while this time of the year. You mustn't give in to the *bise*. That's what it wants you to do." Barry had tenaciously walked to the office every day and hiked alone Sunday morning on the veiled Salève, feeling his way along the mountain paths. He had even gathered some bent-over narcissus for Nini, although picking wild flowers was against Swiss law.

Nini was sure she had put on weight. "I look like a white and oozing piece of over-ripe Brie that no one will bother to scrape from the plate," she said to Barry, self-pityingly. "I can see the pudge forming under my chin."

Nini was lonely. Nicole and Moorehouse had left for New York the day after the lunch, and of course Moira and Iris would never call.

To make matters worse, life was becoming impossible for Barry at the office. Hilary-Moulds hid behind doors when Barry passed through the corridor. Once, when they met by chance entering the office building, Moulds closed his eyes and waved his arms in a prestidigitator-like movement, as if he hoped Barry would dissolve into the city's mists. "He acts as if I'm a tooth-ache," Barry told Nini.

Nini thought it was all her fault for arranging the luncheon. She had over-reached herself.

"Come on, you'll see people at the gallery," Barry urged. "The Belknaps will be there."

Nini thought of Moira gloating over her failure and her fatness. "I'm not going," she said. "The Belknaps hate me, I hate the weather and Hilary-Moulds hates you."

Barry was angry. "I wish you'd forget about my work. I can take care of myself, as long as you can take care of yourself. If you keep moping like this you'll end up in the cuckoo house like Hilary-Moulds's wife. Worry about that. And think how I'll feel then."

Barry took Nini's cape out of the closet and stood by the door, holding the cape.

Reluctantly Nini put on some heavy waders and the hooded policeman's rain cape Barry had selected for her. The pair walked arm in arm through streaming Florrisante, by the ramparts of the old city, and past the Musée Athenée until they reached the Grande Rue and the tidiest antique shops in the world.

Nini had never liked these shops. No higgledy-piggledy cluster of dusty objects to be found here: silver spoons were arranged on Sheraton tables like exhibitions in a museum. Nothing was ever really for sale. If she asked the price of a Sèvres candlestick or a strip of old Chinese wall-paper, a supercilious underling would pronounce an impossible sum and say, in the same breath, that the owner had ordered him to remove it from the display that morning. Nicole had told her that these shops and galleries, with the eighteenth-century Sèvres, the signed French furniture and the Rembrandt etchings, were really owned by banks. The shops were a portion of their capital, long-term assets that would never be moved, "unless someone invades Switzerland."

As they walked down the Rue Verdaine to the Galerie Artisana, which specialized in the work of young, unknown painters, Nini could not stop thinking about the lunch at Priay. The constant blowing and the rain made her memories seem worse.

"There are more suicides during the *bise* than at any other time of the year," Barry interjected cheerfully, happy now that Nini was at his side. "Look at the statistics in the *Tribune de Genève.*"

Hilary-Moulds's behaviour at the lunch had been inexplicable, Nini thought, as she walked along. Why did he act so badly, she asked herself for the thousandth time. He was grouchy from the beginning and accused the owner of the restaurant of serving corked wine. Although Moorehouse was the host, Moulds sent back three bottles, saying, when he tasted the fourth, "This is probably the only decent bottle in the place." Nini thought the restaurant was perfect. The clientele were discerning locals – trenchermen from Lyons and the Savoie. No UN delegates; just farmers and small shopkeepers who came *en famille* to the restaurant after communion. The men had mourning bands on their sleeves and the women wore thick navy suits, which had been made to endure for a decade of Sundays. The children sat like monks, chewing silently through eight courses and four hours of dining. It was the kind of place she wished Eleanor could have seen.

The owner introduced Nini and Moorehouse to his Algerian sous-chef, who was preparing *quenelles de brochet en soufflé* for the ambassador. Yves Marius wanted to live in Geneva, not France, but was unable to procure a work permit from the Swiss. He knew that diplomats, because of their legal immunity, were automatically granted permits for their domestic staff by the authorities. But Hilary-Moulds perversely refused to meet Yves Marius, ate his food without comment and would not even admit that he was looking for a chef.

Instead, he baited the Dhroshkys. The United States was weak because President Kennedy was influenced by people who weren't really American. "For instance, you two," Hilary-Moulds said. "One of you has a Russian father and the other was born on the rue du Bac a block away from Sartre and the rest of the Marxists. The Soviet Union can and will do exactly what it likes with the third world, at the UN and unilaterally. The Americans are powerless. You Dhroshkys should really not be in such a position of influence. It's quite a joke that your institute is named after an American."

Barry was incensed. "Moorehouse's family has been in New England since Plymouth Rock. His origins, in any case, shouldn't matter a damn."

Nini was surprised that Hilary-Moulds thought the Thoreau Institute had such influence. "It's as if," she said to Barry later, "Moulds believes that Moorehouse is personally responsible for every vote taken against the Americans at the UN. It was so strange. He seemed to be accusing them of being Soviet spies. Like the Rosenbergs or something."

Barry, too, was puzzled by Moulds's McCarthy-like accusations. "It's inconsistent with his own conduct. He's always hanging around the Hungarians and the Poles, concocting little schemes."

The Dhroshkys' reaction was even more surprising. Nini thought Nicole would have been justified if she had slapped Hilary-Moulds's face, but she just kept filling his glass with wine. When Nini and Moorehouse walked away from Hilary-Moulds to the car, Moorehouse gave what she thought an unsatisfactory explanation of their lack of reaction. "Nicole and I always refrain from arguing with our guests. Just good manners. No matter how obnoxious the guests' opinions."

At one point during the lunch, Moorehouse had tried to change the subject. He said that Moulds was fortunate to have someone of Barry's calibre working for him. "Another cross to bear," said Moulds, and then he put his arm around Nini. "She's too good for him. The wrong people always marry each other. I've never met a couple who weren't mismatched."

"Now," Nini thought as she walked to the exhibition with Barry, "I have to face Moira, who probably knows all about the luncheon. Iris, the *grande patronne*, will have told her everything. Hilary-Moulds was annoyed," Nini decided, "because we failed to invite Iris. That's why he was so nasty to the Dhroshkys and to Barry and me. And now he's in the middle of recommending promotions of his staff to Ottawa. I can just imagine who Iris would like to see as Number Two. That's why Hilary-Moulds won't talk to Barry at the office. He's planning to give him a terrible rating and ruin his whole career."

Nini would never share such thoughts with Barry. Before, she had accused him of over-reaction, but now she was afraid that he was right.

When the Pikes arrived, the gallery was crowded and smelled of damp clothes and gardenias. The owner of the gallery, who was not a profligate man, had actually bought a few plants for the occasion. The humidity and pungency of the opening flowers gave Nini the sensation of being in a greenhouse. The crowd was mostly Swiss. Nini recognized her dentist. People stood with their backs to the paintings, drinking wine and ignoring the artist, a fat Dane who sat in a chair, a little away from the crowd, with an unhappy expression on his face. The owner, a lean Swiss, came up to Nini and explained that the artist did not speak French or German. She noticed that there were no red "SOLD" dots on his pictures. The Belknaps were the only people looking at the paintings and Barry guided her away from the owner, who had begun exclaiming over a large, blue-coloured oil.

"I don't know what that picture has except a lot of square footage," Barry said. "Be polite to Moira. The morale in the office is bad enough. Then you can buy all the pictures you want."

Stephen approached Nini. "What does the expert think of the Dane?" he asked. "Barry told me you bought three of his drawings a few months ago. His style has changed, apparently. Do you like it as well? The poor fellow. I think he's getting rather short shrift from this crowd. They don't think he's a good investment, but the prices aren't too bad."

Instead of the paintings, Nini looked at Moira, who was more pregnant, sloppier, and sadder than usual. Perhaps Iris had not told her about the disastrous luncheon. That would have perked her up, Nini thought.

A few of the paintings were self-portraits. Nini glanced at one and said to Moira, "He's not as good a portraitist as you, Moira."

"I hate sarcasm," Moira replied.

"You know I'm not being sarcastic. I told you before that you were a good portraitist."

"Moira really didn't think you were being sarcastic. It's just that something unpleasant has happened," Stephen interjected. "Moira's a little upset."

Moira looked ready to hit Stephen.

"A little upset," she said, her voice trembling. "Trust Stephen to minimize anything that happens to me."

Stephen opened his mouth to speak, but there was no stopping Moira's anger.

"Moulds slashed my portrait," Moira said. "When Iris showed it to him, he laughed. 'How ludicrous, go find the scissors,' he told her. Then he cut it up right there in front of her. If I were Iris, I would have walked right out on him. But you know what she did? She went to Devonians and bought him the carpet instead. Talk of self-abasement! And she's still hovering around."

Moira's eyes were ablaze. Stephen had abandoned any hope of silencing her. "His old pal, Roland Neville, is coming to Geneva soon, from Budapest," Moira went on. "Iris is arranging a big dinner, the Maharajah, the Dhroshkys and all. You're sure to be invited. He told Iris that he's in your debt forever. The *Pikes* found him a new Algerian chef." Moira spit an alarming amount of saliva on Nini's pink silk cable-knit sweater when she pronounced the name "Pikes" but continued rambling without pausing to apologize.

"'Simply marvellous,' she says. Iris is delighted. I'm waiting for her to ask me to return the money for the portrait."

Moira was speaking so loudly that other people in the gallery began to look at her with curiosity. As soon as they noticed her agitation, they turned away.

For a moment Nini thought that Moira had invented the story for some inexplicable mischief-making reasons of her own. It was preposterous that Hilary-Moulds would say he was in the Pikes' debt, that he had hired Yves Marius or that he dared invite the Dhroshkys for dinner. The picture-slashing, however, was more than preposterous – it was appalling. And Moira's voice was filled with bitterness and pain. For the first time the idea of being a possible name on any party list of Hilary-Moulds's was not pleasurable to Nini.

"I don't understand," she said. "How could he do such a thing?"

Moira was crying.

"I want to go home," she said to Stephen, and pulled him toward the door.

"Hilary-Moulds must be mad," Barry said. "He must be going mad and there's nothing I can do about it."

Nini decided that she would buy one of Moira's paintings.

19

About a month before Neville's trip to Geneva, Atilla Berendi, his contact in the Hungarian foreign office, met him for their monthly lunch at the Bor Pince restaurant. They usually ate hot boiled ham and discussed Neville's problems with the local staff that the Hungarians forced on him. Then they would talk about "ways to *détente*" or peaceful co-existence with the dessert and coffee. Neville always recognized the beginning of the peaceful co-existence conversation when Berendi took out his cigarettes and said, "My country, Roland, with its very special relationship with the Russians, and yours, with its relationship with the Americans, there are possibilities for you and me personally in this. We could do something to ease the situation."

Sometimes Berendi would reach into his pocket and take out a paper outlining his thoughts on achieving a better understanding between east and west, a way of breaking the prevailing diplomatic stalemate. Neville considered Berendi a bit unusual for a Hungarian. Although he was a staunch party man, Berendi was capable of going beyond straight doctrine. This was one of the reasons Neville met him so often. Berendi was human; he understood there would have to be some give on the part of the Russians as well as the Americans. Berendi even made fun of the AVN and once expressed a strong desire to see the Russian soldiers off the streets of Budapest. Neville thought Berendi was one of the few people in the Hungarian foreign office who might be called an independent thinker. He enjoyed the discussions about what honest brokers like Neville, the Canadian, and Berendi, the Hungarian, could propose to the "big boys" as negotiating points.

But for this lunch, Berendi changed his pattern slightly. He ordered brandy at the end of the lunch, although Neville protested that he disliked drinking brandy during the middle of the day. He barely listened while Neville told him about his difficulty with the Hungarian receptionist at the embassy, who spoke neither German nor English and garbled every message. Ignoring Neville, Berendi said, "Drink the brandy. It's good stuff." Then he pulled an envelope from his briefcase without waiting for coffee.

The envelope contained photographs taken near Lake Balaton, at a resort town not far from Budapest, where Neville and Janos had spent their only weekend away from the city. They were bedroom pictures, soft porn. Neville decided, after looking them over, that the camera wasn't sufficiently sophisticated for the high relief, the precise detail needed to really shock. Neville and Janos, however, were instantly recognizable.

"Roland, don't get upset, please." Berendi's voice was mollifying. "I personally don't disapprove of homosexuals. You know how liberal I am. As long as you don't pick on the children. But my chief is old-fashioned and thinks your behaviour unbecoming for a diplomat. He has ordered me to send the pictures to your foreign office because one country should help another and exchange useful personnel information. I told my chief that I'm sure Neville's family knows about his sexual preferences. The family won't care, I said. Believe me, Neville, I don't approve of this at all. But he insists they must see the pictures as well. Only so they can influence you to change. My chief is not strictly communistic. He believes in strong family ties. I have some addresses here."

Berendi looked unhappy but was determined to get through this unpleasantness. Slowly, he read the correct names and addresses of Neville's mother, sister and nieces living in Toronto, as if he were punctiliously checking a mailing list of Herend-ware bon-bon dishes being sent out as official gifts from the Hungarian tourist office.

"If you don't wish your family and superiors to be bothered with such things, it can be avoided. You co-operate with us and we co-operate with you. In fact, I don't honestly think anyone on our side would really ask you to do anything. Definitely not now. Maybe in a few years. Perhaps never. And only something very minor."

Berendi was speaking softly. Neville looked around the restaurant. His Number Two was seated a few tables away talking to the American counsellor—they paid no attention to him, nor did anyone else in the restaurant. This was Berendi's regular table for meeting foreigners. Tomorrow he'd be promoting peaceful co-existence with the Swedish ambassador.

"Would you like strawberries?" Berendi asked. "They told me they would keep two portions for us especially. They run out so quickly. You see, no one else is eating strawberries. But we shall have them."

"Oh, yes. Let's have strawberries," Neville said, "with whipped cream, too." And without pause he continued, "You are an idiot, Berendi. I don't care who knows about my sexual preference. I don't consider it anything to be ashamed of. I would be shamed and dishonoured, however, if I spied for the KGB or the AVN. Blackmail, for God's sake. How stupid can you be? When Ottawa finds out that I don't give a damn, I'll probably get a promotion. You're doing me a favour."

146

Neville honestly did not care about the pictures. He was proud of being a homosexual. He was a member of an elite that had enriched the principles of humanism since civilization had begun, that had fought off barbarism as the pretorian guard had done. He believed in a code of masculine intimacy and friendship, more lasting and honest than the shabby accommodations made by heterosexual society. People had to breed to survive. But as far as Neville observed, most marriages were shams, intellectual and emotional losses for at least one of the spouses. He belonged to an old tradition and the pictures were just another irritant from the hordes.

Neville's Number Two and the American counsellor rose and made their way toward the door. The American inclined his head to Berendi and Neville, as if to say goodbye. Neither man responded.

Berendi looked rueful. "No one is asking you to be a spy. You shouldn't jump to such conclusions."

Slowly and deliberately, Neville ate his strawberries, then put his napkin on the table and rose.

"Do what you want with the pictures. I'm a diplomat and shall continue to be one. You cannot harm me." His words came out in a soft hiss so that not even the diners at the next table were aware that he had spoken.

Berendi remained seated and ordered another brandy, watching Neville walk out of the restaurant. He carefully arranged his papers and put them back in his case.

Later, Neville didn't feel quite as confident as he had during their conversation. He wondered if he was being too optimistic about Ottawa's reaction. He knew there were some people there who would agree with his philosophy, and who acted upon it as well. But he also knew that friends could be cowards. However, when he heard nothing from headquarters for the next several weeks, he left for Geneva, feeling fairly sure that the Hungarians had decided the game was not worth the effort. He had to admit to himself that he felt sickened. The idea of being spied upon by some evil, sanctimonious dwarf, by all those psychopathic morons, was difficult to bear. He wondered how long they had known. He refrained from saying anything to Janos and saw him as usual. It really didn't matter now.

20

Barry was going over all the back files, deciding what had to be shredded and what had to be kept, when Stephen walked into his office. It was a tiresome job but someone had to get the excess paper out of the way. The office lacked the filing space to keep more than six months' worth of paper at one time. And it was a quiet period. Hilary-Moulds had gone off to Vienna with Iris for a trade meeting.

Stephen sat down.

"You're so meticulous," he said. "Let Otis sort that stuff out. He's got brains enough for that kind of decision. Or just throw everything in the shredder. You ought to follow my example. I'm doing something far more interesting." He held up a thick, leather-bound book. "*Middlemarch*, by George Eliot. When everything is foul I seek out the Victorians for comfort. Refreshing to read about the psychological behaviour of a pedantic cleric. She really has him pegged."

"Do you know," Barry asked, ignoring Stephen's literary tastes, "if Moulds is really in Vienna? Headquarters tried to reach him at the meetings and his hotel. He hasn't been sighted." Barry looked to Stephen for comment, but Stephen was intent on examining Barry's letter opener – an unusual piece that Nini had unearthed in her rounds of the antique shops. Without much hope, Barry continued.

"You should have gone to Vienna with him, anyway. He doesn't even know our negotiating position. Seven government departments consulting with banks, with industry, with mining companies, and the telexes are still sitting on Iris's desk. He'll mess everything up. Someone with a knowledge of the talks should have gone. You know the problems. And so do I, for that matter. But you get on with Moulds. I don't."

Stephen had lost interest in the letter opener. He put his feet up on Barry's desk and lit a cigar.

"You don't understand the ambassador, Barry. He doesn't want either of us hanging in too close." Stephen concentrated on shaping his lips into a tight "O" and succeeded in producing a lazy smoke ring.

"You really care more about the job than I do," he continued. "And whatever you may think, Moulds doesn't give a damn about me. He treats me like a flunky. You scowl when he asks you to do something silly. I don't. In any case, this sort of conversation is just what Moulds would like."

"What do you mean?" Barry asked, dropping six fat files in the shredder pile without even looking at them.

"It's part of his policy of destabilization. Haven't you noticed his technique? He blows hot and cold with all of us – and it's not whim. It's a deliberate psychological policy. I would have bet a thousand on the black that he would have chosen you to go. After all, you found him a chef. But I would have lost my bet. He doesn't want you to get too confident."

"Confident!" Barry exclaimed in disbelief.

"Yes, confident," Stephen affirmed, and without allowing any time for Barry to react, he went on. "You won't find him in Vienna anyhow. God knows where he is. He's always saying he'll be in Vienna when I know damned well he isn't. Forget about Vienna."

Stephen contemplated another smoke ring and Barry asked, "What did he tell you about the lunch?"

"Only enough to make the Belknaps feel inferior. He was 'grateful' that you introduced him to Dhroshky. Your wife, as usual, was the perfect diplomat's companion. And, if it weren't for the Pikes, he would never have got rid of Juanita."

Stephen leaned forward to tap ash in the clean ashtray on Barry's desk.

"A conscious policy of destabilization," Barry repeated. "You may have something there. Believe me, that lunch with him was a gruesome experience. He was impossible. I don't even exist as a servant any more. As far as Moulds is concerned, I'm not part of his staff. You know, Nini and I didn't even know he hired the chef until Moira mentioned it at the *vernissage*? Nini's been in a state since that lunch."

"Nini's feeling badly?" Stephen raised his eyebrows.

"You wouldn't believe what I'm going through with Moira. Moulds may as well have slashed her face when he slashed the painting. All she does is lock herself in the studio and cry."

Stephen showed no signs of being disturbed about Moira's distress.

Barry said, "I don't believe he did it because he didn't like Moira's portrait. I think he was getting at Iris. A little destabilization for her. Maybe she was becoming too sure of herself. He slashes her present, then takes her to Vienna. If, in fact, he's there," he said as an afterthought. "Convince Moira that the violence was directed against Iris, not her. Moira shouldn't allow herself to see it as an artistic judgment. It's too crazy for that."

Barry got up and looked out the window. Mont Blanc was hidden by cloud.

"Convince Moira?" Stephen asked. "We never talk. When she's not crying, she's sleeping. When she's not sleeping she locks herself in the studio, supposedly painting. She thinks everything is my fault. 'Hilary-Moulds is part of your life,' she says. 'Why does he have the power to reach out and destroy me as well?' She calls me his court jester. She hates being a diplomatic wife, or any kind of wife. She hates Moulds. There is nothing about my life she doesn't resent. It drains her creativity. Maybe it's money. I don't know. We need more money."

"You shouldn't go to the casino at Divonne so much. She knows about the gambling," Barry said, then instantly hoped he didn't sound too priggish.

Stephen swung his feet off the desk and stood up, facing Barry.

"I've only lost a few thousand. I need some kind of outlet, too. I've done a lot for Moira. Why do you think we rent such a big house? It's expensive but there's a studio for Moira, a place to escape from the rest of us. What do you suppose her painting equipment costs? So far, the only money she's made is Iris's two hundred dollars. Hardly pays for the canvas and the turps. It's not that she's too busy taking care of the kids. They may as well go about the city with begging bowls – or be pickpockets. Street urchins. I've been called four times by the police to pick up the two-year-old wandering alone in Parc Bertrand. They found him in the traffic, the middle of a *rond-point*, twenty cars honking. Once he got lost in the Grand Passage. The fabric department, I think. Moira puts a tag around his neck with my name and office number on it. Not hers. She's too busy painting to collect him. Too lazy to take any responsibility. Life was just bearable before this picture business. She had some interest in me and the children. Now Moulds has finished her off. You're lucky to have Nini for a wife. She belongs in one of my Victorian novels."

Stephen stabbed out his cigar on the top paper of Barry's in-basket, leaving a brown mark on the document.

Barry thought it best to get away from the subject of wives.

"Moulds is coming back from wherever the hell he is in

two days. I suppose he'll meet Neville at the airport. Neville's coming to visit him the next day."

"Who knows," Stephen said. "It depends on whether he likes to destabilize old pals, too. Anyway," Stephen concluded, "I don't mind going to meet Neville. He's a good fellow. You'll like him."

21

Geneva International Airport, at Cointrin, scarcely met the demands of passenger traffic. This morning, anxious, unshaven migrant workers, Levantine men of affairs who smelled of expensive French aftershave, women in Dior ocelot and women wrapped in black homespun, were lined up in triple rows in front of the Swiss customs and immigration desks. Every bag was being opened, every sausage scrutinized. Several old women in black shawls and stockings were crying in Portuguese or Sicilian as the customs officers picked disdainfully over their paraphernalia.

Unless someone from the Mission met him, Neville would be forced to wait in the queue, perhaps for several hours, behind fifty or more of the impoverished jet-setters, until it was his turn to move up to the desk. Only then could he show his diplomatic passport and at least avoid the baggage probe. He was especially pessimistic because he stood behind a hairy man wearing an Astrakhan cap and holding a fistful of dubious looking documents that were probably worth a half-hour investigation from the Swiss officials.

Neville tried to resign himself to the wait, but he was angry. If Hilary-Moulds was unable to meet him, he should have sent Belknap or Pike or Otis to hurry him through – as a normal courtesy from one ambassador to another. He kept looking through the large window that separated the imprisoned passengers from the free men of Geneva, hoping that a familiar face would appear. He had only moved up twice in twenty minutes, tripping each time over the hairy man's brown paper bundles.

Suddenly a small door at one side, marked ENTRÉE INTERDITE, was opened by a policeman and Hilary-Moulds himself swept into the passenger barn and found Neville immediately.

"All my fault. I'm late and your plane was on time. What a nuisance you've had this wait. But I told the boys at the Mission I wanted to meet you myself and some last-minute business detained me. We'll have you through in a jiffy."

A policeman and Julio accompanied Hilary-Moulds and the trio guided Neville past the lines. The ambassador whispered something to the customs man, who nodded, and they hurried Neville out of the airport and into Hilary-Moulds's limousine, which was parked illegally in front of the main entrance. Neville just managed to feel the warm air of Geneva on his neck before he got into the car.

"Don't worry about the luggage. Julio is taking us to the offices at Chateau Banquet. He'll drive right back out for your things. There's no point all of us waiting for the pushing and grabbing. Just give him your baggage chit and he'll see that it's all right. I hope you don't mind going to the office before your hotel. I have to speak to Iris about something."

Neville was pleased that Hilary-Moulds had met him personally, and forgave him the delay.

"Go right ahead. I've never seen the Mission and I've nothing to do at the hotel, anyway."

"You do look well, Roland. Your disease doesn't seem to have aged you. I've aged. I'm the one with the troubles. Had to fly back early from Vienna and visit the Beau Rivage. Don't say a word about it to anyone. They all think I've been in Vienna the whole time. I even took Iris for a weekend's skiing at Lech, and then had to leave her stranded.

Couldn't explain what was wrong. But you remember. It's the same old thing."

Neville wasn't sure whether Moulds was talking about his wife or his own ailments and thought it best not to question him too specifically.

"You look well; are you all right?" Neville thought that Hilary-Moulds was fatter than before, and his colour high. He did not remember him having such a florid complexion.

"It's absolutely nothing. Just the old contusions. Not something I want talked about."

Neville knew what he meant and decided it was safer to ask about his wife.

"How's Beatrice?"

"I didn't even see her this time. The doctors say she can't tell her own face from the clock on the wall. What's the point? She's in comfort, at any rate. If she can feel comfort. She'll probably live on like this for another forty years. I'll die before she does. They say she's a paranoid schizophrenic, whatever that means."

Hilary-Moulds was fortunate that he had the North money to keep her in comfort, Neville thought, but he refrained from saying so.

They drove up to the chancery and took the elevator to the eighth floor. Moulds directed Neville through the hall into his personal office.

"Make yourself at home. There's some whisky in the open drawer. I'll only be a few minutes."

Hilary-Moulds's desk faced a huge window overlooking Lake Geneva and the view of the jet d'eau and of the small pleasure boats, with their coloured sails, drifting on the water, was magnificent. The office was restrained to the point of austerity – grey carpet, grey upholstered sofa and a security shell in the corner that was precisely the same shade. Regulation security shells were always hospital green. Neville was mildly surprised to see one in Hilary-

Moulds's private office. He wondered if he could get away with having one painted brown and placed in his Budapest office. Obviously not. Only Hilary-Moulds knew how to wangle these things. He was probably the only ambassador in the service who managed to have a security shell coloured to his own taste and placed in his office.

Neville would not have been surprised if his initials had been discreetly engraved on the top drawer.

Another attempt to reflect the individual taste of the occupant – besides the matching grey security shell and sofas – were framed photographs on the opposite wall, pictures from Hilary-Moulds's past postings. They were carefully arranged in columns and labelled according to country and time. London, 1937, Paris, 1946, Budapest, 1952. Neville first looked at the old London photographs to see who Hilary-Moulds thought worthy of being put up on his walls. Apart from the standard group picture of the chancery staff, there were signed photographs: "For dear Hugh," "In memory of the best of times and the worst of times," "To my companion Hugh," and so on, from Lords Mountbatten and Beaverbrook, King George, Queen Mary and others. But from his father-in-law, Lord North, there was a mere "to Hugh." There was no picture of Beatrice. Neville skipped the Paris photographs and went directly to Budapest to see if the high and influential in Hungary at that period were still around, or if they had been liquidated by the time Neville arrived. Would Attila Berendi have had sufficient power in 1952 to get on Hilary-Moulds's walls?

The Hungarian column was disappointing. Far fewer pictures, and faces that meant nothing to Neville. They were taken before the '56 uprising and Neville guessed that most of Hilary-Moulds's important contacts had had their comeuppance. He looked at the picture of his friend with his chancery staff, locals and Canadians. Hugh had definitely aged, and the locally engaged staff would be entirely different, since there had been several changes of personnel before Neville's arrival.

Then Neville choked. He removed his glasses, peered unbelievingly at the picture, wiped and replaced the glasses and stared hard, his body trembling. There was no mistake. He was standing in the back row with the locals, the receptionist, the chauffeur and the cook. He must have dealt with immigration or consular matters as the locally engaged clerk. He had not aged at all, though Janos would have been only eighteen or nineteen at the time.

Barry Pike made it a practice to try to meet all the senior officers. He wanted to put a face on the card in his private index of officers and he knew that Neville was alone in Hilary-Moulds's room. Given Hilary-Moulds's evasion tactics, Barry had not expected to be introduced, but he thought he might take the opportunity of his superior's absence and welcome Neville himself. But just as Barry left his office and began to lock the door behind him, the ambassador walked wordlessly by and rejoined Neville. As Barry stood in the hallway, he heard their voices. The words were indistinguishable but it sounded as if they were arguing. Short, sharp barks from Hilary-Moulds and a kind of hissing from Neville. After a quarter of an hour, Hilary-Moulds locked his door and walked out with Neville. Barry was sitting at his desk with his door open. Neither ambassador spoke as they walked through the corridor.

It would be better, Barry thought, if he didn't try to present himself. Instead, Nini could call Neville. She knew how to do these things with more grace. She would happily show Neville around the Geneva shops and then bring him back to the apartment for dinner or a drink.

The present moment was not propitious, Barry concluded. It seemed as if Neville had been destabilized by Hilary-Moulds.

22

Hugh Hilary-Moulds's invitation list was sitting on Iris's desk. She was carefully writing out cards for the Belknaps, the Pikes and Neville. Even though the Canadian contingent was "family," Hilary-Moulds told Iris that they deserved handwritten cards like everyone else on the list. "But you don't have to write one to yourself." Hilary-Moulds laughed. "Just come a little before, so you can greet the guests and help the ladies with their coats."

"Do you want me to arrange the seating plan now?" Iris asked.

"I have to think about it a bit," was the reply. "Leave it with me. I don't want anyone turning his plate upside-down, like the French ambassador because he thought he was too far down at the table. The silly man walked out before the soup was served. It was a private party, too."

Iris was pleased that Hugh was inviting the Belknaps to the dinner. She had not heard from Moira since she told her about Hugh's reaction to the portrait, and she hoped the invitation would make Moira friendly again. She missed Moira, who had often asked her over to share a tuna casserole when Hugh and Stephen were away, unlike Nini Pike, who treated her, she thought, with strained, condescending politeness.

When Hugh had slashed the portrait, Iris was certain the

159

act was a sign that he did not need her anymore. Afterward he was sullen for several hours, asking her only once how she had the bad taste to want to hang such a grotesque joke on his walls. He had told her he looked like a parody of Winston Churchill in his dotage, sitting on Onassis's yacht wearing a Panama hat. He was furious when he learned she had given the photograph to Moira to copy from. "Now everyone knows we went on vacation together. Absolutely ruinous for morale. Where's your sense of discretion? The whole Mission is riddled with insecure, envious people, just waiting to take advantage of me."

Hugh had always been irritable and changeable, but this was the culmination of all his bad tempers. She marvelled that she had managed to control herself, apologizing without crying, saying as calmly as she could that it would be best if he sent a request to headquarters that she be posted elsewhere immediately. Obviously she was of no use to him. As soon as she said this, Hugh's mood changed. He asked her to forgive him. He was only vexed because he looked too old in the portrait. Moira was such a rotten painter. "We shall go to Vienna, just ourselves – forget Pike and Belknap – and after the conference we'll get in a little skiing at Lech at the Grand Hotel."

Hugh's birthday had finished well: Iris and Hugh had chosen the carpet at Devonians together. Hugh said she was the most generous woman he had ever known, generous in spirit. No one else would have been capable of such a gesture. Beatrice would have steamed and screamed and stamped. After the experiences he had had with his wife, discipline and control were the qualities he most cherished in women.

Iris had another reason to be in a good mood. For a while she had thought Hugh was favouring Barry Pike because of the discovery of the chef and the new contact with the Dhroshkys. Iris had always preferred Stephen. He accepted her authority gracefully, flirting a little to get around her.

Barry thought he was God's own messenger and thundered when she was supposed to go to Vienna because, he implied, she was too inexperienced to understand the substance of the work. Pike failed to recognize that it was unnecessary for her to worry over negotiations. Hugh knew all that. Who did Barry Pike think he was, questioning her competence and Hugh's professionalism? Everybody said the ambassador was a superb negotiator. Her rôle was to smooth his way, unpack his bags, check him in at the hotel and organize his papers. That was all Hugh really needed, and Pike would never stoop to it.

On the day of Hilary-Moulds's dinner, Iris was hard at work at her desk, preparing drafts of the evaluations and ratings of the officers in the Mission. Yesterday, rather formally – and gratifyingly, for her – Hugh had asked her to step into his office and give him her opinion on Pike's and Belknap's work performances. Her advice was always worth listening to, Hugh said. When Iris threw her favour to Stephen, Hilary-Moulds agreed absolutely that Belknap should be promoted to FSO 4 level, rather than Pike, and become the senior man. He told Iris that the rating should be sufficiently positive to ensure that the promotion board back at headquarters would have little choice but to promote him. She was writing out the report for Hilary-Moulds, attempting to imitate his style. Hugh hated the bother of drafting promotion reports. It would take Iris a couple of days to evoke Hugh's distinctive tone.

But as important and challenging as was her task, Iris kept thinking about the dinner and wondering if she had spent too much money on the dove-coloured chiffon gown, made by Nini Pike's dressmaker, Saturnia. Saturnia told her that the gown was more classic, less flamboyant than Madame Pike's. *"La vôtre fait plus femme de diplomat,"* Saturnia assured her. *"Mme. Pike porte le tangerine, beaucoup moins chic que le gris."* A sober colour was certainly more suitable, especially considering she was the hostess. Although Iris had not seen the seating plan, she guessed Hugh had put her on the immediate left of the guest of honour, the Maharajah.

Without knocking, Barry Pike walked into her office looking harassed. "I need the talking points the ambassador used during the trade discussions in Vienna to update my analysis, Iris. The telegram has to be completed today. We've had a flash telegram from headquarters asking for an immediate report. There's been a question in the House of Commons and the minister needs a report by tomorrow."

The man was really irritating. Stephen would have joked around and asked what she was wearing to the party.

"Why on earth would I have the talking points?" she asked.

"I'm not saying you actually have them." Barry tried to sound placating, but he was exasperated. "They are not in the registry, so they must be in the ambassador's security shell. I don't want to disturb the ambassador, and you are the only other person who has the combination."

"But Otis and the security guards must have the combination," Iris said, genuinely astonished. "They take care of all that. You ought to know the procedure by now."

"You mean you haven't got the combination?"

Iris shook her head.

"You've never had it?"

"Never."

Barry was white. "But Otis said the ambassador told him you had it. He was certain. I even asked him again today."

"Well, I don't."

"But why would the ambassador lie to Otis?" said Barry.

"Hugh never lies. Only you would accuse him of that. You're so goddamned suspicious, always prying, always pushing. I'm delighted you're not going to get your promotion. I can hardly wait till I finish typing up Hugh's ratings. It's going to be Stephen, not you. You know what rating you're getting? Eight! Give my regards to your wife. I hope

162

she enjoys herself at the party. And now, get out of my office."

Barry left without a word and went directly to his own office. He gathered his papers, locked his door and walked down the corridor to the comcentre to put away the documents and his key. Sloan opened the iron grille and Barry handed them over.

"Where are you going?" Sloan asked. "Never seen you buzz off in the middle of the afternoon, like Belknap."

Barry stood there thinking for a moment.

"Mr. Sloan," Barry said very carefully, "I think you should know the ambassador did not give the combination of his shell to Iris. He is the only one in the Mission who has it. Please tell Mr. Otis, if you see him this afternoon. I'm going home."

Sloan stared at Barry, and briefly his taciturnity gave way. "What the hell could he have in the shell if he doesn't even trust his own bitch? And what am I supposed to do about it? Otis will tell me to screw off. He's afraid of Hilary-Moulds. That man would eat his shit if Moulds ordered him to."

Barry agreed with Sloan that Otis had become obsessed with Hilary-Moulds. It was hardly an obsession based on love. Hilary-Moulds treated Otis as his permanent victim, not even bothering with his usual destabilization tactics. The more cruel Hilary-Moulds was to Otis, the more fascinated Otis became with the man. Stephen had described the relationship as a devilish possession. "Otis loathes Moulds, but he doesn't know how to exorcize him. He'll have to drive a parking pole through the ambassador's heart just to get rid of him."

"If Mr. Otis refuses to report him, I'll write to security myself," Barry insisted to Sloan. "D.L. II will likely send a mildly chastising letter. But a report should be sent. It's the principle of the thing."

Although Radcliffe was sitting near the grille, the teletype machine was making too much noise for their conversation to be heard. Even so, Sloan moved closer to Barry and whispered.

"You'll get bugger-all for your trouble, Mr. Pike. Moulds will fry your eyeballs if you send that report. And headquarters don't like it when a junior complains about his boss."

"I still think it must be sent."

"Well, sir, you know your duty. But don't expect any thanks."

"I don't," said Barry.

He left and Sloan silently locked the two doors.

Nini was sitting at her dressing table getting ready for the party, washing her diamond brooch and earrings in rubbing alcohol, when Barry told her about his conversation with Iris and the business of the security shell.

Nini felt as if a great fist had just squeezed the oxygen and blood from her heart.

"He is evil. Truly evil. He's hiding something and he's afraid you'll find out what he's hiding."

"I don't know that he's evil," Barry rejoined. "I do think his behaviour is erratic to the point of being unbalanced. And I'm not saying that because of what he's doing to my future. It's more than that. He doesn't even follow his instructions from headquarters. Yet no one complains. He's too important." Barry paused, swirling his drink so the ice cubes made tinkling sounds in the crystal glass.

"About the shell, I don't know. Maybe he has some dirty books inside. Maybe he's writing his sexual fantasies and doesn't want anyone to find them. Who cares? Anyhow, I'm exhausted. I'm going to lie down on the couch," he said, and headed for the den.

Nini waited a moment, then followed him into the den. She noticed that Barry had been losing weight – his thin frame looked almost porous. This was the first time she had ever seen Barry lie down in the middle of the afternoon and on a working day at that.

"It's all over," he said, hearing Nini's footsteps on the parquet floor as she entered the room. "I'm finished. We may as well pack up and leave." His tone was that of a man resigned to defeat.

Nini was angry.

"How can you say that? Just because one ambassador doesn't give you the rating you deserve? What about the dispatch you wrote about demographic movements in the Soviet Union? Everyone at headquarters said it was brilliant. I know Hilary-Moulds was lukewarm, but the prime minister wrote 'penetrating and profound' on the margin. They're not going to forget that."

Nini waited for Barry to defend himself. When he did not, she said, "Well?"

"You don't understand the system," Barry said wearily. "Iris said I was getting an eight. Eight is not on the fast track. The officers are rated from one to ten. Eight doesn't sound bad. But she may as well mark down three. Hilary-Moulds is just too smart to give me too poor a rating. Then questions would be asked." He sat up and spoke very slowly so Nini would get the full force of his argument. "You see, it works like this. There is only room for a couple of promotions a year in each rank. Only outstanding officers get promoted. The competition is terrific. And an outstanding rating is only given to those who receive at least eight and a half. Some receive nine, or even ten. As a rule, at least a dozen officers in the service are rated by their ambassadors as outstanding, and only two or three are chosen from that group at each level. With my eight, I'm definitely out of the running. And losing a promotion at this time in my career sets me back indefinitely. I can't become head of a division unless I receive my promotion now. When I go home, they'll make me responsible for the legal aspects of protocol or something. My dispatch counts for nothing. Moulds will say it's a flash in the pan, that my work is generally uneven, or some such bullshit. According to my index cards, a lot of officers start off as high-flyers and then bog down for the rest of their lives. Just because they received one poor rating from an ambassador.''

Barry let himself fall heavily back onto the sofa so that he was once again prone. Nini would never have believed such a response from him. It frightened her.

"Moulds can't be *that* influential at headquarters,'' Nini pleaded. "There must be other factors taken into account besides his rating of you. Or rather Iris's. It's just not fair!''

"Look, Nini, who said this was a fair trial? There's no defence. Hugh Hilary-Moulds is both judge and prosecutor. He's got the connections.''

"But –'' Nini interrupted.

"No buts.'' Barry overpowered her. "He flies back and forth to Canada. He knows everyone on the rating board. He knows every mandarin in Ottawa, and all the ministers. They all go to that Five-Finger Fishing Club and decide who's up and who's down. Informally, of course. Over a few drinks and between painting canoes. He can ruin me everywhere in government, not only the foreign office. A whisper here and there that young Pike is brilliant but erratic will finish me in government. That's all they have to hear. Mediocre but steady is always better than brilliant and erratic in the bureaucracy. I tell you, it's all over and I don't know what to do.''

"Well, you're not accomplishing a damned thing lying around here like this!'' Nini cried, her voice rising to a dangerously high pitch.

Barry did not move. He made no answer. Nini wished she hadn't spoken.

The only other time Nini had experienced such fear was during the weeks before she met Barry, when she first knew she was barren. Now, however, the sensation was far more intense.

What was it that Moira had said about Hilary-Moulds? "Why does he have the power to reach out and destroy me, as well?"

Barry was Nini's "work," her painting. She could not face the idea that Barry would become a drone, like her father, envying bitterly, from a distance, those who had succeeded. The image nauseated her. If Barry believed that his life had been destroyed, how could she continue with her own? But he was exaggerating. Just for a moment, he had lost his balance.

Nini decided to call Nicole. The Dhroshkys knew how brilliant Barry was. They would put everything back into focus. "Don't be silly," they'd say, "Barry's bound to be a famous man. He's just over-reacting." Nini was sure she could prove to Barry that everything would be all right.

She went to her bedroom, placed her jewellery back into the box, locked it and rang Nicole. The Dhroshkys had just returned to Geneva and had asked her to come for tea. Nini had previously refused, saying she had too much to do getting ready for the party. But now she hardly felt like brightening her diamonds for a public execution – with her husband as the victim.

Before she left, she peeked into the den. Barry was still lying down, his eyes open, staring at the ceiling. He did not turn his head to the door, though surely he heard her. Nini walked out of the apartment, hardly knowing what she was doing, and rang the Dhroshkys' bell.

She found Nicole and Moorehouse in the sun on the balcony, drinking Campari.

"We've begun the partying early, Nini. Have a drink. No tea today. Maid's and butler's day off. I'm mixing."

There was a large tray of bottles in front of Moorehouse.

"A Negroni, with lots of gin, please."

Moorehouse filled a large tumbler with gin, added a

touch of Campari and a dash of soda. He and Nicole looked as if they had been at a health spa instead of in New York: sleek, tanned and content.

"So, Nini," Nicole asked, "tell me what you're wearing tonight. Long, of course?"

"Long tangerine taffeta. I don't really know why. It's what a tart might wear to a respectable party. I couldn't care less."

"I bought a Valentino in New York. Black and white, like a domino. A little much for this evening, perhaps."

"I think it's sensational," said Moorehouse. "You'll spellbind the ambassador. Hilary-Moulds likes to entertain beautifully dressed women. He's very discerning."

Nini was repelled by the two of them sitting like pashas against their overstuffed patio cushions. She drank half the Negroni at once. Abruptly, she put her glass down on the table, spilling the liquid on the linen cloth. She realized she would get no satisfaction or reassurance from the artificial thrust and parry of the Dhroshky style of conversation.

"Spellbind Moulds? What hypocrites you two are. How could you go to his party, after the way he spoke to you in Priay? You're a new breed of social climbers. I know what you're up to. You want a few blacks on the board of the Thoreau Institute to give it international respectability. And Moulds is a big pal of the Nigerians. You think he'll push the Africans your way. Well, he's not all that influential. He's just another ambassador with a reputation based on myth rather than truth."

Nicole replied sharply. "What business have you questioning our relationship with Hilary-Moulds?"

Moorehouse put a restraining hand on Nicole's shoulder. "Let Nini have her say."

Nini deliberately drank the rest of her Negroni, then helped herself to some pure gin and gulped it down.

"Hilary-Moulds is a fraud. My respect for intelligent people like you drops to zero when you don't and won't see through him."

"Obviously something unpleasant has happened to your husband," Nicole said evenly. "Has Moulds refused to promote him?"

"Oh, you're clever. Of course, I'm biased. But there are other things, too. He even has his own security shell in his office and won't let anyone else have the combination. Not even Iris. Barry says that's against the rules. He slashed Moira's portrait, which borders on the psychotic. He tells everyone he's going to Vienna, yet no one believes he's really there. And he never follows instructions from Ottawa. No one at the Mission knows what he's up to. And you two admire him enough to swallow his insults and buy a Valentino dress for his party."

Oddly enough, when Nini finished her tirade, Moorehouse looked even more pleased with himself than before. Nicole was excited. She put both her hands on Nini. "You are right to worry. I've always said to Moorehouse that Nini Pike has sound instincts."

Nini's head was buzzing from the drink and for a moment she couldn't speak. Moorehouse leaned in very close to Nini, taking the glass from her hand. Nicole sat back, keeping her eyes on Nini.

"You say," he said, "that he has his own security shell. No one else has the combination? And that he's always disappearing to Vienna?"

The lift from the gin was gone. Nini had passed the peak of her anger.

"Oh, he's probably writing about his sex life under a pseudonym. If I know Moulds, he'll sell it and make a fortune."

It was almost five o'clock and the nannies and children were crossing the road from the Parc Bertrand below. A parade of *poussettes* with their little parasols entered into the building. The sight always depressed her.

"Sex life," Nicole said dryly. "Indeed. I wonder if he'll mention his anal contusions. They do other things at the Clinique Beau Rivage besides take care of crazy rich women. Moulds goes there for this chronic trouble of his. A very common thing for homosexuals."

Nini thought Nicole had gone mad.

"What do you mean, anal contusions? How do you know he's a homosexual? Does the Thoreau Institute fund the Clinique Beau Rivage, or what?"

"Pay no attention to Nicole," Moorehouse said curtly. "She likes to make people think she knows more than she does. It makes her feel important. When she talks about something she knows, then she's worth listening to. Not this time."

Nini had never heard Moorehouse speak so roughly, especially about his wife. Most uncharacteristically, Nicole took her chastisement silently. She looked mortified.

Nini had seen the Dhroshkys react strongly to the name of Hilary-Moulds before. They had been exceptionally eager to lunch with him. She remembered Moorehouse's gold pencil swiftly marking the date. Nini was anxious to pursue Nicole's comments, but Moorehouse's reaction had deflated Nicole entirely.

He said, as if to calm Nini, "I'm sorry about your husband. I truly think he is the best officer in your Mission. That's very hard luck."

The telephone rang. It was Barry telling Nini to come home. They and the Belknaps, Iris and Roland Neville— "the family"—were supposed to be at the party earlier than the other guests.

She barely said goodbye to the Dhroshkys, sensing that Moorehouse was anxious for her to go. As soon as she got in her apartment she ran the bath so Barry would know she was home. There was no question in Nini's mind that Nicole knew exactly what she was talking about. Moorehouse

170

was angry because Nicole had revealed too much about Moorehouse and herself.

Nini began to see her relationship with the Dhroshkys in a new light. Why did Moorehouse seem so interested in Moulds's security shell and in his trips to Vienna? Why should the head of a scholarly institute react so intensely to the internal administration of Canada's UN Mission?

"They've cultivated me because I can tell them about Hilary-Moulds," Nini realized suddenly. "I'm only their conduit, the channel to the person they really want to know about. The Thoreau Institute must be linked in some way to the CIA. They're watching him. That's why they need my gossip, my information. The Dhroshkys think our ambassador is a spy. He's a traitor. But he'll never be caught. There's no evidence. Just bits and pieces. No one will ever find out. What if Hilary-Moulds becomes head of NATO?"

She shut her eyes and slid deep into the bath, as if the water would cover up the horrible idea.

It didn't matter to Nini that the Dhroshkys had become her friends under false pretenses. She felt not in the least bit wounded. Nini cared about only two facts: one, that Hilary-Moulds was a traitor; and two, that Hilary-Moulds was destroying her husband.

He is evil, Nini repeated to herself. He's like some flying creature in a nightmare brushing his poisonous wings on one and then another. She wondered if Moira or Neville or even poor Otis saw Hilary-Moulds as a nightmarish thing. Iris had felt those wings as well. We'll duck and squirm, Nini thought, hoping the wings will miss us. But Hilary-Moulds will succeed and poison us all.

Nini knew she ought to tell Barry about the Dhroshkys, but considering the state Barry was in just now, she knew she had to clear her thoughts before she could share them. He'd just accuse her of fantasizing. Where are your facts, he'd say. Maybe Nicole was just being snide, and Moorehouse was embarrassed.

But Nicole had been too precise. Anal contusions. If she were merely guessing, she'd have said that Moulds was faggy, or something like that. And Moorehouse. Every time she had mentioned Hilary-Moulds's name in the past few months, he had lost that sleepy air and looked as if he wanted to take notes. "Let Nini have her say," he had told Nicole. Moorehouse was pumping her. And then he was afraid Nicole had given away too much when she mentioned the clinic.

Nini was too upset to soak very long in the bath. But she would not share this with Barry. She would tell him about Hilary-Moulds in time. Or maybe not. "Barry cannot accept evil," she thought. "I can."

23

"The family" obeyed the ambassador's request and came half an hour earlier than the rest of the guests. This time they were gathered in "le grand salon," which had been furnished at government expense by government decorators. Neutral beige and green chintz on the brand-new Sheraton-style chairs, the same pattern on the drapes, and a beige wall-to-wall carpet. Expensive hotel-room decoration. Nothing offended, nothing delighted. All traces of individuality had been deliberately eliminated.

Nini wondered how she could be so sensitive to the blandness of the room while feeling so wretched. The ashtrays had maple-leaf insignias and there were Eskimo carvings of bears and walruses, huge grey hunks, modern corruptions of a former art. Oh, the subtle ways these decorators had of showing the flag, she thought.

A corner of le grand salon was garnished with a large, drooping *ficus*. Drooping trees and drooping people, she thought. Even Hilary-Moulds drooped. He was drinking a large martini and doing his best to talk as little as possible to Stephen, who kept looking nervously at Moira. Moira had dressed defiantly in a fringed Oaxacan poncho and a short plaid kilt, as if she'd come in from buying horse meat at the boucherie chevaline and hadn't had time to change. Moira liked the ethnic look and never minded mixing countries.

She was talking to Roland Neville, the only person in the room to whom she showed no hostility.

"Have you noticed," she said loudly, "that Mr. Hilary-Moulds has no Canadian paintings on the walls? Don't you think it unpatriotic for a Canadian ambassador to display foreign rugs instead? He has them hanging in le petit salon."

Neville, looking uncomfortable, muttered something, then quickly drained his martini and grabbed another from the waiter's tray. Last week Nini had taken Neville to the Pharmacie de Genève to buy his syringes and insulin. Now, watching him, she wondered how much a diabetic was allowed to drink. She thought he had looked morose even before Moira's conversation, and she noticed that he and Hilary-Moulds had not exchanged a word.

"He could have had a Canadian painting for nothing," Moira continued. "But he slashed it with his own scissors. He must despise everything from his own country. He's one of those *depaysé* ambassadors, totally cut off from his roots. An expatriate. I ask you, how on earth can such a man represent Canada? He's not fit to be an ambassador."

Stephen literally ran toward Moira and pulled her away from Neville. Moira gave him an exultant look but remained silent after that.

Neville, in the meantime, edged toward Nini, who was sitting by herself drinking Perrier water. Barry was wandering around, trying not to look grim, peering at the walruses and whales.

The atmosphere might have been marginally less lugubrious if it were not for Iris. No one knew quite what to do about Iris. She stood far from the others by the fig tree. The dove-coloured chiffon was perfect – it could have been designed by Grès. Iris's face was turned away from the company, and the art-nouveau silver comb given to her by Hilary-Moulds gleamed in her hair.

Everyone knew she was crying.

The seating plan had been displayed on an embossed leather stand, nestled among fresh violets in the entrance hall of Parc des Cèdres. As Julio took their coats, Nini and Barry glanced at the map to find out their dinner partners, and to learn which of the important people Hilary-Moulds had asked had accepted.

Nini was seated beside the guest of honour, the Maharajah, traditionally the place of the hostess. Mrs. Schwartz, the *New York Times* correspondent's wife, and Lady Cutting were to the left and right of Hilary-Moulds. Neville, Stephen and Barry were carefully seated according to strict protocol among the least eminent ladies.

Iris's name was not on the board. She had no place at all at the table.

"Destabilization," said Barry, *sotto voce*. "He practises it on everyone. Even Iris."

"But what is she supposed to do?" Nini asked. "Wait in the kitchen while we eat?"

It was impossible to continue their discussion because Hilary-Moulds appeared and greeted them with sickening effusion.

"Ah, Nini, flamingo taffeta this evening. A very appropriate colour. Asians appreciate bright colours. Perfect for the Maharajah."

When the real guests arrived, Iris, at a sign from the ambassador, went out to the hall and greeted them. A humiliating function, since they all could see, from the seating plan, that she was not a real guest, merely the office secretary, inexplicably overdressed for her minor duties at the party.

She re-entered the salon and mingled, accepting compliments on her dress from Nicole, chatting about refugees with the Maharajah in his dinner jacket and golden turban, comparing skiing holidays with Edna Schwartz. Although she had stopped crying, she walked jerkily and her mouth was twisted into a smile. Five minutes before the dinner, Iris disappeared.

Hilary-Moulds slid over to Nini and took her aside.

"Iris decided it would be better if Yves Marius prepared a tray for her in the upstairs library. That way she can look in on the servants from time to time to make certain things go smoothly. She insisted, you know. I offered to place her at the table. But she's terribly anxious about the party. Much too anxious. So I didn't press."

Nini was revolted by Hilary-Moulds's duplicity, and remained so throughout the dinner.

When all of the guests had left, Hilary-Moulds cajoled "the family," excepting Iris, into staying on to taste his oldest Armagnac. Nini assumed that Iris had gone home.

Hilary-Moulds, Nini noticed, had rudely ignored Neville, not even introducing him to the guests. Moulds's behaviour to Barry was marginally better. Apparently he no longer considered Barry a threat; Barry was finished, in his eyes. Among "the family," only Nini and Stephen had been treated with courtesy.

Hilary-Moulds was in an expansive mood. He even asked Barry and Stephen what they thought of Lord Cutting's reaction to the party, although he then answered the question himself. Cutting had congratulated him on the meal, a good sign. And the food had been superb. Soufflé of sweetbreads, *pintade farcie, crème brulée* with fresh raspberries. He had to thank Nini for all that, and she had been absolutely superb with the Maharajah. He jostled Barry in the arm and said he'd better watch out.

"The Maharajah's got his eye on your beautiful wife. And when he likes a lady, they say he's irresistible. She'll probably get a little bracelet tomorrow morning from Cartier. Just to say thank-you."

Hilary-Moulds was drinking his second large Armagnac and his words were becoming a bit slurred.

Neville was matching him drink for drink, but it had not made him more talkative.

Suddenly Moulds stood up, weaving slightly.

176

"You know, my friends, my doctor tells me that I should rest a little after a party. I do have high blood pressure. But I want to continue our conversation. Belknap still hasn't told me what Schwartz was whispering about during the coffee. I just want a short snooze and then I'm coming right down. You must all stay and have another drink. We haven't had a really decent post-mortem."

Everyone knew that Hilary-Moulds had a habit of taking naps during a party, even at other people's homes. It had become quite usual for him to excuse himself to the hostess and then reappear completely refreshed. Hilary-Moulds went upstairs and the Pikes, the Belknaps and Neville resigned themselves to an unpredictable waiting period.

After a few minutes of desultory conversation, with Moira and Neville remaining resolutely silent, Nini said, "What about Iris? Do you suppose she left?"

Moira shrugged. "Who knows? Who cares? She's probably upstairs ironing his shirts."

"If she is upstairs," Nini said, "I think she should join us."

Stephen agreed. "Go on up, Nini, and bring her down for a drink. He's treated her shamefully."

Nini took off her shoes, so as not to disturb Hilary-Moulds, and checked the rooms upstairs. There was no sign of Iris, her purse, or her coat. After a search, Nini came down without her.

The group waited almost an hour. Hilary-Moulds did not reappear. Barry could not stand it any longer.

"Neville, maybe you'd better have a look. Just to see if he's all right."

Neville disappeared and came down with the news that Moulds was fast asleep.

"Less g'home." Neville had finally begun to slur his words. He looked sick.

The Pikes, the Belknaps and Neville decided that the ambassador was out for the night, and they left together.

Nini and Barry were still in bed when Julio called them at

8:15 the next morning. Julio told Barry that Hilary-Moulds was dead and that he did not want to stay by himself in the house with a corpse.

Barry got dressed and called Stephen. The two men went over to Parc des Cèdres. Nini and Moira stayed home.

24

Neville sat on an uncomfortable slatted chair drinking *eau de vie de poire* at la Potinière, a small café in the middle of le Jardin Anglais.

It was four in the afternoon and he was surrounded by old women sipping tea and children fooling with their melting ice cream in silver-stemmed *coupes*. It was as unseasonably warm as it had been the last time he had been in Geneva, a year ago, when Hugh Hilary-Moulds had died. The petals of the tulips along the walks were splitting and dropping from the heat.

Neither Hugh nor Nini Pike would ever have recommended la Potinière for drinking *poire*. They would have insisted that he go to an *auberge* discovered by Nini, thirty kilometres from Geneva, near one of those orchards where pears actually grew into liqueur bottles fixed on the branches. But it was the wrong season, thought Neville. The trees would just be flowering, and he doubted if they would put the bottles up so early in the spring.

Whatever the season, Barry Pike would not have been concerned that Neville had chosen the wrong café to order *poire*. He would merely have said that it was unwise ("unwise" was one of Pike's favourite words) for a diabetic with emotional problems to drink eighty-per-cent proof white alcohol in the late afternoon.

179

A year ago it would not have occurred to Neville to think about Barry Pike's opinions.

Barry Pike had, a year ago, been Neville's junior. Neville had got the impression from Hugh, when they talked together the day before Hugh died, that Barry was not a rising man. Neville had judged him to be a sombre, disapproving fellow who made a better marriage than he deserved. But at that point, he had only met Pike once, in Hugh's presence, which might have been the inhibiting factor.

It was amazing, Neville thought, how one could so misread character. Pike had talents that both he and Hugh must certainly have missed. The prime minister and the undersecretary had recognized those qualities quickly enough when they came to Geneva for the meeting of the Eighteen-Nation Disarmament Conference, shortly after Hugh's death. Soon after the visit, Pike had been recalled to headquarters by the under-secretary, at the request of the prime minister, to become head of personnel in the external affairs department—an astonishing promotion for the slow-moving foreign office.

But it was an extraordinary period, and extraordinary measures had been taken. Everybody was saying now that Pike had judgment and discretion as well as toughness and ambition. Neville had to admit that he himself only shared the last quality with Pike.

It had been said that the prime minister needed a trained surgeon, a man who knew how to cut without pain or embarrassment to the government. As the new head of personnel, Barry Pike became that surgeon. Twenty-one operations—problems—had awaited him in external affairs. And Roland Neville was one of them.

The worst part of being fired by Pike, Neville reflected, had been having to listen to him, still junior in rank as well as age, justifying the "departmental decision." Pike had spoken of his behaviour as reflecting "emotional difficulties," and had made a ridiculous pretense of sophisticated understanding.

Neville believed Pike to be truly shocked, and hated him for it.

Neville had become one of the department's twenty-one problems after his return to Budapest from Geneva. When he arrived in Hungary after the death of Hilary-Moulds, he said nothing to Janos about seeing the Hungarian in the photograph in Hilary-Moulds's office. They continued to make plans about their future in New York and now met practically every weekend at the same hotel near Lake Balaton, the hotel in which they had been photographed. Neville saw no purpose in telling Janos about the blackmail attempt. After all, Janos had kept his own secret: he had not mentioned working at the Canadian Embassy.

Why the security police did one thing and not another had always been a mystery to Neville. He would never understand their motives in waiting so long before sending the pictures to Ottawa. They were inefficient in many ways, and their decision-making processes must have been highly bureaucratized. Berendi would have had to deal with at least three layers of the hierarchy.

When a telex arrived from headquarters in Ottawa asking Neville to return forthwith for interviews, he knew immediately that the photographs had finally been sent. He hoped he could clear everything up by explaining his position. He had done nothing treasonable.

The day before he left, Janos came to see him at the embassy. It must have been the first time Janos had set foot in the office since Hilary-Moulds's time.

Janos told him that the pictures had been sent to his colleagues at the opera and that he had been fired from the company. The police had threatened him with a long prison sentence for capitalistic deviation unless he convinced the ambassador to help the Hungarian government. He was to become a non-person in his own country. No way of getting out, no way of living decently where he was. And it was all Neville's fault. Janos, weeping, accused Neville of emotional treachery and of destroying his life.

Neville had had many affairs during his life, and had always managed to shift from one to the other without sloppy emotional complications. He had thought of each lover as a new experience, and had swiftly left him when the euphoria disappeared. Before Janos, love had meant excitement and rebirth. But Neville was getting old, too old to attract someone as young, fresh and intelligent as Janos. He knew that, in his world, youth–adolescent good looks–was the key to all. Neville realized this was probably his last romance and he wanted it to go on forever. If only he could have taken Janos home. Eventually he would have lost the dominance in the relationship. But Janos would still have been good to him. How stupid the Hungarians were in their strategy. If only they had used Janos as their weapon and not alerted Ottawa by sending the pictures, Neville thought, he might have done much–far too much–to keep Janos. But once headquarters had learned about its security risk in Budapest, Neville could do nothing to help himself or Janos.

Neville went back to Ottawa the day after seeing Janos, and never went back to Hungary again.

The sessions with the security people at headquarters–Defense Liaison II Division was their euphemistic title–had not been as distasteful as the interview with Barry Pike. D.L. II merely insisted upon the repetition of minute details–names, places and events. They thought there was a chance that Neville had really given something to the Hungarians, then had become frightened and had backed off. It was possible, they felt, that the photographs might be a Hungarian punishment for ceasing to co-operate, not retribution for honourably resisting blackmail. There would always be that question in their minds. Neville's word did not count.

The D.L. II people treated him impersonally.

Pike, in personnel, was the moralizer, the man who explained to Neville why he was not fit to be a diplomat.

"I realize," Pike said, "that you told them to send the photographs to us. You felt that if you were open about your sexual preferences, there wouldn't be a problem. But that is just not so. You may feel that you can resist blackmail because you don't care who knows that you are a homosexual. But what if one of your friends is threatened? In most countries, people cannot afford to be as brave as you believe you were. Do you know how you would react if you were responsible for the destruction of someone else – someone you cared for?"

Neville was certain that Pike was referring to Janos, and he found the oblique accusation unbearable.

Pike shifted his argument to a less emotional sphere.

"We can't send you to the Soviet Union or to any Eastern European post because you are vulnerable, whatever you may think, to intimidation. We can't send you to any Muslim country because in places like Pakistan, they cut the arms off men found practising homosexuality. That is their usual crime-prevention measure." Barry said this with distaste.

"You may be posted to Washington, New York, London or anywhere in Western Europe, to places where civilized people don't mind overmuch about sexual preference. Obviously, this provides us with a situation where you get the best posts while someone else who isn't a good prospect for blackmail is sent to the hardship posts."

What a bureaucratic prig, thought Neville.

Barry had more to say. "Personally, I don't believe it's fair to punish the discreet and steady officers by giving them the most difficult embassies. I can't have a personnel policy based on rewarding the least reliable."

Barry quickly turned his gaze away from Neville as he said "least reliable."

"We are not exactly firing you," Barry went on when Neville said nothing. "We are telling you that you will get no further promotions and that you will not be trusted with any substantial assignments. My advice is to get out of external affairs and into a field where you can be with whom you like. Try the universities or journalism. But stay away from diplomacy."

They never spoke again after that interview.

Neville discovered that twenty other men – ambassadors, junior officers, communicators, cipher clerks – just happened to be planning to leave the ministry in a gentlemanly fashion. They were all given a year's grace to find jobs – except for one colleague, who was already in jail. And they were all told their usefulness was limited within the department because they were homosexuals.

Neville later discovered that a Canadian security guard, a heterosexual, had been found spying for the KGB by the British in Tehran. The man was forced to leave external affairs, but was never prosecuted. Another heterosexual, a medical man, had been caught planting bugs in his own embassy and reporting on the moral weaknesses of his Western colleagues to the Soviets. He left the government with his pension. Neville knew of three officers, heterosexuals, who had had affairs with a Bolshoi ballet dancer, a housemaid in Prague, and the wife of a Communist party member in Warsaw, all female agents of the KGB. The three men had been allowed to continue their careers in the ministry.

Neville concluded that Pike disapproved of homosexuals because they were homosexuals, not because they were security risks.

This was Neville's last week as a diplomat.

He had come to Geneva as an adviser to the Canadian

delegation for some insignificant trade negotiations. No one seemed to care if he attended the meetings or not.

This café would have to serve him as a conference hall. The children had left, the sun was down and now the adults were drifting in. It was the aperitif hour.

He ordered another *poire* and thought that Hugh Hilary-Moulds had had better luck.

25

Barry Pike was, as people had described him to Neville, a man of judgment, ambition and discretion. Indeed, at no time had Barry ever volunteered or supplied information about security difficulties, although it was plain to many involved in government that something unusual was happening. Occasionally, Barry was still asked why so many able men had left the ministry. His answer was that it was nothing more than coincidence. They had all found better positions in banks and universities.

But Barry was becoming increasingly restless as chief of personnel. Shortly after his two-year anniversary in the position, he described his job to Nini as worrying about other people's egos, and said he was fed up with the shifting and appointing of ambassadors – "a bunch of prima donnas" – around the world. They discussed the possibility of Barry leaving the foreign office, going into a corporation or even entering politics. Nini thought Barry would be a good politician, but he saw too many risks.

Jack Fowler, director of the national party, official king-maker, compulsive poll-taker, had been worrying about an approaching by-election located fairly close to Ottawa, in the county of Derby-Nepean. The seat was occupied by a member from the opposition party. The government party had not had a member from Derby-Nepean for the past fifteen years. Fowler thought he had found a way of stopping the rot.

Given one or two new factors, Derby-Nepean could possibly be a swing riding. One factor was already there: the county had become, increasingly, a bedroom riding to Ottawa. Those who worked in Ottawa were generally public servants who traditionally voted for the party in power. The local Derby people, however, the farmers and small businessmen, could still be depended upon to vote for the opposition.

And that was where the second new factor – Barry Pike – came in. Fowler had met Barry at three or four large interdepartmental meetings, and the prime minister had told Fowler that Pike was an impressive man. To Fowler, however, the most significant thing about Pike was that he was from Derby.

On their return from Geneva, the Pikes had bought a summer cottage in Derby not far from Nini's parents' house. They renewed their old Derby contacts, used the small-town lawyers, tradespeople and real-estate agents and spent money at local hardware stores and lumber yards when they renovated their cottage. Derby opinion was that the Pikes had not become snobbish just because they had lived in Europe. Fowler was certain that the local Derby farmers and tradespeople would vote for one of their own. But he had to convince Pike to leave his government job and run in the by-election first. He had had no trouble convincing the prime minister that he wanted Pike to run. The PM told him moodily that he wished his present cabinet ministers were as able as Pike.

Fowler was a big, dark man with black eyebrows that met in the middle, but his savage appearance belied his amiability and democratic ways. His Christmas party for the parliamentary cleaning ladies had become a lauded public event: Fowler dressed up as Santa Claus and distributed atomizers of Joy perfume, bought at his own expense. The most junior of reporters were always lunching with Fowler while he plied them with questions, first asking their opinion on an obscure amendment to the Railway or Bank Act and then soliciting their comments on the "feel" of the nation as a whole. "It's you newspaper people that know what's going on. I get stuck too much in the capital," he'd say flatteringly.

Fowler tended to confine his luncheon dates to members of the press, out-of-towners from the weaker constituencies, and the prettier parliamentary assistants. He bothered with middle-management public servants only if they were working on sensitive domestic questions that could affect the polls for several weeks. But he would invite anyone to lunch, no matter the person's prestige or position, if he thought that person could be useful to the party.

He was already waiting at his regular table at the Four Seasons dining room, where he ate daily, when Barry arrived. Barry had never been alone with Fowler before and wondered why the powerful politician would seek him out.

Fowler didn't waste his time.

As Barry sat down, Fowler said, "We are very grateful to you, Barry. The prime minister thinks we are in your debt. And so do I. Might have been hurt in the next elections if something had surfaced. Just look at the trouble they had in England with the Burgess and Maclean business." He looked meaningfully at Barry, letting the gratitude sink in.

The Four Seasons dining room was busy stretching its collective neck to see with whom Fowler was lunching today. It was not unpleasant, Barry thought, to be the centre of attention.

"Not only are you an able man, Barry," Fowler continued when he judged his pause sufficiently meaningful, "you're a man who knows this country. You have real roots. You haven't been ruined by the foreign service. On the contrary, I understand that you and your wife have chosen to live in your hometown. I know about the Pikes and the Sullivans."

Fowler was playing with the forks and knives as he talked.

"Very well known families in the area, very well liked. And I'm damn glad you are continuing the tradition. We move around too much in North America. Lose our friends, our connections."

The waiter brought them lunch without anyone ordering. Mouton Cadet and rare steak. Everyone knew that the Four Seasons served indifferent food and that Fowler – and Fowler's guests – ate and drank the same thing every day. The waiter had a bus-boy bring some fresh cutlery to Fowler's table.

Barry did not have to wait long for Fowler to get to the point.

"We want you to run in the by-election in Derby-Nepean. The prime minister specifically asked me to approach you. And I agree with his choice. You're a winner – you'll cream the opposition."

Fowler smiled disarmingly and put two thousand dollars in cash on the table. "You know I like to bet," he said. "It's yours if you lose." Fowler allowed the money to rest on the table for a few seconds, then in one swift, precise motion he swept it up and replaced it in his billfold, saying, "But you'll never see it." He went on rapidly now, scarcely giving Barry time to eat or think. "Derby's becoming home to public servants working in Ottawa; they'll like voting for another public servant. But more important, you have roots. You and your wife have the respect of the locals – the Derby people who vote against us, damn them. You'll win on your name alone, Barry. Small-town people like to know their candidates. Naturally, you'll have to resign from your job in the government. Give up your pension. But the PM told me that you're not a person who's afraid of risks. I'm a poker player. And I think you like the game, too."

Barry had no intention of becoming a member of parliament who sat on the back benches with nothing to do. The job he had now was far more interesting, powerful and secure. And he told Fowler exactly that.

Fowler smiled, as if he had heard this a thousand times before. But Fowler had smiled a lot during the lunch. Practically everyone in the restaurant came up to his table to shake hands. The conversation was constantly interrupted by Fowler's politely rising, asking about wives, vacations, new jobs, and the headwaiter's granddaughter's wedding. But each time Fowler sat down he continued his argument with Barry without a break in his thoughts. Barry would never understand how the man had also managed to eat everything on his plate.

"You'll run, you'll win and you'll be in the cabinet," Fowler hammered on. "We need you more than you need us. We haven't had any representation from that region for more than fifteen years. You'll have to be in the cabinet. I'll even get the PM to give a speech in your constituency. He's never done that for any MP in his life – but you have my personal guarantee. The caucus will be pissed off, naturally. But you're a Derby man with a good local reputation. And you're smart." Fowler tapped his temple, as if pointing out the location of the brain.

"You'll win, all right. And you'll be a minister. A junior minister at first. But no back bench. Not for Barry Pike. Where's the risk?"

"No risk," Nini said. "There's no risk at all. How can you lose? Your grandfather baptized every farmer in the region and my father knows where and how to touch for the campaign funds. He's always loved being the bag-man at election time. It's part of the Sullivan tradition. And now he'll be doing it for his daughter. We have no money problems. And I don't care about your pension."

They were sitting at the kitchen table in their Derby house, drinking tea.

Barry was still cautious. He said that Fowler promised a cabinet position to every candidate. "That's part of his job. He has to be a bit of a con man to convince anyone to run. Politics isn't all sweetness, Nini. Think of the newspapers, the criticism. What's more, I'm confident I can go to Washington as ambassador eventually. Give me about six or seven years. You would like Washington. It's just a matter of waiting."

Nini replaced a ginger-snap she was about to eat. She couldn't believe what Barry was saying.

"In less time than that, in five years, if you have any gumption, you'll be prime minister. And I'd like that much better. How rigid, how cautious you've become in the foreign service. Diplomacy hasn't broadened your sights. You and your index cards."

She rose and poured a couple of ounces of Glenlivet into her tea.

"Why on earth would you want to become an ambassador, a Hilary-Moulds? You can have real power as prime minister and appoint whomever you want, wherever you like. Give Washington to the Belknaps."

She drank her tea in one gulp.

"Stephen and Moira can play bridge with the congressmen and run after the senators. That's what ambassadors do. All prestige and no power. High-class lobbyists. Let Moira give the tea parties and burst into tears when the cabinet wives don't show up. It's depressing to hear you talk about pensions and risks. I married you because you were ambitious. You wanted to change things. What are you going to change in Washington? Jack Fowler offers you the biggest chance in your life and you fuss and fret like an old woman. What do you know about risk?"

"And what risks have you taken, Nini," he asked sarcastically, "except for marrying me?"

Nini ignored the question but she did change her tone, placing her arguments on a more logical footing so that

Barry would be convinced. The liquor had clarified her thoughts.

"Look, the prime minister is over sixty-five. He wants to retire. And the cabinet is full of mediocrities. The party needs new faces, fresh blood. The PM doesn't even bother listening to his ministers' advice: he's bored with the whole lot of them. And so is the country. But he listens when you speak. And so will everyone else. Tell Fowler you're interested in the leadership. Not only a cabinet seat."

"I would never talk to Fowler about such a thing," Barry said in exasperation. Then he added, "It's much too soon."

"Well, maybe not now," Nini agreed quickly, jumping up and pacing as she continued. "But I believe Fowler about the cabinet position. This area hasn't had any representation from his party for ages. He has to make you a minister. And once you're in the cabinet, you'll be able to cultivate the other ministers, especially the French Canadians. My God, Barry, just think, you'll be the only English-speaking cabinet minister who can speak French. You'll have the Québec voters eating out of your hand. The PM is French-speaking, from Québec. The next PM has to be English-speaking. The opposition will never find a decent leader. An Anglophone minister from Fowler's party who speaks French will carry Québec and English Canada as well. And there's only one minister who will fit into that category. You."

Barry rose and drew the curtains, as if he were afraid of someone listening to the conversation.

He said she was jumping to incredible conclusions. But he found her arguments compelling. Above all, he knew she would never forgive him if he refused Fowler's offer. It would be better to run for the by-election and lose than live with Nini in Washington as ambassador without having taken the risk. He would have lost all her respect.

When word got out in Derby that Barry Pike might be a

candidate, Fowler took a straw poll and the results surprised even him. When Pike announced, some months later, that he was definitely a candidate, Fowler took a more precise poll and bet Barry another thousand that the opposition candidate would lose his deposit. Barry said he didn't believe in reading chicken entrails.

Nini's mother gave forty coffee parties in two months, inviting the dairy farmers' wives, the wheel-chair invalids from the "chronic hospital" and even the women over eighteen from St. Mary's, a home for unwed mothers. Mrs. Sullivan made her last party exclusive. Only the most influential were invited and the effect was predictable: each woman present felt so honoured to have been asked that she left thinking Barry Pike was a saint.

Nini went everywhere with Barry in a pick-up truck, listening to complaints about the poor roads (which were under provincial, not federal, jurisdiction) and planting placards with Barry's name in cow pastures. She went to every local Saturday-night dance and danced polkas with the lumberjacks, who smelled of sweat and Brut in equal proportion.

It was, as Fowler promised, a shoo-in. Barry paid him three thousand dollars the moment his election was announced. The day after the election, Barry became a minister and entered the cabinet. The Ontario caucus was disgruntled, but everyone agreed that there had to be a minister from Derby and that only Pike could have won the election.

On the night of his new appointment, Barry and Nini celebrated by opening a couple of bottles of vintage Dom Perignon she had brought back from Geneva. It was a special night. Nini looked happier than she had ever been.

In the past, Barry had always confided in Nini but he had never mentioned the firings to her because it was a top-security matter. She knew that Barry had had to get rid of some problem cases, but had not known the reasons. The

whole business still bothered Barry. What with the new
ministerial job and the champagne, he felt he needed Nini's
reaction, even after the fact. She was, he knew well, the only
person in the world who wanted everything to be right for
him. Barry believed she was more realistic than he was, in a
selfish sense, but the selfishness was always for his benefit.
Nini had no instinct for what Barry called public policy, but
she did have strong views on what was good or bad for
Barry Pike.

Nini was surprised that Neville had been silly enough to
take a lover in a police state like Hungary. She would have
thought Neville had more sense. Still, she was uneasy when
Barry told her about the general policy of firing homosexuals. She had liked some of the men who had been fired,
and she asked Barry if he had spoken to them with consideration, especially Neville. "If you spoke in a way that
would make them hate themselves, they will transfer their
hate to you. You don't need twenty-one enemies now that
you're in politics."

Barry said he hadn't relished the job but, given the cir-
cumstances, he had been pretty blunt.

"How is it," she asked, "that you were easier on the men
who had affairs with women agents?"

He explained that it was felt by Departmental Security
and the RCMP that the homosexuals had a greater potential
for trouble. He had only acted upon their advice.

"It sounds as if you're passing the buck," she said frankly.

After consideration, Barry admitted that there might have
been some unfairness.

"I don't believe you handled it as well as you might have.
You get this righteous tone in your voice, just like your
grandfather. And it can be most offensive. I don't know
why I ever married the son of a preacher. I hate the breed.
Did you sound righteous with Neville?"

Barry didn't answer, but he wished he had softened his

tone, especially with Neville. He should have consulted Nini before the firings, even though it meant breaking security.

Roland Neville, he had just learned, had been hired to write a political column that was being syndicated in a number of major newspapers across the country.

26

It really was Queen Victoria's fault.

She chose the town as the capital of her most northern colony because it was compromise ground between the English and the French.

After the good timber had been chopped down, Bytown should have remained an inert village near a military canal that continued far beyond the populated area, emptying into the St. Lawrence at the American border.

Then Bytown was given another name, an Algonquin name – Ottawa – again to avoid aggravating the English and the French. That's when the Queen's new industry began to attract workers other than loggers. The populated area eventually grew; soon there were half a million people.

In this government town, there was a right way of going about life and a wrong way. The rules had not been pinned to the doors of Parliament – but everyone knew them by heart. Everyone was dependent on the big factory for financial and emotional sustenance, everyone from the men who removed the dead elms in the national capital parks to the wife of the prime minister. The difference in income between the prime minister and the most senior member of the elm-cutting crew was negligible. And the incomes of public workers were on public record.

In a government town, distinctions of any kind are

avoided; they cause envy and suspicion. Yet there was little here that was suspect. The government was free from venal corruption, and there were no secret police to knock on doors at midnight.

Take a cocktail party, given on neutral embassy grounds by a diplomat with an entertainment allowance and tax-free alcohol. The politicians of the reigning party would stand in a circle facing inward, initiating conversations only with their own kind, relishing their power. There was no question of noblesse oblige. Relishment ended and resentment began if a voice outside the circle were overheard praising a member of the opposition or – even worse – a non-elected official.

Officials at the same cocktail party would stand discreetly in corners, in groups of not more than three, discussing some new foolishness that might embarrass the party in power. Their voices sounded smug but they felt diminished because no one bothered to ask for their advice. Members of the opposition would smile, speak warmly to everyone who had a vote and wait for revenge. The townspeople – doctors and business people who serviced the government – moved aimlessly about, not adhering to the powerful people. After a bored sentence or two, the politicians and officials would return to their circles and corners and the townspeople would drift with the diplomats.

Ambassadors were appointed to the capital because it was a comfortable retirement post. They searched for honest butlers and skilful partners at duplicate bridge. Aside from the cocktail parties, they kept to themselves in well maintained mansions, paid for by cheques signed in other government towns.

Camouflage was necessary because there was suspicion, resentment and destruction of the ego. In this government town, the camouflage was sameness and plainness, reinforced by an astringent heritage of English Puritanism and American populism.

But the principal reason for camouflage was the journalists. A government town attracts journalists from across the country, and the journalists must prove to their editors that they are working.

At a cocktail party, the journalists would sit by the bar, waiting and hoping for a top person, preferably female, to speak and act without discretion after the fourth martini. If she stuck her head out of the fox-hole, it would be knocked off by a journalist's bazooka. The zealous captain of these search-and-destroy missions was Roland Neville, the acknowledged arbiter of integrity in the capital. He'd write about the corrupt (and very occasionally the just), relentlessly attack the papier-mâché policies and ridicule the statements of those who held positions of power. The other journalists considered him their highest priest of virtue because he would never lunch with Fowler or even one of Fowler's running dogs, appointed officials who could poison a journalist's mind while pretending to impart information. The just men, in Neville's column, were the fallen angels, the disgruntled junior ministers, the public servants who were far away from those who made decisions. Neville would spend a lot of time with these grievance collectors, who were a rich source of colourful material. A few journalists would admit privately that Neville might be sloppy about a few facts, but they all pointed out, sanctimoniously, that Neville was the first to smell smoke.

None of the *paparazzi* cared if a real fire existed. Real fires were slow-burning; their causes were obscure, and would take too much effort to expose. And they were too complicated to explain. The editors, in any case, never wanted more than a paragraph or two of titillation.

Neville and the other journalists were also on the watch for profligacy on the part of those in power. It was wrong to be a spender. No one got anywhere, in this town, by picking up a restaurant bill. A wife who wore silk organza and emeralds to a cocktail party, instead of polyester, was merely the wife of an irrelevant diplomat or a prosperous merchant who sold men's suits to the government people.

The right way to live was to work long hours and be seen skating home along the canal. No one criticized you if you had a summer cottage, as long as the electricals were enfeebled and the eaves were full of bats.

The town was not without innovations. The latest signs of sophistication were vast abstract murals in the lobbies of government buildings, and spinach quiche for dinner in the homes of government people. But no one was supposed to criticize either the murals, for messiness, or the quiche, for sogginess.

In a government town, everything physical looks controlled. The snow on the old military canal was cleared in winter for skaters, and recreational boating was permitted in summer, motorboats excepted. Two huge rivers formed a restrained pattern, encircling and bisecting the town. Here and there were neat waterfalls.

Very close to one of these waterfalls, at the point where the two rivers joined, there was a big grey stone house surrounded by hedges and a handsome iron railing. Occasionally a Mountie stood at the gate, but not every day. This was the residence of the prime minister, on Sussex Drive. In the spring, a tourist or two would peep through the hedges entwined with wild grape leaves and snap pictures of the daffodil beds on the lawn. The prime minister's residence, unlike the White House, was not open to the public. Only guests and friends knew what it was like inside.

And no one dropped in on Nini Pike without an invitation.

27

Nini had gradually come out from under the covers and perched herself on top of the butterfly bedspread, sitting upright with her legs tucked under her body. She was wearing a blue satin robe, trimmed with maribou at the hem, which draped over the side of the bed.

Nini must be uncomfortable lying in between the sheets with all that fuzz, Eleanor thought. She looks like a movie heroine in one of those thirties screw-ball comedies about millionaires. The fact that Nini was twenty-five years older than Lombard or Harlow didn't spoil the comparison in Eleanor's eyes. Nini was slender and her hair hadn't faded, like the hair of so many other aging blondes. Her complexion was fresh, except for a few lines under the eyes and the usual sagging at the corners of the mouth. Looking at her, Eleanor wondered when Nini would ask her which doctor in Canada did the best facelifts. If Barry were to stay on as prime minister, Nini would certainly want a facelift.

It had stopped snowing and a few weak rays of sun blinked on and off like an SOS signal through the bay window, shadowing and lightening Nini's face. She looked livelier, almost happy, and Eleanor was glad she had stayed.

Doreen came in the room with another maid; each carried a tray. "So you've finally come out from under. I'll just put a cloth on the table by the window so you and the doctor can have a comfortable lunch."

Doreen busied herself in the room as she continued, brave enough to gloat but not brave enough to look Nini in the eye while she gloated. "Nothing worse than eating in bed, I always say. All you have to do is take a couple of steps. I'll bring your sheepskin bedroom slippers."

As soon as Doreen spoke, Eleanor knew that Nini would not get out of bed. If Doreen had kept her mouth shut, set the table and left them alone with the lobster and the wine, Eleanor was sure that Nini would have managed to creep to the window after Doreen left. But now it was a question of honour.

"Two trays, Doreen," Nini said perfunctorily. "One for Dr. Campbell near the chaise longue. Bring up a little folding table. I won't eat off that tray, Doreen. Bring me the invalid tray with the sides and transfer the plates. Then I won't have crumbs."

Doreen threw a conspiratorial, disgusted glance at Eleanor.

"Mr. Pike called. He said to tell you that everyone is coming for the wing-ding tonight. Mr. Fowler, Senator Gross and all the wives. *Everyone*." Doreen snapped out the sides of the invalid tray with more noise and flourish than necessary and went on. "It's a miracle the weather cleared. What dress are you wearing? Marie, here, will iron it for you. It should have been ironed yesterday. But you wouldn't let us near the closet."

"Don't iron anything. I'm not going downstairs this evening. And I'll inform the prime minister of my plans myself."

She gathered her robe about her and slipped under the covers again.

When Doreen walked out of the room, Eleanor thought she ought to have slammed the door a little louder. Nini went back to staring at the butterflies printed on the underside of the bed canopy. Eleanor couldn't stand her childishness any longer.

"Did I say you weren't spoiled? I take that back. Get out of bed. If you walk up and down this room a couple of times you'll be perfectly able to be the *House-and-Garden* hostess tonight."

"I can't, and I won't. God will punish Barry if I go down for dinner."

Eleanor couldn't recall Nini ever mentioning God or his wrath. In Derby they had been taught that the use of the word "God" was in bad taste. Only the girls who went to the Jehovah's Witnesses and grew up to be waitresses talked about God as if they were afraid of Him, like mean Pessel with the badly stitched hare-lip whose father had the Massey-Ferguson tractor dealership. Immigrants, Eleanor knew from her practice, used the word colloquially without invoking fear. She could tell a patient's ethnic background, even if there was no accent, by the way he would use the word "God."

She decided that Nini was afraid of drinking too much in front of her guests.

"Do you mean you will get drunk and embarrass Barry?"

Nini sat up. She was outraged.

"There are two things that will be believed of any politician's wife, and one of them is that she has taken to drink. I may be known for a sharp tongue but my insults are always deliberate, never the result of too many martinis. I know enough not to lose my control in front of people like Jack Fowler and Gross."

Eleanor was encouraged by this. Despite their differences, she had always respected Nini's code. Nini did many things for Barry that other political wives would have refused to do. Nini was an old-fashioned wife, a member of a dying breed. Eleanor would never reproach Nini because her ambitions filtered through her husband. Nini had her standards. She visited hospitals and tried to pretend she was at ease with the deformed and the dying. Only Eleanor knew Nini well enough to understand that Nini found these duties terrible. She did it because she believed Barry might gain a few votes from afflicted families and professional do-gooders if the newspapers mentioned that the wife of the prime minister had been to a home for the mentally retarded. Others might have thought this cynical on Nini's part, but Eleanor knew differently. The visits were indeed motivated by selfless devotion, but Barry, not the recipient of the visit, was the object of that devotion.

Unlike Barry or even Eleanor, Nini did not have the ambiguous instincts of a missionary whose self-importance swells when he or she hands the natives their ration of dried milk. Nini genuinely felt sorry, but she derived no personal satisfaction or salvation from being a sister of charity, a great white goddess or a den mother. She had not a taint of the evangelical within her. But she played these rôles for her husband's sake.

"I know you have superb control, Nini. So why punish yourself?"

"Because God never punishes me. I'm the spoiled one. You have just said it now."

God again. Eleanor was worried. Perhaps this meant total collapse. As a last resort, Eleanor decided to appeal to a solid aspect of Nini's personality: physical vanity.

"Your legs must be all shrivelled from lying in bed like that for so long. Walk around the bedroom with me. I won't tell Doreen that you got out of bed."

With reluctance, Nini pushed a skinny white leg out from under the covers and looked at it with distaste. There was a fine mat of brown hair from her ankle to her knee. The unshaven leg upset Eleanor even more than the talk of God. Fastidious Nini, who covered her undies with silk satin squares, hadn't shaved, waxed or burnt off the hairs on her legs for six weeks. It was as if Eleanor had stopped brushing her teeth.

She went over to the bed and hauled Nini out, putting one arm around her waist for support. Nini leaned against Eleanor's shoulder and together they walked from one end of the room to the other. Nini paused in front of a small round table covered with a long, mauve velvet skirt. The table top was a Victorian cluster of *pots pourris* in silver bowls and photographs framed in chased silver.

Princess Margaret, Queen Juliana of the Netherlands and the late emperor of Ethiopia, Haile Selassie, holding a Pekinese dog, had all inscribed personal greetings to Nini and Barry. Nini thought it was too provocative to show the royal testimonials in the more public rooms downstairs. They only made people like Senator Gross's wife jealous.

"Princess Margaret is fatter now," said Eleanor.

Nini agreed and sighed, thinking of better days when the princess had her figure. She pointed to the Pekinese.

"Although he was a boy, he was called Lulu. The emperor brought him to dinner. The dog ran under the dining-room table and urinated on Barry's leg during the soup. Watercress. Barry kicked him in the stomach and he screamed like a woman. The emperor stared at Barry. Barry stared back. The emperor would not remove the dog. Barry refused to apologize. He was the only royal person who dared bring a dog to Sussex Drive. The others miss their animals, of course, but they don't impose them on their hosts."

As they gazed at the Lion of Judah and at Lulu, Nini in her blue marabou and Eleanor in corduroy knickers and woollen socks, Doreen threw open the bedroom door. It was the first time she had seen Nini standing in six weeks but Doreen was beyond sarcasm. Her eyes were protruding from their sockets and she was heaving and gasping like a dying carp on Honey Harbour Beach.

204

"Mrs. P., something awful has happened downstairs. Nutt won't go."

Nini steadied herself by placing a hand near the photograph of Queen Juliana.

"What do you mean, Nutt won't go? It's the rule. I write it down every time there is a party. Get him out, Doreen. You know how to handle him."

"Mrs. P., you'll have to speak to him yourself. He doesn't listen to me anymore."

"I haven't spoken to that man in five years. I certainly am not going to start now."

"I can't get him out like the other times, Mrs. P. It's because you're sick and won't come downstairs. He says you're not in charge. He says we have a power vacuum at Sussex. He says that he's giving the orders now. He's going to run the place like it should be because Mrs. P.'s dying from cancer. He says he got that straight from the mouth of Dr. Campbell."

Doreen gave Eleanor a disapproving glance. Her tone escalated into hysteria as she continued. "It started when I yelled at him for chasing away the new gardener. He was making such a pretty job of the flowers, too. Copying your picture book exactly. I ran after the little fellow and I begged him to come back. My, but he was rude. He said, 'Tell the old fart to fix the flowers himself.' He meant Nutt," Doreen explained. She was embarrassed as she spoke the last words. But, distressed as she was, she knew it was important to report as accurately as possible.

Nini owned an eighteenth-century volume of coloured engravings of flowers, which stood propped open on her grandmother's harpsichord in the front hall. The plates showed *strelitzia* and other exotic blossoms. The book was opened at a different page every day, according to Nini's instructions, and every day a different plate was displayed.

Doreen continued.

"The gardener slapped Nutt across the face with the

freesias and dumped the rest of the flowers on the front-hall floor on purpose because Nutt was complaining so much about the leaves and puffs on the carpets."

She paused to let Nini and Eleanor absorb the information.

"But there's worse. He gave me this piece of paper."

She took a page of Sussex notepaper from her pocket and handed it to Nini, watching her face. The paper said:

Verbal abuse to gays at 24 Sussex
Pikes prejudiced against alternate lifestyle

"Mrs. P., he's coming back to the residence tonight, with picketers, members of their local chapter. He's their president and that's what's going to be written on the signs. He said it's going to be front-page news tomorrow."

"Picketers. Homosexual picketers," Nini said. "I knew it. I knew Neville would begin his attack. He's put him up to it. They're kind of a clique, they all know each other. Did Neville talk to the gardener when he came to see me six weeks ago?" she asked Doreen.

Doreen was surprised.

"As a matter of fact, they did speak. Nutt told me the little fellow idled away quite some time with Mr. Neville just before he left."

"All our old friends from Geneva have turned against us," Nini said. "It doesn't matter *what* Barry does for them. He made Stephen Belknap ambassador to Washington, and Moira picketed the residence."

"Moira picketed the residence because Stephen was appointed ambassador to Washington?" asked Eleanor.

"Not *because* of that." Nini was getting exasperated. "She and those environmental women, the so-called liberated ones. Moira organized a consumer rally and picketed us because the supermarkets put pork in the hamburger meat. The newspapers said, 'Wife of newly appointed Canadian ambassador to Washington, Moira Belknap, pickets Sussex Drive. Old friend of PM's wife.' They took her picture. Let them all die of trichinosis, I say—demagogues in denim skirts. And Barry actually sent the Belknaps to Washington, even after that. He's soft."

Nini's telephone rang. Eleanor answered, letting Nini and Doreen worry about the picketers. She listened for quite a long time, said thank-you and hung up.

"Well," Eleanor said slowly, "I guess there won't be any demonstration tonight. There might be something in the papers tomorrow, but not about gay rights. That was Constable Mackinnon. When he was walking around the grounds on his afternoon check, he found a body lying in the back yard, halfway down the cliff by the river. The head was bashed in. The body has been identified. He believes someone murdered your little gardener."

28

Most foreign offices list the capital cities in climatic order for the benefit of their nomadic personnel. Ottawa, according to these post reports, is the second coldest capital in the world, outranked only by Ulan Bator.

The winter had been longer and colder than most. Although it was April, the snow on the Ottawa River was thick and the ice firm, still safe for cross-country skiing. The steep cliff behind the prime minister's residence descended from the lawn to the edge of the river—nature's provision for the prime minister's security. But it is not the Canadian way to cloister the back yard of the prime minister with forbidding iron fencing, or to hide plain-clothes policemen in the snow banks. Man-made security at the Pikes' was not obvious. A few years back, the Mounties had wanted to install a televised surveillance system because some elderly Eastern European immigrants began to ice-fish on the river, but Nini had refused. "Three old men standing around a hole waiting for a carp? Impossible to stare at them for more than fifteen minutes without falling asleep." Barry had agreed that ice-fishing was not a spectator sport and that the policeman watching the television set would soon let his attention stray.

Other action occurring on the river was negligible. On weekends a few skiers who didn't want to bother with the twenty-minute drive to the Gatineau Hills would lope along the river until the wind or boredom drove them off. Expert cross-country skiers like Eleanor considered the river too flat to be challenging, and preferred the more difficult manipulations of trail-skiing. To Eleanor, the river was just a broad, cold space without the surprise curves dropping into narrow, icy slopes around fallen cedars that made skiing in the woods so interesting.

Barry, however, liked the convenience of skiing on the river and was the first to break the snow with his skis; he made a path behind the house down the cliff. Later, despite the disapproval of the Mounties, Barry had some workers from the National Capital Commission go over the path and widen it with a plough so it would be easier for Nini to manoeuvre.

The gardener's body had been found lying against a boulder not far from Barry's path. He had walked halfway down. He was wearing boots, and his feet had sunk at least ten inches in the snow, making huge burrows and ruining the path for skiers. Someone else had come up from the river; the laborious "V" marks of climbing skis were fresh in the new snow. The two had met on the steepest angle of the cliff, and had left the marks of their struggle. All around were craters and burrows and the tracings of out-of-control ski poles. Yet it was surprising the gardener had died: the snow was deep enough to have broken his fall. His body must have rolled down with great speed for his skull to have hit the boulder with such impact. The police believed that he had been pushed directly toward the rock.

The skier had left the body where it stopped. He had gone off the path only to pick up his fallen poles, then returned and skied to the river. He had left a trail for half a mile on the river and then continued up a public path, which led to a small parking area below Rockliffe Park, much frequented by novice down-hill skiers and sledding children because of its mildly hilly terrain. He must have removed his skis and driven away in his car. Nothing else was known.

"We'll have to cancel the dinner party," Nini said with satisfaction. "The newspapers will say it's inhuman for the prime minister to entertain the same day someone was murdered on his grounds."

"Don't look for an excuse," said Eleanor. "You're not in mourning for the fellow. He's not part of your live-in staff. Have you ever laid eyes on him?"

"Never," Doreen said. "She's always been upstairs. He arrived here just a day before the operation."

"Anyone can climb up that path," Eleanor added. "The murderer came from the river. I'm not a politician, but I think it would be wiser if you acted as if the affair had nothing to do with the Pikes. I'm positive Barry won't want to cancel the party."

Eleanor was correct. Barry called and told her that a press release had already been drafted, saying the gardener was a new employee who only spent two hours a day at Sussex, working for the most part in the greenhouse. The police were continuing their investigation, assuming that the location of the accident was mere coincidence. "Accident" was the key word.

However, for security reasons, the path was going to be obliterated because of the resulting publicity.

Barry told Eleanor that he'd drop in later to see Nini. "I'm depending on you to get her out of that room. Tell her if she doesn't come downstairs tonight, Fowler will think she's a drunk."

Eleanor waited until Doreen left before she passed on Barry's message.

"I don't care what Fowler thinks."

Nini climbed back into bed, covered herself up to her chin with her eiderdown, slid up onto her cushions and uncharacteristically began a nervous plucking of her marabou feathers. "I've told you everything about Geneva. You've

210

survived that. Now I suppose it's time to tell you about Neville and the blackmail."

Eleanor eased back on the hated chaise longue and waited.

"At first I refused to see him," Nini said. "I told my secretary that the man was a pollutant. Then he wrote me saying that he wanted to discuss the old days in Geneva, when we were friends. I told my secretary that I'd rather see him in a law court. I've always wanted to sue him for the things he wrote about Barry. But Barry doesn't believe in suing reporters. That's Fowler's influence. Then he sent me another note enclosed in a double envelope: 'Private and Confidential, for Mrs. Pike. To be opened by hand.' It had one line. 'Hugh Hilary-Moulds.'"

Nini's fingers plucked frenetically and blue feathers floated toward Eleanor.

"I was waiting in the library downstairs when Nutt showed him in. I could scarcely believe it. He looked exactly the same. Loud suit. His freckles hadn't faded with age. Neville obviously takes good care of himself. Perhaps a small paunch. But then journalism is basically an easy life – no real responsibilities like Barry has to contend with. After all, they don't have to do anything – just criticize."

Nini looked directly at Eleanor but when the doctor made no comment, she continued.

"At first Roland was complimentary. It was back to 'Roland' and 'Nini,' you see. We had a sherry and he reminded me how good I had been to him in Geneva.

"'On my last visit you took me to the Pharmacie de Genève to buy syringes and insulin. What a place. Three floors selling everything from artificial prostheses to portable radios. I did buy a radio, although you told me not to waste my money. You said they would go down in price. I should have followed your advice,' he said.

"Then Nutt brought in two lunch trays. I didn't want the

table set, but Neville didn't seem to notice the slight. He just kept talking as if we were a couple of old friends reminiscing.

"'I was absolutely befuddled in that store,' he said, 'after Hungary. It was shocking to have so much choice; the abundance was overwhelming. And the crowds. In Budapest there was nothing to buy, nothing to push people aside for except old turnips and tainted meat.'

"Neville lifted up one of the napkins and stared at the fish and then he continued.

"'If it hadn't been for you, Nini, I would have wandered for hours like a confused old man. But you smoothed my way and I finished my purchases in fifteen minutes.'"

Nini shook her head, then forced herself to go on with the story.

"I began to eat without waiting for him.

"'Of course, the Swiss are more efficient than the Hungarians,' Neville said. 'And it helps not needing a prescription for insulin. They just shove the bottles across the counter like aspirin. Fifty diabetics must enter that store a day. An exaggeration. But I still think it's an amazing place. Never been in one like it since. The drug-store on Boulevard St. Germain in Paris might be just as big. But the Swiss, I think, must sell more medicine.'

"Neville had brought a small briefcase with him. As he talked he started to unzip it, but when a thought occurred to him he'd close it again. He did it three times," Nini emphasized. "I found this most unnerving.

"He told me I had been very sympathetic. He said, 'You must have realized the shopping was all rather too much for me. You thought I was taking a terrible risk with my health, living in Hungary where there was no decent medical treatment. I remember you saying that. And then you asked me all about my diabetes. You told me that diabetes was in your family and that you worried about inheriting the disease. I described my injection routine to you. I even showed you how to put the syringe in the bottle and with-draw insulin.'"

"Did you tell him that?" Eleanor asked.

Nini nodded her head.

Eleanor knew there was no history of diabetes in Nini's family.

Nini glanced at Eleanor, waiting for a reproach, but Eleanor said nothing. Nervously, Nini talked on. "Suddenly, Neville stopped eating, stopped talking about diabetes and finally opened his briefcase. He had refused wine and was drinking tomato juice because he said Perrier water gave him a bloated feeling. He took out some rather yellowed newspaper clippings and put them beside his plate, not offering to show them to me at first.

"'Did those television people call you?' he asked. 'Some academic has convinced the CBC to do a show on important post-war Canadians—when the country really had something going, when first-class people were in charge.'

"He stood up and stared at Barry's collection of Russian history books as he spoke. I was furious by this time, listening to him make veiled insults to Barry while he made himself at home in our library. But I had to let him keep talking. I remember he was browsing through one of the older volumes on the shelf when he said, 'A researcher actually remembered that Hugh Hilary-Moulds had been a leading diplomat and possibly the next head of NATO. So they decided to do a retrospective on Hugh. Or is retrospective a word used only for painters, Nini?'

"Of course, I didn't answer him, but he couldn't have cared less. He just kept talking, casual, sweet-tempered Roland," Nini said sarcastically. When she resumed her reporting, she imitated Neville's casual tone.

"'All his old friends have been called. Perhaps the producer was too intimidated to call the wife of the prime minister for a cameo shot of her relating personal memories of old Moulds. Naturally, it's not going to be on prime time.

The show will most likely be slotted at 7:00 A.M., after the Spanish lessons. But my interest was piqued when they rang me, and I volunteered to talk on the show.'

"He sat down again and kept rattling those yellow papers at me while he talked. He was getting terribly excited by this time, bounding up and down from his seat, blinking those pale eyes. The words started rushing out of his mouth.

" 'I realized that I had to say something intelligent about Hugh,' he said, 'even if it's just for the tube. I decided to do my own research. There had been this curious business when Hugh died. An autopsy. I read about it in the *Tribune de Genève* while I was eating perch at the Creux de Genthod. You recommended the restaurant, Nini. And it was superb. A bad mark for me. I should have been too upset to remember what I ate. I notice that we're eating perch today. Makes me nostalgic. Only ocean perch, of course, not from Lake Geneva.' "

Nini had picked up one of her magazines and was flipping its pages as if she were imitating Neville's rattling of the newspapers. Eleanor saw that it was an unconscious gesture.

" 'You can imagine my reaction, finding out about Hugh's death in the newspaper,' he continued. 'I had dined with all of you at his home the night before and yet nobody bothered to call me. I was very angry. And hurt. But most of all mystified. Why an autopsy? We all knew that Hilary-Moulds wasn't in the best of health. High blood pressure. And that evening he really was drinking. The poor bugger had put on twenty pounds since I last saw him. I was shocked at his death, but you have to admit he was a prime candidate for a heart attack. I called your husband from the restaurant, but he was very secretive. No information for Neville.' "

Nini interrupted herself, threw down the magazine,

reached out to the end of her bed for another and began to rip up the pages of *Vogue*.

Eleanor said, "Go on."

"'I was rude,' he said, 'and told Barry the autopsy was ridiculous, that he was a meddler, just stirring up trouble for no reason. Then I left for Hungary and heard nothing more about Hugh. Well, after speaking to the television people, I thought I better have another look at that article. Not remembering the precise date, I asked the *Tribune de Genève* to send me every issue from that week. Clippings almost twenty years old. Here they are. Newspapers won't do that for everyone. But journalists do receive some privileges from other journalists. Professional courtesy.'

"He started fingering the papers, jabbing at a paragraph here and there.

"'Did you know, Nini,' he asked, 'that there had been another article about Hugh's death? First time I ever saw it. That article gave the reason for the autopsy. A pin-prick in his buttocks. I would never have argued with Barry if he had told me why he asked for the autopsy. Unlike the *Tribune de Genève*, Barry wasn't exactly punctilious about professional courtesy—even though I was an ambassador, a close friend of Hugh's and much, much senior in rank. But that was a long time ago. I have to admit that Barry was right to be suspicious. I owe him an apology.'

"Neville shoved the clipping in front of me and underlined with his forefinger the part about the pin-prick."

Nini placed her finger on a page of *Vogue*, imitating for Eleanor his insistent pointing.

"'Look here, Nini,' he said. 'It says the doctor commented that perhaps the laundry left a small pin in his shorts. Ridiculous. Hilary-Moulds never sent his underwear to a commercial laundry. You knew that. He had a laundress come to the residence twice a week. I even sent my laundry to Parc des Cèdres while I was in Geneva. Iris said it would be cheaper than the Hotel de la Paix. And there were never any pins.'

"'Well, I certainly didn't put any pins in his shorts,' I screamed at Neville. 'What are you trying to say?'

"Neville smiled and put the clippings in a cardboard folder and replaced them carefully in his briefcase, zipping it up again.

"'Of course, you didn't,' Neville said. 'That would have been a prank, a practical joke. Not your style at all, Nini. But you did go upstairs that evening to look for Iris. You were feeling sorry for her. I don't know why. She never cared for you. She told me that she had recommended that Stephen be promoted instead of your husband. And that Hugh had agreed. I think you knew about that rating report.'"

Nini's bed was covered with shredded paper and blue feathers. She had torn up as much of her marabou as of the *Vogue* magazine.

"'And yet you were sorry for Iris,' Neville went on. 'Even Moira was indifferent to Iris's whereabouts. And she had been her friend. You know what I believe, Nini? I believe that Hugh Hilary-Moulds was murdered. Wouldn't you agree, Nini, that the murder of such an eminent man ought to be public knowledge?'"

Nini was tearing what was left of the magazine into neat, narrow strips as she repeated Neville's words to Eleanor.

"'Wouldn't you agree, Nini, that it's my duty to appear on a television show, produced in Hugh's honour, and detail my suspicions – describe who was with Moulds just before his death, how they felt about him and their movements in the house? You must admit that my speculations will increase the show's appeal. When the producer finds out that I suspect Moulds was murdered, it might even be re-slotted in prime time.'

"Neville lifted his hands to prevent me from interrupting, although I had no intention of doing so.

"'I'm aware that the toxicological report was negative.

I've read right here in the second article that the doctor pronounced him dead of a heart attack. But I think differently and you know differently. Insulin poisoning does not show in toxicological analyses. Many laymen know that. What a perfect way to kill a man who is not a diabetic. I have, of course, no proof he died that way. All my evidence is circumstantial. But I shall share my suspicions with the public. I will repeat everything I am saying to you now on that television show. If I were you, I'd sue.'"

Nini began to gather all the torn bits of paper into a pile beside her pillow. As she recounted Neville's words, her voice took on his sanctimonious tone.

"'The trial will be a sensation. Here's Nini Pike, the prime minister's wife, suing Roland Neville because he has linked her to a possible murder that occurred twenty years ago. I might even lose a few thousand dollars. Or maybe not. Can you prove your innocence? You will be in a peculiar legal position. I don't think you'll go to jail. But Barry will be finished. No one would ever elect him prime minister again. Who knows? He might have been an accessory. Does he know how Moulds died?

"'You sit there so silently, Nini. What are you thinking? Why did I bother to see you today if I was going to ruin your husband anyway? Perhaps you believe I have a sadistic streak and want you to break down in front of me. Not at all.'

"He stood up and looked down at me.

"'I'm not going on television to talk about murder and poisoning because I want to humiliate you. Or for the sake of being sensational. We have enough of that sort of thing on television already. Nini, we knew each other a long time ago, and I won't forget that. But there are more important things in life than personal feelings. This country is devastated by your husband's leadership. He cares as much about democratic principles as Idi Amin does. Barry has got to go. I realize that you think I hate him because he brought my diplomatic career to an end. You have always believed that my columns denouncing him were personally motivated. But that's untrue. All my life I've worked for peace, as a diplomat and now as a journalist. And what do I see? My prime minister condemning the Soviet Union for aggression and imperialism when we have finally attained a period of *détente*. He's totally isolated. No other head-of-nation has spoken out like he has. Your husband's a war-monger, a Red baiter, obsessively anti-Russian. He's a dangerous man. And a lousy prime minister. He must step down for the sake of the country. Nini, I don't want to involve you in this degrading television business—degrading for both of us.'"

Nini paused, stared down at the mess on her bed and went on.

"'I've come here this afternoon,' he said, 'to tell you that you have a choice. You have the power to make Barry quit. Don't say anything to him about Hilary-Moulds. Say that you're tired of political life. I know Barry loves you. If you're determined enough, he'll get out. I promise that I'll never open my mouth. I'm not a sadist. I didn't come here for the pleasure of seeing you beg or plead. You can't possibly believe that of me. We both have the same ideals, the same goals. I would never have had lunch with you unless I thought we could find a solution to the problem. Think about what I say. And trust me. I'll wait for your call. I really don't want to go through with this. Hilary-Moulds should stay put in his grave.'"

Nini swept all the strips of paper onto the floor. "He was such a son-of-a-bitch," she said.

Several minutes passed. Eleanor waited, then said, "And?"

Nini drew a deep breath, grateful for the break, but aware that she must finish the story. She did not, however, sound calm when she continued.

"I don't know how I managed to get the words out, Eleanor, but I told him that what he said was preposterous, that he was a contagion and it was ludicrous to think I could stop him from spreading his foulness. I told him that my husband was the best prime minister the country ever had. In an instant that mock look of remorse vanished from his face, as if my words had released him from the pain of a restraining scruple.

"'Don't get carried away, Nini,' he said. 'You went into Hilary-Moulds's room when you went upstairs to look for Iris. What business did you have there while he was asleep? I can think of only one thing. Iris told me. She even sent me a letter. Do you know where Iris is now? In Washington. I wrote her a few weeks ago and she replied. I told her I was doing a little research. She writes that she was rather surprised when you opened Hugh's bedroom door and closed it behind you. Do the right and proper thing, Nini. Tell Barry. He'll resign.'

"Then he walked out of the library and I haven't seen or spoken to him since."

Suddenly Nini jumped out of bed and held the blue marabou away from her body. "It's a disgusting robe," she said. "I look as if I'm moulting."

Now it was Eleanor who looked exhausted. She put her head back on the chair and closed her eyes as if her energy had to switch off in order for Nini's to flow.

"I suppose you can blame me, in a way," Eleanor said. "I did bring up the subject that summer in Derby, before your marriage. We discussed the perfect crime. I was the pedantic medical student, so eager to impress. I think our victim of insulin poisoning was your art-history professor."

"I would have found out some other way. Roland Neville mentioned it to me in Geneva, as a joke. He's forgotten. Ironical. He remembers everything else, but he's forgotten that. Tell me what to do, Eleanor. I don't want Barry to know I murdered Hugh Hilary-Moulds."

29

A particular rise in front of the East Block on Parliament Hill had become sacred ground in Ottawa because of some intersecting underground heating pipes. Spring arrived on the hill first. The inhabitants of the city, starved for any colour other than the dirty grey of the stones of the neo-Gothic government buildings and the dirty white of left-over snow, would gather around this spot where the snow melted earliest. They would come in threes and fours to worship some crocuses – blue and yellow vernal gods nurtured into premature birth by the serendipitous engineering plans of a hundred years ago.

A procession of hooded monks wearing splendid mahogany-coloured capes that swept the snow walked in single file on the road above the crocuses. Not because this was a holy place. They were members of a bizarre sect from no established church, and had obscure grievances against the world, the government and Barry Pike.

They had chosen this spot two years before because it provided an occasional audience for their pickets. The false monks, despite their placards, were appropriate to the setting. But today there were other people gathered, people inimical to the sacred place, camera-men perched on tops of trucks, lounging print reporters and the rough men from television and radio, their microphones cocked. They wanted Barry Pike to tell them about the death of his gardener.

Barry's limousine was nearly blocked by this swarm, and half a dozen policemen were attempting to clear his way. The monks shook their fists in unison at Barry, as they had done four times a day for the past two years. The reporters ignored the monks but Barry waved back; he always looked forward to their greeting. He felt less benign toward the journalists because he was pretty sure they would distort a banal death into a conspiracy, perhaps an assassination plot devised and ordered by the prime minister himself. He looked at his schedule as the police leaned into the scrum. He had Question Period coming up in the House, then an orderly news conference about the constitution and a visit from two Western premiers about wheat-pricing policy. The death of the gardener should have been the least of his worries. But he knew Nini was lying mournfully in bed and would certainly take the gardener's death as one more signal that she didn't deserve to be happy.

Barry had been terribly worried about his wife and was feeling guilty about being so busy. He thought he'd better skip Question Period in Parliament and instead reassure Nini. As he rode to Sussex Drive, he read what few facts the police had discovered about the gardener's background and death. His eyes widened slightly. He went over the report once more, then sat back and thought. He tapped Otis, his executive assistant, who was sitting in the front seat, and asked him to call for some documents. Otis picked up the telephone in the car, spoke briefly, then told Barry he would have them the following morning.

"Now," Barry said. "I want them at Sussex not later than forty minutes from now. It's always tomorrow with you, Otis, never today."

Otis sighed, picked up the telephone and put more urgency into his request.

Barry had hired Otis against his better judgment, out of

misplaced loyalty. Otis, as Barry had predicted twenty years ago in his personal index cards, had not been promoted beyond an FSO 3. Disappointed, he had left the foreign ministry and volunteered to work for Barry during his early election campaigns in Derby. It seemed that Otis could find no work in between elections and Barry, prevailed upon by Fowler, had taken him on. It had been a mistake.

Nini had warned him that Otis wouldn't do. He was idle, had no sense of priorities and was always disappearing when he was most needed. Sometimes Otis was at the Press Club, sometimes in the Caribbean, and once he went shopping for sweat-socks at ten o'clock in the morning on a work-day. Barry experienced only two sensations when he had to deal with Otis: irritation and guilt. Irritation because Otis was incompetent and guilt because Barry always felt sorry after he shouted at him. The guilt made it difficult to fire Otis. Barry gazed in distaste at the back of Otis's head; his hair grew only at the nape of the neck, in a straggly fashion, and not at all on his skull. Apparently, Otis did not want to cut the tangle around the neck for fear it would disappear permanently like the rest. As Barry stared, a thought occurred to him. When he spoke, his voice was surprisingly soft, as if he were reminiscing, which was not his usual manner when he wanted some information from Otis.

30

A psychiatrist colleague had once told Eleanor that psychotics who are disconnected from common human emotions, who murder at random and without motive, experience intense relief after confession. Eleanor was interested to see that Nini, who certainly did not belong in that chamber of horrors, had voluntarily risen from her bed, plugged in her electric rollers, and was now staring into her dressing-table mirror, fretting about imaginary signs of debilitation. As she waited for her rollers to heat and patted and creamed her face, Eleanor understood that Nini had returned to the world, although nothing had been resolved except her decision to admit guilt. Of course, Nini was a natural-born confessor. In Derby, Eleanor had been her priest, then Barry had taken over. If Nini had been alone in life, like Eleanor, she might well have become a Catholic. Eleanor lived alone, but not consistently and not now.

When Nini's mother told her, a few years back, that Eleanor was sharing a house with a young nurse, the news suited Nini very well. Until then Nini had felt a heaviness, even an undertone of artificiality in their friendship. Her habit of confessing to Eleanor had been an odd kind of emotional obligation. Now their relationship had lightened, and Nini's confession of Hilary-Moulds's murder had been made without the sense of paying off a debt. If Eleanor had any religious beliefs, they were in reticence and order. Nini was aware that their new and more satisfactory relationship would vanish if she asked the most casual question about Eleanor's personal life.

Eleanor admitted to herself that this had been the first time in her life that she had listened to Nini without an irrational sense of resentment. Eleanor genuinely wanted to help her, and, watching her primp, Eleanor decided Nini was strong enough to relate the details of the murder.

"Why did you tell Neville there was diabetes in your family?" Eleanor asked.

"I never even thought about killing Moulds when I took Neville to the Pharmacie de Genève," Nini replied. "I didn't go with him to learn about insulin. I just wanted to be hospitable. He really was quite helpless. The idea only occurred to me after I saw how easy it was to buy insulin. I wrote down the name of the insulin while he paid. There was a bottle sitting out on the counter. Then I lied about my family. I wanted to find out how he used the syringe."

"When did you buy the syringe and insulin?"

"A week before the party. As I bought it, I thought, 'This is my safety net. If things become worse, I have my protection.' I considered injecting myself. I didn't know if I could live and watch Barry's destruction. But there was the other choice. It was also in my mind. Hilary-Moulds's death. How marvellous that would be for the Pikes. I used to wake up praying each day that Moulds would die of a heart attack."

Nini wiped all the cream off her face, picked up the tweezers and began carefully plucking her eyebrows.

"I made my decision on the day of the party. Barry came home and told me it was all over. Moulds had destroyed him; he was powerless. Totally powerless. I had never seen him so low. Barry's a natural optimist. It was so uncharacteristic for him to say he was without hope. I had to do something. Even then I wasn't sure I had the courage to go to that party with the syringe. It was my conversation with

224

the Dhroshkys that gave me the strength, the moral certainty. Moulds was a traitor. He had broken all the rules. I wouldn't be killing him for selfish reasons only. There would be others he would destroy."

Nini touched the rollers to see if they were hot and started to put up her hair.

"I think, Eleanor, if we had been at war, I would have received a medal – in a private ceremony, of course. What if I had worked for the underground?"

"How did you carry the insulin to the party?"

"Obviously I didn't want to take both the bottle of insulin and syringe with me. Before I left, I filled the syringe almost three-quarters full. I tried to fill it completely at first, but the insulin began to drip through the needle. I wrapped the syringe in Kleenex and put it in a paper bag. I stuffed it in my patent-leather afternoon purse. An evening bag would have been too small."

Nini finished rolling her hair, picked up a bottle of nail polish and tried out the colour on one nail.

"I never let go of that bag for an instant. The big purse looked odd with my evening dress but most people don't notice such things, especially Barry. I just hoped and waited. I had no conscience about killing him. I was just worried about being caught. I was excited, but my mind was clear. And I didn't drink any alcohol; the gin I had at the Dhroshkys had worn off. So you see, Eleanor, I can't plead temporary insanity or drunken rages. My intention was to kill Hilary-Moulds. When he decided to go upstairs, I took it as a gift from God."

The colour didn't please Nini; she quickly wiped the polish off with a Kleenex and chose another bottle.

"Naturally, I was worried about Iris. I thought she might be sneaking around. And I did look for her. But she knew every corner of that house. I hadn't the time to open closet doors and linen cupboards. I went into his bedroom; he was fast asleep, snoring. I took the syringe out of my bag and jabbed him quickly, through his trousers. I was terrified the prick of the needle would wake him. I put the syringe back in my bag and ran out of the room and downstairs. When I got home I threw the needle and the insulin bottle down the common garbage duct in the apartment building. They used to pick up the garbage early in the morning."

Nini had now painted all the nails of one hand and held them up, satisfied with the colour.

"You have to admit, Eleanor, until now it was a successful murder. I can't imagine why Iris didn't give me away when Barry ordered the autopsy. She loathed us both."

"About what time did you go upstairs?"

"It must have been two o'clock or so. We didn't get home till after four; we sat around so long at the residence waiting for Moulds to descend. And we had to drive Neville to his hotel. The alcohol finally got to him; he was swaying when we dropped him off and the car smelled of Armagnac."

"It is odd that Iris didn't say anything," Eleanor agreed. "I think you should call and ask her why."

"Are you mad? I haven't spoken to her in twenty years. I haven't even seen her at a distance since Hilary-Moulds's death."

"But," Eleanor insisted, "Barry must have had something to do with her. She was around during the autopsy and afterward, wasn't she? How did she behave?"

"Surprisingly efficient, but withdrawn, I think Barry said. She was at work the next day and made all the arrangements for shipping the body home. The ideal secretary in a moment of crisis."

"What about the promotion ratings?"

"Nothing could go forward without Hilary-Moulds's signature. I don't think she even finished writing them."

Nini proceeded with the work of polishing the nails of her other hand.

"Headquarters immediately appointed Barry as senior man," she went on, "the chargé d'affaires at the Mission. Iris had to take her orders from Barry after that. We didn't think she had mentioned the ratings to anyone except Barry. Stephen hadn't a clue that he was supposed to be the chosen one. She must have told Neville, of course, but he was in Budapest. She was whispering madly to Neville at Moulds's party, not long before she disappeared. I realize now that it was about us. Iris gave away my motive. Anyway, Iris stayed on for a few weeks and then asked for a cross-posting. Barry was delighted to recommend the idea to headquarters. I think she went to Germany. And we went to Ottawa." Nini paused. "I had no idea she was in Washington with Moira. I can't possibly call her. What would it accomplish?"

Eleanor was frank.

"Look, Nini, confessing the murder to me is not a solution. Neville is determined to let this out. Things can't be any worse for you. He's going to use Iris's testimony, if you can call it that. She's his prime witness. You're much better off to hear the story from her own lips than to accept Neville's version. You must keep one step ahead of him. You can only prepare your defence if you know how strong the evidence is from the prosecution. What have you to lose by calling her?"

"She'll gloat," Nini said. "Or maybe she'll refuse to talk to me."

"Or maybe not. You're being childish."

"I am. I am," Nini replied. "It's my vanity. I really haven't any choice, have I?"

"One more thing," Eleanor asked, "just before you call. Didn't the second newspaper report say that Hilary-Moulds was found with his pants and shorts tangled about his tasselled shoes? And yet you say you injected him through his clothing."

"Well, I did think that was peculiar. I never took down his pants. I didn't have time. And I would have been too afraid, anyway. When I read that bit in the newspaper, I assumed he must have thrashed around a bit afterward and removed his pants for comfort."

"You say the syringe was around three-quarters filled?"

"I think so." Nini paused, thinking. "No, by the time I stuck it into him, probably less. It started out three-quarters full but the thing kept leaking in my purse. Also I dripped some insulin on his trousers – so probably less than three quarters. I was afraid they would find traces of it on his clothing," Nini continued, "but when Julio called to tell Barry that Moulds was dead, I still felt enormous relief. I have never had any regrets, Eleanor."

"Nini, can you remember the kind of insulin you used? Was there a name on the bottle? What did you ask for at the Pharmacie?"

"I asked for protamine-zinc insulin – PZI. I remember copying the name down from the bottle on the counter when Neville bought his supply."

Then Nini took a deep breath and picked up the telephone.

31

Until the Belknaps moved to Washington, Moira and Iris had not met since the death of Hilary-Moulds. Shortly after her posting in Germany, Iris had left the foreign service and attempted to become what is euphemistically called a small entrepreneur. When her boutiques and book-shops failed because of poor location and insufficient capital, she reluctantly returned to her secretarial work in the foreign service. Iris was already in Washington when the Belknaps arrived. All Iris wished for was a renewal of friendship with Moira. She was certain, however, that Moira was still holding a grudge because of the picture-slashing incident. Being the ambassador's wife, Moira could snub Iris without qualm. Meekly and shrewdly, Iris offered her services as social secretary to Moira, who felt duly placated and flattered by the gesture. She wondered if Iris would offer her the same efficient devotion that had been Hilary-Moulds's due.

During their first meeting, on the terrace by the swimming pool of Moira's residence, no mention was made of portrait-slashing or of the death of Hilary-Moulds. Iris was relieved to notice that Moira's clothes were clean and did not look as if they had been designed for some other use, like table-cloths or camel covers.

After some edgy reminiscing, Moira spoke about the subject at hand.

"What will you do, Iris, as my social secretary? I am not a social person. Unlike the other ambassadors' wives in Washington, I don't play tennis, I can't play bridge and I told Stephen that I won't organize charity balls for senators, congressmen or anyone. I paint."

"Do you still paint portraits?" Iris asked warily.

Moira acknowledged that she liked doing that best. "They're my specialty, since Geneva. I owe that to Nini Pike. She told me then that portrait painting was my greatest strength. Admittedly, Nini isn't really as knowledgeable as she pretends to be. I don't think she ever got her degree. But she always had an eye, quite a connoisseur's eye."

Iris interrupted. "Why don't you paint portraits of the people you're supposed to entertain or play bridge with? You paint and I'll sell. If your sitters look fresh and young and the price is high enough to impress, we'll make money. Have you sold any of your portraits?"

Moira shook her head.

"You will if you follow my advice. First, ask some prominent woman to sit for you. Ask Nicole Dhroshky. Paint her portrait for nothing. She knows everyone. Her husband is director of the CIA. Once she has a portrait of herself, looking fresh and young, hanging over the mantelpiece, everyone else will want a Moira Belknap, too. That's the way this city works."

Nicole Dhroshky recalled that the only good words Nini Pike had had for Moira concerned her abilities as a portraitist, and accepted Iris's offer out of curiosity. Moira copied a John Singer Sargent pose. Nicole was leaning against a table, wearing a black velvet evening dress with a thin shoulder strap slipping erotically onto her bare arm. In Paris, at the turn of the century, the slipped strap had created so much scandal that Sargent was forced to withdraw it from view. In Washington, Moira's portrait created the precise touch of decorous suggestiveness to appeal to the senators' and cabinet secretaries' wives who saw it in Nicole's dining room. Every woman wanted a mutedly erotic portrait of herself. Strapless and backless ball gowns were pulled out from cedar closets and Moira painted the ladies with her delicate brush. She avoided puckers, creases and overhanging flesh. Iris discreetly arranged the fees, taking a substantial commission for herself. Belknap portraits soon became so fashionable that Moira received commissions from corporation chairmen in New York and Ohio who wanted to exude erotic masculinity. Moira painted the men in track suits and tennis shorts and made them into contemporary heroes.

As their success increased, Iris decided that Moira needed professional packaging. She rented a house in Georgetown as a gallery, a show-place for the portraits. Moira had urged her to start off modestly, in some out-of-the-way, upstairs place, but Iris had learned from her bankruptcies. The rents in Georgetown were so high the numbers were meaningless to both women, which made it easier for Iris to ask the bank for a loan. She received it.

"If you ask for too little money," Iris explained, "a little person deals with you. He won't have the imagination to say yes. If you ask for a lot of money, they'll pass you to his superior, who will be much more intelligent."

She hired a decorator who created the atmosphere of a private club. There were leather wing chairs; the spines of Barrons, the Wall Street Journal and the Economist were fastened to the special sticks used in Viennese coffee houses. Iris paid pretty congressmen's daughters the minimum wage to pass around Chinese tea, wine and imported wellwater from Norway. The oak floors were covered with Hugh Hilary-Moulds's carpets. Iris knew he would have hated the idea of people walking over them. Moira had been surprised to see the carpets, but prudently asked no questions. Iris jacked up the prices of the portraits to cover the cost of the interest from the loans. Gratifyingly, the higher the price, the more paintings people bought. All but three of Moira's portraits had been sold.

The current show was hung with early Belknaps, portraits of nobodies. Moira and Stephen had been posted to Yaounde, Tel Aviv, Mexico City and Peking and Moira had painted anyone in these places who had been willing to sit still. The Senagalese market women, Jewish old-clothes hawkers, Yucatan waiters and Chinese sweepers could have formed part of a pre-Raphaelite frieze. Moira's attention to detail, her technique and her dream-like colouring placed her style directly in the romantic school of painting. Until Iris had taken over, the portraits had been lying in a warehouse in Ottawa. Now they might have been the early works of an itinerant Burne-Jones or Rossetti, so great was their popularity.

Only one portrait in the show had been specifically commissioned. Moorehouse Dhroshky stood in a business suit beside the American flag in his office. Iris had hung the picture in the place of honour above the gallery's fireplace.

The decorator had built a partially hidden inglenook by the fireplace where Iris could go over her accounts. She was perched on the edge of a leather chair wondering if Moira could paint quickly enough to keep up with the demand. No matter. Iris was already padding the gallery with nineteenth-century landscapes, grazing bovines and misted-over Irish ruins that attracted clients as much as the portraits did. Iris had never been so content in her life.

When the telephone rang and Iris heard Nini's voice, she felt no envy or rancour. Nini was a potential client. She probably wanted a Belknap for Sussex Drive. A portrait of the prime minister's wife would have excellent promotional value. Nini expressed surprise at Iris's new occupation. Iris decided she would give Nini a special price.

"I spoke to Moira," Nini said. "She says you've made her

famous. I told you she was talented. But you had the vision and took the risks. Wonderful publicity for Canada. Barry will be proud."

Iris's hopes rose – a commission ready to pop.

"Why don't you let Moira paint you, Nini? A portrait of the prime minister's wife would become part of the country's heritage."

"Why not?" Nini replied. "But there's just one little thing I have to ask you about. It's difficult after so many years. I'm speaking of the night when Hugh Hilary-Moulds died. Just a question of clarification. Do you remember any particular details from that party, or is it all a great fuzz in your mind? I scarcely remember anything myself."

"I remember everything," said Iris flatly. "That was the night Hugh humiliated me. He killed me. I was a corpse before he was. Worse than that, I was his monster. Since then I have never let myself be manipulated by anyone. I don't think I'm monstrous anymore."

Nini was encouraged.

"Roland Neville told me he wrote to you about two months ago. He's going on television. He will be making insinuations about Hilary-Moulds's death."

"What insinuations?"

"Well, he believes that Hilary-Moulds was murdered. Did you ever mention my name to Neville? Or write to him?"

Iris was furious at herself. Why did she tell Neville that Nini had been in Hugh's room? Neville hadn't said anything about murder or television. He had just mumbled something about memoirs for the archives. And she had been only too glad to provide a little gossip. Oh, the danger of trying to impress a journalist with inside knowledge.

"What did he tell you?"

"He said that you saw me go into Hilary-Moulds's room and close the door. Is that true?"

"Yes. But he never told me he would use the information against you."

"Why didn't you say anything when Barry ordered the autopsy? It would have been appropriate then."

"I told you. I was released by his death. I owe my life to his death. I was happy. I didn't care who went in his room or how he died. And besides, you weren't the only one in Hugh's room. Neville was in there, too."

"That doesn't matter," Nini said. "Barry told him to check and see if Moulds was sleeping. I don't know about Neville. I went upstairs to look for you. I thought Hilary-Moulds's behaviour had been contemptible. And we all wanted you to join us downstairs. Everyone was on your side. But I couldn't find you."

"I was upstairs and I saw both you and Neville. But," Iris said quickly, "I never went into Hugh's room. And Neville stayed in there longer than you. I wondered what he was doing. In any case, I refuse to get into this mess. Why should anyone know who went upstairs and why? Neville can say what he likes on television. But I'm going to call him right now and say that I will deny everything. It's his word against mine. He'll look like a malicious tattletale. We must not let him intimidate us. I don't need this garbage now."

"But you can't," Nini said. "You can't deny anything. He's got your letter." Without realizing what she was doing, Nini hung up.

32

Barry walked into Nini's bedroom with a bemused expression on his face. Both women were sitting on the window seat and looked at him with apprehension.

"Out of bed, Nini?" Barry was pleased. "Anything wrong with her clinically, Eleanor? If not, she's coming downstairs tonight."

"Physically, Nini's fine. Even though she hasn't moved for six weeks. It's a miracle she hasn't got phlebitis. But she says no to the dinner party," replied Eleanor.

"Tell us about the gardener," Nini interrupted impatiently. "We have to know more about him. Who is he?"

"It's curious," Barry answered. "I made the discovery myself. His name was familiar."

He looked dubiously at Eleanor.

"I should ask you to leave the room, Eleanor. This information comes from security files. Eyes only. It will be embarrassing for certain people and their families if it ever becomes public."

"She's not the public." Nini was irritated. "Eleanor is far more discreet than I am."

"That's true," Barry admitted. "And you'll tell her everything after I leave." He looked from one woman to the other, as if confirming his own observation, then proceeded.

"Well, here's the information we have so far. First, the gardener was a recent Hungarian immigrant named Janos Molner. He was forty years old, came to Canada four years ago when exit visas became easier to get as a result of *détente*. Hungary has changed since we were in Geneva, Nini. Other satellite countries are still much the same."

"Could Janos Molner be the same Janos who was Roland Neville's lover?" Nini asked excitedly. "Nutt saw them talking once outside the residence. You must have looked in the files about Roland Neville's affair in Budapest," she rushed on, not waiting for confirmation. "I bet you still have the photographs – I bet you even identified the body with them. I wonder why he didn't change his name?"

Barry sat down heavily on the Louis XVI ballroom chair, not noticing Nini's raised eyebrows or Eleanor's bemused expression. He was unsure as to how much Nini had told Eleanor about Roland Neville. He disliked the idea of her gossiping about government secrets. He would not forget again that Nini had always remembered everything he ever told her.

"You should not have mentioned Roland Neville's troubles, even to Eleanor. I realize he hasn't exactly been our friend. That he's wickedly unfair to me in the newspapers. But he deserves discretion and privacy, like the rest of us. You told me long ago that I treated him too harshly, and now you're revealing things that are nobody's business but his own."

"Well, it's too late to keep any secrets from Eleanor now." Nini would not be drawn into quibbling. "What else have you found out?"

Barry gave up.

"Of course, the police are worried that he's a spy. I don't think so. The atmosphere is much freer in Hungary now, compared to the early sixties when Neville was ambassador. The KGB used to be hanging from the trees, and it's still the same in Czechoslovakia, unhappily. But I'm sure the

Hungarians wouldn't use somebody who's already in our files without a name change, even if they were ambitious enough to spread their network as far as Ottawa. In any case, Otis was helpful, for the first time."

"What does Otis know about Janos?" asked Nini, surprised.

"Remember that shell in Hilary-Moulds's office? The one he wasn't supposed to have? After Moulds died I was appointed senior man at the Mission. We had to open his shell. Otis was the security officer, if you'll recall. We found correspondence between Hilary-Moulds and Attila Berendi, then a senior official in the Hungarian foreign office. The content of the letters was innocuous. But, of course, there were two unanswered questions.

"Why should Moulds be corresponding with Berendi? And why did he consider Berendi's letters significant enough to lock in his non-regulation shell? At the end of one letter, there was a peculiar postscript from Berendi. 'Janos sends his regards.' Otis actually remembered that. The letters were suspect in the extreme, but Moulds was dead and there was nothing we could do except file them away until now." He gave Eleanor a worried look. "This will be damaging to everyone if it gets out."

"Stop worrying about me," Eleanor said. "If Neville's indiscretion became public, I think it would hurt you more than him. The press would say you deliberately leaked the story. I know what's at stake."

"Why don't you have Otis's job?" said Barry. "He's useless. Wanted me to connect Molner with Neville publicly. For revenge. Otis has never heard of backlash."

"I told you Otis had the political instincts of a retarded Chihuahua," Nini said.

"But how did Janos ever get into Sussex?" Eleanor asked.

Barry shrugged. "Nini knows better than I how slow the security people are to do their work. You hire a laundress and a few weeks later they tell you she's an illegal immigrant or something. Very inconvenient. He was only here six weeks before he died. Maybe he *was* a plant. Neither Nini nor I ever met him. But I'm inclined to be skeptical. We have no proof that he was anything other than one more victim of the KGB. Poor fellow managed to get out of Hungary and had to work as a labourer here, instead of an opera singer. Happens all the time," Barry said as he stood. "But he was a homosexual and some of them go in for what is called 'rough trade.' Probably picked up a stranger in Rockliffe Park, where they hang out, who beat him up during a quarrel. I certainly hope the death was an accident. If the press decides he's a spy, they'll blame the Mounties for allowing him into the residence or say they killed him. But whatever they print, it will only be a seven-day wonder. Don't worry, Nini. It all will be forgotten shortly. Poor bugger."

Barry was now standing on one leg, eager to be off.

"Unfortunately, there are two provincial premiers waiting in my office at Parliament Hill to give me hell about grain elevators. I have to go."

He turned to Nini.

"I expect to see you downstairs at eight tonight. You look very well indeed."

33

Yves Marius was churning the *calvados sorbet* by hand. Normally he would have used the electric churn, but today he was suffering from too much stress. Tears filled his eyes, then dropped into the sugary crystals of ice. Other people jogged when they were upset – he churned. He was supposed to have been left alone today. That had been the rule since he had come to Sussex Drive – that the staff, even Mrs. Pike, would leave him alone during the preparation of an important dinner. He was supposed to be the master, the captain of his kitchen. Only two people were allowed in, the vegetable peeler and the dishwasher, and they knew well enough to keep their mouths shut and eyes averted in his presence, like dutiful nuns.

But today, Yves Marius was the victim of a power struggle. Worse, a mutiny. An abusive Doreen, dragging a reluctant Nutt, had invaded Yves Marius's kitchen and taken it over. Doreen had thrown out the peeler and the dishwasher. She had ignored Yves Marius's protests, treating him as a no-account person, humiliating him in front of his underlings. Then she had flung Nutt back and forth, dangerously near the big copper basins on the wall.

Why had Doreen brought Nutt here? Yves Marius moaned to himself. Why couldn't she fight with Nutt in her own room upstairs? He should go on strike, refuse to cook.

But he felt he had to remain loyal to Mrs. Pike. Besides, he had an undeniable curiosity to remain and see what the fight was about.

"Go, go, go," Doreen screamed at Nutt. "I cannot take you snuffling and shuffling around here any more like an old, useless dog nosing up our skirts. You were supposed to leave Sussex by noon sharp. Those have always been Mrs. P.'s orders. Instead, you hung about and bothered that gardener, and now he's dead. I don't know how we'll ever get through this dinner if I have to keep tripping over you. Now get out. What do you think you're doing here, anyhow?"

Nutt was undisturbed by Doreen's battering. He lit a Monte Cristo, which he must have stolen from the prime minister's humidor, sucked on it noisily, then, to Yves Marius's horror, spit the end off into a plate of *zuccini en eventail.*

"My job," said Nutt slowly, "is to butle. I'm going to butle tonight. No matter what you or Mrs. Pike says. I earn my keep better than some of those young good-for-nothings, like that gardener. No one's going to say Nutt shirks his work."

"Butle!" Doreen could hardly bring forth the word. "You don't know how to butle. Look at your dirty fingernails. You haven't moved one muscle in this place for five years."

Yves Marius gave a little scream and pulled away his churn just as Nutt tried to dip his fingers in the sherbet, presumably to help himself to a taste.

Doreen was working up to her climax.

"You're a curse on this house. If you had been out of the house, that little gardener would still be alive."

She picked up a cleaver and threw it at Nutt. The pitch went wild and the cleaver fell on a tray of Yves Marius's hollowed-out apples, scattering them over the counter and onto the floor.

Doreen was at the breaking point. The day, so far, had

been awful. Apart from Nutt's presence, the major irritant had been the police. They delayed her chores for more than an hour, asking questions she couldn't answer and soiling the carpets and tile floors with their dirty, heavy boots. She was sure they suspected her of killing the gardener. She was the one who had asked him to arrange the flowers. The police had even picked up the big bouquet in the hall and sloshed their hands inside the vase. Mrs. P. was lucky. The prime minister had given orders that she wasn't to be disturbed by them. They had left only fifteen minutes ago and Doreen was feeling savage.

"If I didn't know you so well," she yelled at Nutt, "I'd say you murdered the man. But you're too lazy to murder anyone. You're a number-one trouble-maker. Why didn't you go away this morning?"

Doreen was really losing control, Yves Marius thought, as he re-assembled the apples. She was breathing heavily and there were tears in her eyes. The sight of Doreen's breakdown mitigated his own feeling of humiliation.

Nutt smiled. "That's the trouble with women. Fall to pieces at little things. Go on, call me a murderer. You're the one that threw the hatchet. Can't expect much else from a woman at your time of life. It's the hormone loss. You can't help yourself. I understand women, although I'm a bachelor. That's why I stay single. I'd never fly with a woman pilot, bet your life on that. They can go bonkers at the controls. It's either too many hormones once a month or not enough after fifty."

Nutt enjoyed having the floor and made expansive gestures, first at Doreen, then at Yves Marius. "You haven't enough hormones, Doreen. That's your problem, and it makes you crazy. Look at Yves Marius there. He gets on with his job. No hysterics, no fuss. Picks up his apples and doesn't say a word. Hormones is everything when you deal with a woman. No bloody mystery about it. Lucky we men don't have them." He looked fraternally at Yves Marius.

241

Yves Marius did not return the look. It wouldn't do to encourage Nutt. Nutt had won the first round, but the fight wasn't finished.

"I'll give you hormones," said Doreen. "I'll see that you never set foot in Sussex again. Female harassment. I know the rules, too. I'll get you on female harassment."

"No, you won't," Nutt said suddenly. "That's what the gardener said. Harassment. He'd get me for harassment. Might as well have said female harassment. Now he was the exception that proves the rule, I'd guess. Wouldn't you say, Yves Marius, that he had hormones? Like a little flower, he was. Little female flower with hormones."

Nutt stubbed out the half-smoked cigar in one of Nini's Spode service plates.

"I guess Mrs. Pike would like to know who killed the gardener on that river path. I could tell the police, of course, but who wants to get mixed up with them? The lawyer puts you on the witness stand and destroys your good name. That's not for Nutt, no, sir."

"What are you talking about, you old fool?" Doreen sounded scared. "Do you know what you're saying?"

"Sure, I do. But I won't say anything if you and Mrs. Pike let me butle."

Doreen was silent.

"Look," he said, mollifying Doreen. "I'll clean my fingernails." He picked up Yves Marius's filleting knife and proceeded to chip away at the dirt. "I want to speak directly to the lady of the house. It's not right her not talking to me for five years. I've never seen the bedroom. All that money spent and I don't even know what's in there. You take me up there, Doreen. And she'll let me butle."

Doreen gave up the battle. Murder cases were out of her jurisdiction. And she was frightened by Nutt's intimations.

"Wait here," she said. "I'll bring you upstairs, but I have to warn her first."

Nini combed out her hair, changed into a sober viyella dressing gown and sat up at her desk, waiting for Doreen to return with Nutt. Nutt was bad news. She was repelled by the idea of having to talk to him, after all these years, in her bedroom.

He entered with Doreen, who immediately went out, leaving him alone with Eleanor and Nini. Nutt looked gleeful and sheepish at the same time, almost touching his forelock yet allowing a little smile of triumph play on his lips.

He looked round at the curtains, the bed and the furniture. "Nice decorations, Mrs. Pike. Spent a lot of money, I guess. It shows."

Nutt began to play with the photographs on the table. He picked up Haile Selassie and planted his finger on the glass, over the image. "I remember that one."

Nini cut him short. "Doreen says you know something about the gardener's accident. What?"

"Well, I didn't exactly see someone bash his head in, if that's what you mean. But he told me who he was meeting at the river path."

"Why should the gardener have told you about his personal affairs? I thought you had an argument with him."

"That's just it, Mrs. Pike. He told me *because* of the argument. He said he would report my attitude to his friend. And that his friend would put it in the papers. He's been here before – he's your friend, too." Nutt looked slyly at Nini.

"Who are you talking about?" Nini insisted.

"That Neville fellow. You know him. The one that writes in the papers. The gardener said that he had an appointment to meet him near the river and that he'd tell Neville that I was persecuting him. That's the word he used, persecuting. And harassment. What do you think about that?"

"Have you told the police about this?" Eleanor interrupted.

"No, sir. They'll make my life something terrible. Besides, Neville's a big name. I'm nobody. They'd make me sweat. But I thought Mrs. Pike better know."

"You didn't actually see the fight? You didn't follow the gardener?" Eleanor insisted.

"No, sir. I was in the house with him when he told me he'd fix me good. Then he ran toward the back. And that's all. Except I guess that Neville fixed the gardener, instead of me."

"You're absolutely sure about this? You're sure of the name and the man?" Eleanor asked.

"Sure enough. He came here about six weeks ago to have lunch with Mrs. Pike in the library. I know who he is. I even saw him talking to the gardener then. Couldn't figure out what they had in common. I think it was the first time both set foot in the house. Surprised me a little."

Nini and Eleanor looked at each other. Then Nini said, "Would you mind keeping quiet just a little more about your information, Nutt? After all, there's no proof Neville actually met him. Or fought with him. We have to be very careful about this."

Nutt knew he had her.

"Exactly what I think, Mrs. Pike. I don't want to get anyone in trouble. All I want to do is butle. I'd like to butle tonight, Mrs. Pike. I'll keep it mum. We don't need any more scandal in this place. You don't want people to think your visitors are murderers. So how about it? Am I on for tonight? And as long as you and the prime minister stay on in Sussex?"

Nini wondered how soon Doreen would quit after she found out that Nutt was resuming his rôle as major-domo obstructionist. To keep Doreen happy, Nini decided, she'd have to pay her more money, secretly, out of her Sullivan money. She'd have to figure out something to keep the two of them apart. But all that would have to be settled afterward.

"And will you say good morning to me, Mrs. Pike, from time to time? I'm the only one in the house who never gets a word from you. Lots of years, too. If you treat me right, so will everyone else."

Nini gave up.

"Of course, Nutt. But hello and goodbye only. I don't like chatting forever about nothing. That's what you never understood, and you always interrupt people. But I will greet you. I can't promise long conversations."

Nutt appeared satisfied. He had an inch; more would come later.

"What about Doreen?"

"I'll speak to Doreen. Just don't toot your horn right away. Let me handle it. Now you go downstairs and behave yourself. Don't touch the crystal or the silver. Stay out of the kitchen. And keep far from Doreen. Tonight you will pass the trays. Rest a little until then."

Nutt had got what he wanted. He was happy to let Mrs. Pike take the responsibility off his shoulders. He touched his hand to his head and let himself out, almost walking backward.

"Neville must have killed Janos," Nini said when Nutt left. "Why did he do it? Because of jealousy?"

"Possibly," Eleanor said. "Or perhaps it was something else. Janos knew a lot about Neville."

"What could he know? Neville certainly isn't afraid of being exposed as a homosexual. He even wrote an article about how he told his mother. And another one of his columns had the heading, 'The Homophile Credo.' What's more, he's received all kinds of letters of support. He's come out of the closet, Eleanor."

Nini wondered if she should use that term in front of Eleanor. She wasn't sure if Eleanor had come out of the closet.

"Not about that," Eleanor said shortly. "I have another idea. I believe we can do something productive. We have

Nutt's statement, and Barry's information was enlightening, too. But there's something else. Do you suppose Otis is still in the residence? Or has he gone with Barry?"

"Otis?" Nini was surprised. "What do you want him for?" She picked up the phone again, asked his whereabouts and replaced the receiver.

"It seems he's still lurking in the library downstairs. He often does, hoping Barry will forget about him when he returns to the office. It looks like he's succeeded. But why speak to Otis?"

"I'll tell you later. I'm going to pop down and talk to him while you put on your stockings. We must visit Neville this afternoon. Don't worry. I'll help you wobble out of the house. We'll go in my car, it will be less noticeable. But we must go now, right after I talk to Otis. How long can you trust Nutt to keep his mouth shut? I know he's impossible to control." Eleanor didn't wait for an answer. Her hand on the door-knob, she said brusquely, "Call Neville when I go downstairs. But don't say I'm coming with you."

"What good will it do to see Neville?" asked Nini.

"We might be able to neutralize him," Eleanor replied over her shoulder as she was closing the door.

Neville had told Nini that he always worked at home. She dialled his number.

When Eleanor returned a few minutes later, Nini was arranging her Valentino scarf around her neck.

"He's expecting me. But what are we doing, Eleanor?" Nini asked. "What have we got on Neville, anyway? The idea of depending on Nutt's word hardly gives me a sense of security. How do you intimidate a zealot like Neville?"

Eleanor was looking rather pleased with herself. "Tell Barry that Otis occasionally has his uses. His memory about certain things is formidable. Come on, Nini, what's there to lose? A few new facts might knock him off balance."

"Might," Nini said. "Might. But not for sure."

Doreen was appalled when Nutt told her that Nini was

letting him be butler tonight and most likely forever. She decided there was no alternative for her except to give notice and was just about to go upstairs to tell Nini when she saw Nini and Eleanor in the downstairs front hall. Nini was wearing her mink coat and heavy Moreland boots and refused to look directly at Doreen.

"I'm going for a drive in Dr. Campbell's car. She says I need fresh air. I can depend on you to see that everything is in order for the party, Doreen?"

"Order? You want order with Nutt poking around? I can't keep order in this house anymore."

Nini's face was strained and white.

"Just for tonight, Doreen. Give me until tonight. We'll come to some arrangement. Be good and let Nutt have his way this once. I'll look after you."

Doreen softened. She could bide her time until Nutt spilt creamed spinach on the senator's wife, or belched in the prime minister's ear. He had already made himself several cocktails of his special potion, Chivas Regal, *framboise* and sweet vermouth.

34

Nini noticed that Neville's years in Europe hadn't done much to enrich or expand his idea of ornamenting a room. His living room looked the same as his apartment had, more than twenty years ago in Toronto during those bleak evenings when she had been his acolyte. Almost no furniture; no vases, pictures or mirrors; only a few utilitarian objects. There was a large module-type divan, some lamps, a table with a tape recorder and tapes, and a few old maps of the Canadian Arctic stuck on the wall with Scotch tape.

The dullness, the severity of the room must be deliberate, she thought. He thinks it's more masculine, but it only shows a lack of confidence. Hilary-Moulds was far less self-conscious about revealing his aesthetic tastes.

The only emotional investment Neville had made in his apartment was the elaborate high-fidelity equipment built into one wall. Nini had read somewhere that Roland Neville played music twenty-four hours a day, Palestrina, Bach, liturgical music, but never a solo human voice.

Neville was surprised to see a tall, strange woman in a cross-country-ski outfit with Nini. Because of her height and solidity, he assumed Eleanor was a police-woman, wearing some kind of odd disguise, who was detailed to accompany Nini wherever she went.

"This is Eleanor. I don't think you've met her. I've asked her to come with me. She's my doctor. I hope you don't mind my bringing her."

Neville wondered if Nini was in such a bad way that she needed a psychiatrist by her side at all times.

"Bring anyone you like. Even Barry. It's your secret we're going to talk about, not mine."

He pushed some records off the divan, then asked them to sit while he carefully removed Nini's fur coat from her shoulders.

"How luxurious," he said with mock admiration, raising his eyebrows and stroking the pelt. "I'll put it in the other room. It will be safe there."

Nini had removed her boots at the doorstep and sat down on the couch in her stocking feet beside Eleanor. Her feet were cold and her toes looked skeletal through her nylon stockings. She wished she had brought shoes. She felt as if she had no clothes on at all.

Neville came back from the bedroom rubbing his hands together.

"I don't get much of a chance to entertain. But what will you have? Gin? Sherry? Coffee? Tea? I can make you ladies a cup of tea, if you like."

"Tea," Nini said.

Anything to delay the conversation, she thought. How were they supposed to make Neville vulnerable? They had no plan at all. It was a rotten idea, coming here. He seemed so sure of himself in his own surroundings.

"I have one of those kettles that whistles," Neville yelled from his kitchen. "Do you like herbal teas?"

"No," Nini said. "Plain tea."

"Herbal tea is better for you, isn't it, doctor? Doesn't stain the teeth. I have some Earl Grey, but it's been here for six months and might have lost its flavour."

The music irritated Nini. Background music during conversations always diluted her concentration and the beat affected her like a neuralgia, but she realized it would be a show of weakness if she asked him to turn it off.

Eleanor was composed, her hands folded in her lap, waiting, just as if Neville were another patient entering her office.

Neville sat on the floor cross-legged, his back very straight and arms akimbo. Nini noticed that although his balance was good, his stomach extended beyond his belt. He had put on some flesh in the past few years.

"Do you recommend yoga, doctor?" Neville decided not to ask for Eleanor's last name.

"I've nothing against it for individuals who evidence no difficulties in the lumbar regions."

"I see from your clothes that you cross-country ski. It's been a wonderful winter for skiers. Snow every weekend," Neville said.

"Yes," Eleanor replied. "I sometimes see you skiing. On the river, behind Sussex street."

"I never ski there. Only in the hills. I find the river too windy."

"Few people ski on the river," she said. "I was sure it was you. I've seen your picture under your byline in the newspaper. Your face is well known. It made my day, seeing a celebrity like you skiing."

"You're mistaken," Neville said, his voice easy. "I only ski in the hills. And I always wear a balaclava. I don't know how you would have recognized me."

"Today was pretty warm for a balaclava. You slipped it off. Probably you forgot."

The whistle shrieked and Neville rose without using his hands. He thinks he's a ballet dancer, Nini thought sourly. She wished Eleanor hadn't made up such a story.

"I did not ski on the river today," he shouted from the

kitchen. Neither woman could see his face. He returned with three mugs, sugar and milk on a tray.

"Sorry, no lemon. Didn't realize I would have visitors today."

He placed the tray on the painted pine table that held the tape deck and some papers.

"Help yourself."

He sounded a little less hospitable.

"What have you decided, Nini? Have you spoken to Barry? Is he going to resign? I presume that's the purpose of your coming to see me. Any purpose would be gratifying, of course. After all, an informal visit from the wife of the prime minister is something any citizen would remember. For the rest of his life. But you don't like me well enough to drop in for an ordinary chat and tea, do you? At one time you did, in Toronto, long ago."

It was exactly the same as twenty years ago when she used to be his student and she thought she was in love with him. The cold surroundings, the suffocating sense that she had come because of her sins and Neville was supposed to punish her. As in the old days, she lowered her head and hoped someone else would speak.

"I suppose you were upset to hear about the death of your friend?" Eleanor blurted out.

"What are you talking about? What friend?" Neville looked startled.

"Nini's gardener. He was killed today behind her house. You must have heard something about it on the radio."

"I don't know Nini's gardener and I haven't listened to the radio all day. I've been working. When I work, I just play my music."

"Were you here in the morning?" Eleanor asked.

"Yes, all morning," he snapped. Then he reflected, and commented slowly, as if piecing together a morning he himself had forgotten, "No, no. I went skiing. Just for an

251

hour. Yes, that's right. I did go skiing this morning. In the Gatineau Hills, though, not on the river. I'm very sorry, but you were mistaken about that."

"But you knew our gardener," said Nini, trying to push off her sense of hopelessness.

Neville twisted out of his yoga position, stood, and drained the rest of his tea.

"No, I didn't know your gardener. Why should I know him?"

"When you came to visit me you spoke to him," Nini replied. "At great length, my butler told me."

"Did I? I don't even remember. If I did, maybe I was just getting a little background colour for my columns – what's it like to lunch at Sussex with Nini Pike," he said sarcastically. "Floral arrangements. Food. Everyone knows you are a famous entertainer. I don't write colour pieces myself. But a few of the women journalists are interested. I questioned several members of your staff as a favour to the social reporters. Then they can write an article headlined, 'Nini Pike, Canada's Most Demanding Hostess.' But I often speak to gardeners, waitresses, commissionaires and taxi drivers in any case, to get their opinions on everything. *Vox populi.* What's the point of view of the little people? Very important for a journalist and politician. Barry would do well to talk to a few cabbies."

"So you do remember speaking to the gardener?" Nini persisted.

"What did he look like? I'll have to think back," Neville replied.

"Come off it, Mr. Neville," Eleanor said impatiently. "The body has been identified. You've known him a long time. Since Budapest."

There was a long pause. Neville gave a start, then almost a moan of remembrance.

"My God. It's Janos. I completely forgot he was at Sussex. Is he dead? How terrible. He used to be an opera singer. He told me he was looking for another job in Toronto, more suited to his musical talents. I thought he had left town. I never saw him after –"

"I don't believe you could have possibly forgotten that Janos Molner was Nini's gardener," Eleanor interrupted. "You spoke to him on a rather memorable day, I think. The day you accused her of murder."

"And who the hell are you?" Neville responded. "Are you really a doctor or someone from the police? Why did you bring her here?" he asked, turning to Nini. "You should have told me before-hand. Then I would have had a lawyer here. Is she accusing me of having something to do with Janos's death? How did he die, anyhow?"

"His skull was cracked open by a rock on the river path behind Sussex. Someone else, a cross-country skier, was with him," Nini answered.

"And the good doctor, or whoever she is, claims to have seen me on the river today," Neville said, outraged.

Eleanor didn't reply.

"What is this? The Star Chamber? False witness and all? You're both being awfully silly." Neville sounded surer of himself.

Nini was worried about Nutt, another false witness. She imagined him giving testimony in court, hiccupping, belching, impressing the judge only with his obvious unreliability. He would somehow embroil Barry in Janos's death. She wished Eleanor hadn't made up that story about seeing Neville on the river.

Neville poured more tea. He looked as if he were determined to get the upper hand.

Then Eleanor spoke.

35

"Never mind what happened on the river today," Eleanor said. "Let's go back to Hungary, to Geneva, to the time of Hilary-Moulds's death. We have to analyze the past, find out what actually happened. Janos's death is almost the end of the story. Budapest and Geneva are the beginning. That's where we can find the source of the truth."

She drank her tea and shoved the cup aside as if its presence cluttered her thoughts.

"Let's start first in Budapest, when Attila Berendi asked you to co-operate with the Hungarian Secret Police – and, of course, the KGB. I'm sure you won't mind me bringing this up, Mr. Neville. Nini told me about your difficulties. And, with the public stance you have taken on gay rights, a discussion of your emotional attachments must be of no consequence. Put plainly, Janos was your lover. You can't be ashamed of that. And now Janos has been murdered, approximately twenty years later. You're not a naive man. Why weren't you more suspicious of him in Budapest?"

Neville lit a cigarette and watched the exhaled smoke rise. When he spoke, his tone was flat.

"My relationship was purely sentimental. Janos couldn't have cared less about politics or government secrets."

"That's ridiculous," Nini said. "You told me yourself that the Russians controlled everything and everybody while you were in Budapest." She remembered with bitterness the lunch they had had together in the sun at the restaurant outside Geneva, when he had given her the first editions and his apology as wedding presents. "How could you have said that and yet be so sure, even today, that Janos wasn't being controlled by Berendi? Maybe he was an unwilling agent. But you were certainly taking quite a risk as a diplomat living in a police state. You know, I actually felt sorry for you when they made you leave external affairs. Now I know they were right."

"Not they, Nini. It was Barry who forced me out. And Janos was not a spy. He went to prison after I left."

"Do you know for certain he went to prison?" she demanded.

Eleanor interrupted. "Admit the possibility, Mr. Neville. Janos could well have been seeing Berendi, or even someone else. Perhaps you forced yourself to suppress suspicion in order to avoid pain."

Neville rose abruptly, walked to the front door and kicked at Nini's boots, which had been standing upright on the mat. The two women sat like school-girls, side by side on the sofa, hands folded in their laps, and watched his movements as if he were a naughtier classmate, misbehaving once again.

"Good, he's angry," Eleanor whispered. Neville observed Eleanor leaning toward Nini's ear, stared stupidly at the boots, then, realizing what he had done, quickly returned to his chair and lit another cigarette.

"What are you two driving at?"

Eleanor didn't look at him. She fixed her eyes on the map of the Arctic on the opposite wall and spoke in a strained manner, as if she were trying to read the map's lettering.

"I want to go back to the second time you went to Geneva, the day Hilary-Moulds met you at the airport and brought you to his office at the Permanent Mission. You were such old and good friends. You told Nini almost a year before, at lunch, that Hilary-Moulds had been your mentor in the foreign office. You admired him. But you did admit to her that you'd never be able to emulate his success. Everyone was mildly envious of Hilary-Moulds at that time. You were just one of the crowd. Perhaps his success hurt you more because you were aware of something the others were not."

Her fascination with the great blue patches of the northern seas came to an end and she looked directly at him.

"You must have known Hilary-Moulds was a homosexual. After all, you took holidays together; you had been at the same school. Can you deny that?"

"I may have known," Neville said readily, "but it was nobody's business but Hugh's. What difference did it make then – or now, for that matter?"

It suddenly occurred to Nini that this was the first time she had ever seen Neville smoke. The sight of the two half-finished cigarettes in the ashtray gave her comfort.

"Surely," Eleanor said, "you must have resented his secretiveness about his nature. Not to put too fine a point on it, his duplicity."

Before Neville could reply, Nini decided to push Eleanor's advantage without, however, knowing her goal.

"She's right. You believed in being proud and open about your feelings. You even confided in me about your homosexuality. And later, you told the AVN to send those photographs to your family and the security people in Ottawa."

"I suppose," Eleanor said, "that was a brave gesture." She sounded sarcastic. "Especially with your friend, Hugh, pretending to be heterosexual in order to further his career. If people had any suspicions about his sexual orientations, he could always point to his mad wife, Lady Beatrice, and his new lady, Iris. You didn't betray Hilary-Moulds at that lunch when Nini told you she assumed Iris was his mistress. Did you find that amusing or discomfiting, given your code of honour?"

Neville's cheeks coloured. He sensed her mockery.

"Hilary-Moulds," Eleanor went on, "had a more success-ful career than you. But never mind; you may not have been that resentful. It was before Berendi's attempt to black-mail you. And life was more difficult for homosexuals twenty years ago." Eleanor contemplated Nini's fallen boots as if they had as much to reveal as the map. "It isn't so easy now," she said slowly. "Everyone has his own way, even today, of sorting out the pattern of his life."

Neville, noticing her abstracted gaze and the softer inflec-tion in her voice, looked at her closely and said, "Are you talking about me or yourself? Just how close *are* you and Nini?"

"Don't be vicious," said Nini, upset.

"According to your principles"—Eleanor regained herself easily—"my sexual predilections shouldn't matter. But it's laughable to accuse Nini of homosexuality as well as mur-der."

"I was just wondering why you should care so much about Nini's problems. Do mere 'old friends' usually stick their necks out like this?"

Eleanor remained unperturbed. "All I'm saying is that your feelings toward Hilary-Moulds had to be more com-plicated, more nuanced than those of his heterosexual col-leagues."

Now it was Neville's turn for sarcasm. "You're speaking from personal experience, of course. But I still don't see what homosexual feelings—or lesbian feelings—have to do with the murder of Hilary-Moulds."

The telephone in front of them rang. Neville pushed aside some newspapers on the pine table, answered and listened. "I heard about it a few minutes ago. You'll have a column for tomorrow's paper," he said, and hung up.

"My editor. He wants a piece on the gardener's death at the prime minister's residence. And I'm lucky enough to be entertaining an inside source right here in my room. Shall I take notes?"

He picked up a stenographic pad and pencil and waited for someone to speak. Oblivious of his gesture, Eleanor said, "Tell me what happened when Hilary-Moulds left you alone in his office."

The pencil and notebook slipped from Neville's fingers without him noticing.

"Nothing."

"That's a lie!" Nini exclaimed. "Barry told me the two of you entered his office laughing and joking – and that by the time you left with Hilary-Moulds your behaviour had changed radically. Barry overheard you quarrelling, too. I tried to talk to you afterward but you had become terribly moody. We all noticed your coldness toward Moulds, especially at the party. I'm certain something he said or did in his office destabilized you. That's what he did to everyone. You must have been feeling pretty shaky, Roland, coming from Budapest with a blackmail threat from the AVN on your tail. They contacted you just before you went to Geneva, didn't they?"

Nini's own feeling of vulnerability in the bleak room lessened as she thought how Neville must have felt. She picked the notebook up off the floor and set it on the table. "You hated him after that quarrel. I wasn't the only one. Everyone hated Moulds sooner or later. Moira was in a state of collapse because he destroyed her picture. And Iris's humiliation came a little later, at the party. I never understood how she recovered from that."

Eleanor was nodding agreement while Nini spoke. Then she broke in. "Now we're getting at the truth." Her voice was harsh. "That office is very significant. I wanted to find out everything about it, how it looked, every possible detail. That's why I called Otis, Nini. Something in that office triggered your fright, Neville. What did you see there? What did Hilary-Moulds say or do to upset you?"

258

Neville removed his glasses and began wiping them with a dish-rag. He held them up to the light, carefully checking the lenses for spots.

When he put them back on, he spoke with some intensity, pedantically pointing his finger at Eleanor.

"Forgive me, Doctor Eleanor. Cut-rate psychiatry is fashionable. But not with me. Especially when we're supposed to be talking about murder. First you insinuate that I killed one friend. Now you question my attitude toward another. What have my feelings toward Moulds got to do with Nini? She killed Hugh. Why don't we talk about her? I still, perhaps foolishly, assume that's why you both are here."

These were precisely Nini's thoughts. She wondered why Eleanor kept stressing Neville's argument with Moulds. Neville seemed to have recovered his temper and began to pour more tea. It was far too strong, and cold. After a sip, Nini compulsively rose, went to the door and straightened her boots.

Eleanor waited until she sat down before speaking.

"I'm just establishing your motive for killing Hilary-Moulds. You wanted him dead as much as Nini, or Iris, or Moira."

Nini, startled, stared at Eleanor and then wished she hadn't revealed her look of surprise in front of Neville. But he did not seem to notice Nini's reaction. His face showed only anger.

"What do you mean, motive? We had an argument. Haven't you ever argued with a friend? Does that mean you want to kill him? Or her? This is idiotic. Let's get on to Nini and the injection of insulin."

Nini couldn't stand his righteous, accusing manner any longer and felt compelled to defend herself.

"You shouldn't care how Hilary-Moulds died. The man was a spy! After his death, Barry and Otis found correspondence between your blackmailer, Berendi, and Moulds in that non-regulation shell in his office. Surely you noticed the shell. You didn't have one in Budapest, did you? And Janos Molner's name was mentioned in the letters. Did you know that he actually worked for Moulds while Moulds was an ambassador in Budapest? The old consular files have Molner's signature. So much for the innocence of your friends. How do they fit into your code of honour? I can assure you that every document concerning Hilary-Moulds's activities in Budapest, as well as Geneva, were sent to D.L. II in Ottawa. Imagine the scrutiny of his personal correspondence and his papers. The police were very methodical, matching names, dates, places from one file to another. It was particularly interesting when your pathetic photographs were sent from Budapest by the AVN. Janos seems to have been very active with our ambassadors."

She had struck a blow and was gratified by Neville's appalled reaction.

"Why isn't this public knowledge, if it's true?" he shouted out. "Haven't you heard of the Freedom of Information Act? How is it that Nini Pike knows this and no one else?"

"But *you* have always known about it, Mr. Neville," Eleanor said quietly.

Nini, stung by Neville's remark, did not hear what Eleanor said.

"Why should it be public knowledge?" she continued. "Who would benefit from the publicity? His mother, his sisters? I'll tell you this. If the public knew Hilary-Moulds was a spy, there wouldn't be any eulogizing television programme about him. The publicity would be quite different. I might even get a little sympathy when you accuse me of murdering him."

Impatiently, Eleanor put her arm on Nini to quieten her.

"Did you hear me, Mr. Neville?" she said. "I'm sure you know—knew in Geneva—that Moulds had been recruited. And I'm sure his connection with Janos is no surprise to you, either. That's what you argued about in the office, but

I'll come to that later. Now I'm quite prepared to talk about what you want – Nini and the insulin injection."

Eleanor looked flushed and overheated in her heavy ski clothing. Her tone changed again. It was more dispassionate; she became the superior Dr. Campbell, dutifully lecturing a patient who was chronically overweight.

"I should really kick you both out. Your insinuations are fantastic."

Neville rose and for a moment Nini thought he was going to order them both out the door. Instead he tried to control his emotions by picking up another tape and inserting it into the high-fidelity machine. It was a Gregorian chant. The droning monks appeared to have a settling effect on his rage and he returned to his yoga position.

Nini did not want Eleanor to talk about the injection. She was suddenly nauseated by the liturgical chanting, which sounded as if it had been specifically chosen to increase the churning in her stomach.

Neville seemed to sense her fear. "Nini killed Hugh for her husband's sake," he said matter-of-factly. "I don't care what the security people have decided about Hugh's alleged activities with the KGB or the AVN. That's beside the point."

"It's not beside the point. It's the reason he was killed." Eleanor spoke as if this was a fact. "Now for the actual injection. An excellent topic of conversation. You told Nini how to use the syringe, didn't you?" Eleanor's voice had become very excited. Nini was totally confused.

"Yes, unhappily for Hugh. After shopping at the Pharmacie de Genève. We were sitting in a café. She pretended to be interested in my illness."

"What kind of insulin did you use?"

"I used two kinds," he answered quickly. "But not any more. I have a more efficient single medication now. In the sixties, I had to go in for a more complicated form of torture."

"Nini said she wrote down the name of the insulin you

bought when you weren't looking. What name would she have written down?"

Nini was panicking. Eleanor was mad to reveal such a fact. She had to restrain herself from clapping her hand over Eleanor's mouth.

Neville looked immensely pleased. It was the first time he had heard any evidence from Eleanor or Nini of Nini's guilt.

"She must have written down protamine-zinc insulin, PZI. I already had a supply of CZI, crystalline-zinc insulin."

"Exactly," Eleanor said. "You only bought PZI. You never mentioned the CZI, did you?"

For a moment Neville was confused.

"No, why should I have?"

"You've forgotten, haven't you?" said Eleanor triumphantly. "Think back a little, about the different properties of PZI and CZI."

Everything about Neville seemed to shrink. His glasses looked too large for his face. He could sustain his squatting position no longer and used an arm to climb into a rather greasy brocade chair that he must have bought from the Salvation Army. He put his hands to his face.

"You've forgotten," Eleanor repeated. "And you're the diabetic. It's understandable. It's been years since people had to use two kinds. But I remember their properties well. I prescribed them to my patients in the sixties. As soon as Nini told me what she had used, I knew Hilary-Moulds could not have died from her injection." Eleanor paused, but neither Neville nor Nini made any move to interrupt her. Nini was fascinated.

"Protamine-zinc insulin, PZI," she continued, "has a very slow rate of absorption. It takes well over eight hours to reach its maximum action. And maximum action is what was needed to kill Hilary-Moulds. He wouldn't have died before noon the following day if PZI had been used. But the autopsy findings stated that he died between three and five in the morning. His body was, in fact, still warm when the doctor arrived. Nini couldn't possibly have killed him. She used the wrong kind of insulin."

Neville didn't look up as Eleanor spoke. He was waiting, as if he knew what would follow.

"Now, if someone had given Moulds a shot of crystalline-zinc insulin, CZI, he would have died when he did – within an hour, or at the most within three hours. Crystalline-zinc insulin has an almost immediate and lethal effect, if the person who administers it knows what he's doing. You had both kinds of insulin. Which kind did you inject Moulds with?" There was silence for a moment. Then Nini spoke, her voice filled with wonder.

"The CZI. Of course. Who knew about it except you?"

Both Neville and Eleanor ignored Nini.

When Neville spoke, his voice was barely audible. It was a last try. "If I injected him, why would I have called attention to the pin-prick?"

"You didn't make the pin-prick," Eleanor answered easily. "Nini did. She amateurishly plunged the needle through his clothes. It must have been rather a messy job to make such a noticeable mark. You figured out that Nini attempted to kill Moulds when you read that piece in the Swiss newspaper. But you, Mr. Neville, are a professional with a needle. And a professional wouldn't make the mistake of leaving a mark. You injected him peri-anally. You took off his trousers and underclothes in order to do it." Eleanor pointed to her own knickers to illustrate.

"That was how he was found. It's impossible to detect the mark of a needle in the anus." Her voice was impassive. "Especially that of a homosexual. Think of the anal contusions Hilary-Moulds must have had. That's why you were surprised to read about the pin-prick. You certainly didn't push a needle into his buttocks. But someone else did. And you decided it had to be Nini. And so you tried to blackmail her."

"He might have died of a heart attack." Neville's voice sounded stronger.

As soon as Nini heard Neville say "heart attack," she exploded. "Heart attack! That's what I said to you when you came to threaten me six weeks ago. Shall we settle for heart attack now?" Nini was still stunned by Eleanor's detective work, but thought it best to press their advantage rather than to question Eleanor in front of Neville.

Eleanor treated Nini as if she didn't exist. "You murdered Hilary-Moulds, Mr. Neville."

Eleanor, the diagnostician, the Sherlock Holmes of medicine, knew how the patient had died but was determined to establish the etiology. Her deductions had to be confirmed by Neville.

"You killed him because of the argument you had in his office. Once I realized that Nini couldn't have killed Hilary-Moulds, I thought of you and that quarrel. I decided to call Otis, who had been the security officer when Hilary-Moulds died. What with the death of Janos and the bringing forth of old files, I thought he might be on top of the subject. I asked him to describe everything in that office, the pictures, the memorabilia. I knew there must have been something there to set off your quarrel. I knew your motive was somewhere in that office.

"Otis, as it happens, was obsessed with Hilary-Moulds. He had the contents of the office totally memorized—and described them to me in detail. A very useful conversation." She paused. "From my point of view," she continued. "Otis said the room was covered with photographs of acquaintances, mostly the famous ones. But there were also the usual pictures of the ambassador taken with his local staff. Janos, as consular officer, was in the Budapest staff picture." Neville's face was wooden, his hands folded in his lap, his eyes fixed on Eleanor.

"Hilary-Moulds left you alone for quite a while in his office," she continued. "And the pictures would have been one of the first things you would have noticed – professional curiosity. What did you make of the Budapest picture? It must have been a shock to see your lover staring at you from the back row. You had no idea till then that Janos had worked for Hilary-Moulds at the embassy. Had you known about their liaison (and I think we can all guess the probable nature of that liaison), I doubt if you would have chosen Janos as a lover. As Nini says, you're not entirely naive. You would have immediately suspected him of being a plant. In any case, you would have been too jealous."

Eleanor held up her hand when Neville tried to interrupt her. "Let me finish. Tidy up. I'm telling you why you killed him. Fact one: Hilary-Moulds was a homosexual, which you knew. And, irksome to you, a successful diplomat in spite of it. Fact two: you were shocked by the picture of Janos. And three: Moulds worked for the Hungarian Secret Service and the KGB – which you learned shortly after he returned to the office. As an agent of the Russians and a correspondent of Berendi's, Moulds must have known about the attempt to blackmail you. Finally you must have been more than slightly jealous of his relationship with Janos."

Eleanor got up and paced back and forth while she talked, immersed in her analysis. Occasionally, she sipped the cold tea, which she seemed to find refreshing. Neville listened, staring down at the table. He's harmless, Nini thought. He hasn't even the energy to respond.

"Perhaps he was still seeing Janos," Eleanor continued. "Moulds had clout with the Hungarians. If he wanted a weekend with his boyfriend, all he had to do was whistle. Moulds used to go quite often to Vienna, which is not too far from Budapest. He might have been seeing Janos at the same time you were. Janos may just have been a pawn between Moulds and Berendi. But Janos knew enough to keep his mouth shut. I don't think Moulds did. I think he let a few sentences slip about your difficulties in Budapest when you questioned him about Janos. He said something that revealed too much."

Eleanor paused and then spoke slowly. "Perhaps you suspected – perhaps you realized – that Hilary-Moulds was the one who had betrayed you to the Hungarians.

"You certainly must have hated him." Eleanor was matter-of-fact. "He shares your lover, betrays you and betrays his country. You followed all the rules, you had a personal and public code of honour and you were likely to lose. He had no sense of personal or public morality, followed no rules except those that were to his advantage, yet he was winning. Vengeance and jealousy are two excellent motives for murder, wouldn't you agree, Mr. Neville?"

It was a *tour de force*. Nini understood why the other doctors called Eleanor in as a consultant when they were stuck for a diagnosis. One fact, and then the intuitive leap. She almost expected Eleanor to tap Neville's lungs, listen for a heartbeat, feel his glands. Neville looked like a very sick man.

He turned his face again to Eleanor. It was slate grey; the inward suffering had manifested itself. He said nothing.

"Did you know," Eleanor continued, after a sip of tea, "that we do have something solid connecting you to Janos Molner's death, as well?"

Nini had been hoping that Eleanor wouldn't bring up the subject of Nutt. But Eleanor went on inexorably.

"Forget about me seeing you on the river. I'm too closely associated with Nini. But Janos actually told someone else that he was meeting you on the river path just before he died. One of your little people. *Vox populi*." Eleanor's voice was sarcastic now.

"Now, what about Iris's letter? Will you return it to Iris? No photocopies, please. Iris wouldn't like that. She's very unhappy about sending you the letter. And what about the television show? Will you go ahead with that? Or would

you prefer to go to court? And I don't mean a trial for libel."
She spoke with assurance, pacing in her stocking feet. "I
mean a murder trial, with you as the defendant. You murdered Janos, of course. Did you mean to kill him, or was it
an accident? He must have contacted you as soon as he
entered the country. Who else did he know?" Eleanor
swung around and stared at him.

"And you have feelings, Mr. Neville. Surely you felt some
guilt about leaving him in Hungary. You probably didn't
have much trouble convincing yourself that he had been a
pawn, not a principal in the Budapest-Geneva debacle. So
you welcomed his arrival. How many young men, after all,
can you attract now? Janos could well have become a permanent fixture in your life. He was more than a last fling
twenty years ago. Now you're close to sixty, hardly an
Adonis. Not even a fading one." She seemed to be examining the lines in his face.

"In Geneva, he meant enough to you that you murdered
your friend, Hilary-Moulds. You have – had been," she corrected herself, "seeing him steadily since he came to Canada. It will be an easy fact to prove. All the police have to do
is pass his photograph around in gay bars, restaurants,
show it to the janitor and neighbours in this building. He
must have visited you here. Did you discuss his relationship
with Moulds? Did he swear that he never cared for
Moulds? That he was forced to become his lover because of
Moulds's influence with the KGB? And did you tell him not
to worry?"

Now she leaned over him, both hands on his chair. "You
knew about Moulds, and you killed him because he was a
perfidious man. You reassured Janos with that precious information. A very interesting thing for Janos to know. Once
you told him you murdered Hilary-Moulds, he could control you absolutely. As you say, he wanted to go to Toronto.
With or without you?"

She paused as if he would answer. Nothing was forthcoming. "Most likely without you, but well financed nevertheless. Hilary-Moulds told you too much and you killed him. You told Janos too much and he was squeezing you dry with no recompense of loyalty or affection. So you had to leave him again, this time lying in the snow behind the prime minister's residence."

She turned away from him and sat down.

Neville rose, walked over to the wall and shut off the music. He came back, looking exhausted, and sat down.

"Who's your witness?" His pudgy face was slack and he sounded as if he didn't care about anything. Nini noticed mist on his glasses.

"Does it matter?" Eleanor answered.

They knew they had him.

"What about the letter, the photocopies?" Nini said.

"You can have the letter. I won't photocopy it. What's the point? It's hardly in my interest. I don't know what's in my interest anymore. Of course"–his voice was breaking–"I deny everything she says. But we're the same, aren't we, Nini? We don't want any trouble." He realized he was crying. "I'm upset about Janos's death, that's all. Sort of delayed shock."

Nini wondered if he was crying because he was sorry he had killed Janos or simply sorry for himself. She tried to imagine him leaving Janos dying in the snow just a few hours ago.

"If I am to trust you about the photocopies," Nini said, unmoved by his reaction, "you'll have to trust me about the witness. I think I can control him. Shall we make a pact? No exposure, no television, no difficulties for my husband."

Neville could only nod.

"We'll agree, then, that Hilary-Moulds died of a heart attack." It was a statement.

"Will there be any association of my name with Janos in the newspapers?" Neville asked lamely.

A shabby thing to say, Nini thought. "I don't control the

papers," she said sharply. "If you keep quiet, so will we. Get my coat. I have to leave now. We're having a rather important dinner party tonight." She remained seated as Neville obediently went to the bedroom and returned with her fur coat. She rose and turned her back to him, slipping her arms gracefully into the mink.

"I hope you'll come for dinner," she said to Eleanor. "I know it's late to ask, but Barry will be so happy to see you."

They ignored Neville and closed the door behind them.

36

"I wish you had told me I used the wrong insulin from the start," Nini said as Eleanor drove her back to Sussex.

"You weren't in control. I was afraid you'd blurt it out before I could trap him. He had to corroborate what you told me so I could build my case. I'm sorry, but I had no choice." Eleanor sounded miffed.

"I suppose I was too anxious to be reliable." Nini realized she sounded ungrateful.

Eleanor turned the wrong way down a one-way street, ignoring the honking and whistling from some men in a garbage truck. She accepted Nini's statement as an apology.

"As soon as you told me about the protamine-zinc insulin, I began to suspect Neville, an insulin-dependent diabetic. He was so certain Hilary-Moulds died of insulin poisoning. But I did bluff about the photograph. I couldn't be sure that Neville actually noticed it in Hilary-Moulds's office. Lucky for me that Otis has nothing in his head except total recall of every detail concerning Hilary-Moulds. Medically speaking, I would describe Otis as an *idiot savant.*"

To Nini's relief, they managed to squeeze around the garbage truck and swung into Confederation Square.

"And you bluffed about Hilary-Moulds betraying Neville and revealing the betrayal during the argument. You can't be sure that happened."

"That wasn't bluffing; that was psychological conjecture based on fact. It's a fact that Hilary-Moulds was an agent for the KGB, or the Hungarians, if there's a difference. He also knew Janos. Hilary-Moulds was in correspondence with Attila Berendi during the same period Berendi attempted to blackmail Neville. Neville and Hilary-Moulds shared the same lover. Homosexuals, men or women, are generally more promiscuous than heterosexuals. And promiscuity leads to jealousy. I have many homosexual friends and patients. Neville was right: my observations are based on experience."

"Do you think," Nini asked, not wanting to hear about Eleanor's experience, "that Janos was really a spy? Why was he our gardener? Who put him in Sussex?"

"Maybe Neville urged him to take the job. Perhaps he wanted some unpleasant gossip about you and Barry for his column. The police might be able to find out if he was still in contact with the KGB. Personally, I think Janos was simply an opportunist. Opportunists have to take their risks. And sometimes things don't work out."

Eleanor stopped in front of 24 Sussex and Nini got out of the car.

"I'm going to call Iris right away. She's probably worried about the letter. You are coming for dinner?"

"I hardly think you'll approve of my clothes," Eleanor replied. "I have only a long tartan skirt and a Ports blouse to dress up in. You once told me you hated the combination."

"Of course I hate it," Nini said. "But Nutt will certainly spill a sauce on you tonight. And then you won't be able to wear it anymore."

Nini hesitated and then spoke in her most neutral tone. "If you have a house guest or someone staying with you, bring him or her along. In fact, it might be better if your house guest was female. We have too many men at the table."

"I have no house guest," said Eleanor shortly. "I'll be coming alone."

Three hours after hearing from Nini Pike for the first time in eighteen years, Iris spoke to her again. She put down the telephone in her Washington gallery and looked up at the portrait of Moorehouse Dhroshky. He had paid the top price, $15,000, for his picture, and Iris had taken a thirty-per-cent commission. Nini said she was definitely flying to Washington the following week and that Moira was to do the first sketches for her portrait. Although Nini hadn't asked about price, she would certainly find out from Moorehouse what he had paid. Iris thought she owed Nini a bargain. "Ten thousand," Iris calculated, "and I won't take one cent commission. Nini will be pleased. Moira will take some handling."

Iris was surprised that Nini had managed to settle the matter in an afternoon. But then Nini had some remarkable qualities; this was not the first time she had surprised Iris.

Iris had been brooding about that letter since Nini's first call. It had been folly to have written Neville, especially knowing what she did.

Nearly twenty years ago, Iris had watched Nini plunge a needle into Hugh's buttocks. She had been hiding in the bedroom closet, armed with nothing except murderous intentions, waiting for Hugh to fall asleep. It was Nini who had had the foresight to bring a needle filled with something lethal. What would Iris have done if Nini hadn't killed Hugh? Smothered him, strangled him? Hugh might have awakened and manipulated her with excuses, then promises. If it hadn't been for Nini, Iris was sure she would have become as mad as Lady Beatrice. Worse. Hugh would never have paid the bills for her to stay at the Clinique Beau Rivage.

When Nini had finished with Hugh, Iris went into another bedroom, hoping he would die soon. Then Roland Neville walked into Hugh's bedroom and Iris was afraid he'd call a doctor. But nothing happened, although Neville stayed there for such a long time. Iris had lost her nerve completely and crept out of the house through the servants' stairs after Neville went downstairs.

Iris decided that she wanted to give a party for Nini at her gallery. A spontaneous affair, with the Dhroshkys, the Belknaps and all the people Moira had painted. It would pacify Moira a little for having to take less money for Nini's portrait. And Nini would be grateful. Iris wanted to please Nini. She had been in Nini's debt for a long time.

A visit to Washington will be a tonic, Nini thought, putting down the telephone. Especially after six weeks of lying around this bedroom. She was looking forward to meeting a different Iris, a welcoming Iris. From Moira she had no expectations. Although Eleanor had reduced Neville to impotence, Nini felt dissatisfied, not with Eleanor or Neville, but with herself. "It's because I like to do things well," she thought, "because I'm a perfectionist." She was dejected because she had blundered in the most formidable task of her life. She was sure that Iris, Moira and the Stayfree Mini-Pad woman would have been better organized and made certain they had bought the correct insulin. But it was too late to compare herself to the new woman. Perhaps they're capable of murder, she thought, but not for their husbands: only for themselves.

Where was Barry, anyhow? It was just an hour before the arrival of the dinner guests. She had almost forgotten why she had asked Jack Fowler and Senator Gross in the first place. Barry was losing at the polls and she was supposed to charm away their hostility so Barry would be elected leader of the party again. She wished she could inject their backsides with crystalline-zinc insulin instead of flattering their egos.

Eleanor will hate Jack Fowler's and Senator Gross's conversation, she thought absently, the greasing of the riding people, the endless theories on how to "update" Barry's image. "Update" was their word. They didn't care about real policy; to them, good government meant handing over the public purse to the section of the population that made the most noise. Good government meant Barry smiling reassuringly on the television instead of telling complicated, unpleasant truths. And then taking an instant poll on his audience appeal. That's what this dinner was all about. Barry was losing in the polls and they were out to dump him. Nini was sick of the whole business.

As Nini opened her closet door to take out her red silk, Doreen knocked and entered, not waiting for an answer. Nini had managed to avoid Doreen and Nutt when she went upstairs but she had heard the sounds of quarrelling and breaking glass.

"Feeling better, Mrs. P.? I see that car ride with Dr. Campbell did some good. The red one was ironed this afternoon while you were out. Shall we go downstairs to inspect the dining room?" Doreen's voice was unnaturally high and Nini guessed that Nutt was responsible.

"If you help me on with my robe, I'll go downstairs with you. Who's serving the wine, Chang or Nutt? Or has Chang quit since Nutt's intrusion?"

"Both are serving the wine."

"What do you mean, both? Haven't they divided their duties?"

"Chang puts a claret glass on the table, Nutt follows and puts down the same. Chang puts the white-wine glass on the table and so does Nutt. Ditto for the sherry, the champagne and the Sauterne. Nutt's drunk, Mrs. P. He doesn't know whether he's working in the prime minister's residence or Mrs. Gilhooley's flophouse."

Nini and Doreen went downstairs and surveyed the dining room. The table was in order except for the multiplication of glasses.

"It looks like we're preparing for a wine tasters' convention," Nini said. "Tell Chang to remove the duplicates."

"Doesn't matter, Mrs. P. Whatever Chang takes off, Nutt

puts back. Sabotage, pure and simple."

The flowers, Nini noticed, were simply and elegantly arranged. Little vases of narcissus and mimosa sat at every place setting.

"The flowers look fine, much better than having a haystack of a bouquet in the centre, blocking everyone's vision. Is this the work of the dead gardener?"

"I told you he was good, Mrs. P. The good people always die first."

"Where's Nutt?" Nini asked, ignoring Doreen's remark.

"In the butler's pantry, drinking."

Nutt was standing on a step-ladder holding a sealed bottle of Crown Royal still in its purple pouch.

"What are you doing with the bottle, Nutt?"

"Getting it down for your people tonight, Mrs. Pike."

"You're going to fall off that step-ladder. Let Chang put the bottles out."

Nutt, bent almost double over the top of the ladder, jerked himself upright.

"Where do you think you are, in a Chinese circus?" Doreen shouted.

Nutt backed down the ladder, one step at a time, holding the bottle in one hand.

"It's been a hectic day for you, Nutt," said Nini. "Why don't you have a nap?"

Nutt unscrewed the cap of the bottle, rubbed the purple wool bag against his cheek like a baby with a soother blanket, and swallowed some rye.

Nini had seen Nutt weaving and unsteady before, but this was the first time he allowed himself to be caught in the act of drinking. It was a deliberate challenge to her authority.

"I don't take naps when the mistress is poking around the house. If the mistress is up, I stay up. Nutt doesn't shirk his work. Even though there's killers around. Could easily have been me that was dead."

"And why wasn't it, I ask God," Doreen muttered.

"It's them fairy terrorists," Nutt continued. "They're after all the men in this house. Look out for your husband, Mrs. Pike. Fairy terrorists are worse than the lady terrorists. More strength. Less hormones. I don't think they have monthlies, like you ladies."

"If you think you're in danger, you're better off at home," Nini said.

"No escape from them anywhere, Mrs. Pike. I'm going to sit down right here and wait for them with this."

He brought out a small rifle from the broom closet and sat down on the floor, bottle in one hand, rifle in the other.

"It's not loaded," Doreen said.

Nini decided she had had enough of Nutt.

"Let's go to the kitchen and see what Yves Marius is doing."

"You can't see Yves Marius. He's chained himself in the kitchen with the peeler and the washer," Doreen replied.

"All three are chained to the wall, you mean?"

"No," Doreen corrected herself. "He put three chains across the door from the inside so Nutt wouldn't come in. Nutt spit in all the sauces. Yves Marius says I'm to signal when the guests are ready to eat. I'll call him on the intercom. Then he'll unlock the chains and slip the food out through the door. He's afraid Nutt will do something bad. To tell you the truth, I can't guarantee Yves Marius will ever come out again with Nutt in this house." She paused. "No one can work here anymore, Mrs. P. No matter how much money you give us. I don't see why you don't tell Nutt off. He was always scared of you before. He deserves to be murdered."

Nini closed her eyes.

"Go ahead, Doreen, murder him. You'll do us all a favour. Just don't tell me about it. Throw the body in the river. Do what you want. But don't tell me. I have to finish dressing."

The red silk wasn't so bad, Nini thought, even though her

arms were bare. In a few years all her dresses would have to have long sleeves. "No one wants to see the flesh hanging from the arms of a fifty-year-old woman," she thought. She put on her diamond earrings. "At least I'll be able to wear my diamonds. Old women and diamonds suit each other." The telephone rang. It was Otis, saying that Barry would be delayed because of a call from Brussels and that he, Otis, was coming for dinner at Barry's request.

The dinner was going to be a fiasco, she decided, with Barry certain to be carved up, instead of the meat, by Fowler and Gross. And Nutt drunk. Why did Barry have to bring Otis? Once she had caught him cutting his roll lengthwise with a knife. And his face always looked buttery when he finished eating.

Doreen entered the bedroom, carefully closing the door behind her.

"Mrs. P.," she half-whispered. "It's eight o'clock. There's a bunch who came right on the dot. Shall I say you'll be right down?"

Nini willed herself into the rôle of the hostess, slipped on her sandals and followed Doreen downstairs.

Mrs. Suzy Fowler, or rather Mrs. Suzy Hatch Fowler (Suzy insisted on using her maiden name) looked very much like the *Cosmopolitan* girl in her black-velvet pant suit, frilly white shirt and bow tie. Suzy was twenty years younger than Jack and worked as an executive assistant to one of the lesser ministers. Barry had wanted to drop the minister from the cabinet because the man was lazy and obtuse, but Jack, no doubt prompted by his wife, had insisted that he be given a second chance. As long as the minister had a job, so did Suzy Hatch Fowler. The Fowlers and the Grosses stood uneasily in the drawing room, which was filled with the dead gardener's freesias and white snapdragons, waiting for Barry and their drinks. Nutt entered with the Moët & Chandon and the *eau de vie de framboise*.

The senator looked unhappily at the champagne.

"Rye and Pepsi for Senator Gross, Nutt," Nini said. "I wrote that down six weeks ago."

"He doesn't need rye and Pepsi," Mrs. Gross answered. "Give him club soda."

Margaret Gross was a sour woman who spent most of her time taking care of her husband's ranch in Alberta while he travelled. Senator Gross only brought forth his wife for ceremonial occasions such as this one. His relationship with his secretary was well known.

The senator ignored his wife and took a rye and Pepsi from Nutt's unsteady tray. Nini was pretty sure it was the same rye bottle that Nutt had been drinking from earlier, with the purple sack still on and slightly stained.

"Is Nutt sick?" Jack Fowler asked.

"Sick," Mrs. Gross said. "Didn't you get a whiff? He smells like a still. This is not the first time I've smelled a man doused in rye." She looked meaningfully at her husband.

"Nutt wanted to be here this evening, especially for Mr. Fowler," Nini improvised. "He likes serving Jack. Isn't that right, Nutt?" Nini pinched Nutt's arm.

Nutt heaved a vaguely affirmative response.

"You do have a way with people, Jack," Nini said, smiling.

Suzy agreed.

"Everybody likes Jack." She looked at him adoringly. "My husband has the true common touch. He should run for office. Have you ever seen him on television? Just like a great big Santa Claus."

"A Santa Claus without the bag of toys, however," Nini said dryly, thinking of the government deficit, which never bothered Jack.

Gross laughed. "Jack would be a fool to run. He has all the power he wants right now. Not like Suzy's boss, a nobody minister. Suzy's boss does have his little bag of toys, though. Gives away money so ethnics can learn how to do step-dancing in church basements, which they know, instead of English, which they don't know."

Suzy's minister was in charge of multiculturalism, a programme that financed such things as folk-dancing and Easter-egg painting. It was thought to be a successful vote-getting device among the new Canadians. Nini wasn't so sure.

"The government subsidizes all those foreign-language papers. Who knows what they say about us? Do we get any credit? I suppose you read Polish?" Gross asked Suzy.

Jack didn't like anyone teasing his young wife and changed the subject. "Where's Barry?"

"He's been delayed by a long-distance phone call from Brussels," Nini replied.

"What's so important about Brussels?" Gross interrupted. "We've come a long way just for a rye and Pepsi."

Nini noticed Nutt struggling with the bottles of champagne. She hoped he'd be able to open them without making a spectacle of himself.

A cork flew out and bounced off Suzy's ruffles. Nutt sniffed at the bottle like a Master of Wine, then, to Nini's horror, licked the bubbles off with his tongue.

"Get out," Nini ordered. "You're disgusting."

He pretended not to hear and began to pour the champagne.

Fowler, feeling some moral responsibility for Nutt's presence because of Nini's fib, was mollifying. He was gullible enough to believe Nini when she had said that Nutt liked him. "We'd all do the same thing if no one was watching."

Mrs. Gross placed her hand over her glass when Nutt came round.

"Leave the room, Nutt," Nini repeated. "Call Chang. Tell him to serve the wine."

Chang must have been listening; he appeared immediately with a tray of fresh drinks and whispered some kind of

Oriental curse in Nutt's ear. The curse had the desired effect and Nutt disappeared.

"I hope we won't see that man again," Mrs. Gross said loudly.

As Chang carefully mixed the *framboise* and champagne together in the glasses, Fowler said amiably, "We'll have a lot of trouble about that gardener's death, Nini. I've got to think of a press strategy to protect Barry. Too bad the fellow was a Hungarian. All we need is a spy at Sussex, on top of everything else."

"Everything else," Nini supposed, was Barry's poor showing at the polls.

Nutt returned, followed by Eleanor. For some reason he decided to announce her name in British toastmaster fashion, although he hadn't bothered with anyone else.

"Dr. Eleanor Campbell, Doctor of Internal Medicine, graduate of Queen's University and Derby High School."

Eleanor managed to push him aside.

"My goodness," Mrs. Gross said. "Why did he introduce her like that? Has she won the Nobel Prize or something?"

"Why should you care how she's introduced?" the senator said. "Now that you know she's a doctor, ask her about your bunions."

Jack Fowler, always a peacemaker, took Mrs. Gross aside before she could retort and questioned her about the benefits of leaving stubble on wheat fields. The west was going through a dry period and Jack was worried about the connection between votes and top-soil. Mrs. Gross was a farmer's daughter.

The door opened slightly and Otis peered through, looking right and left into the reception room, not knowing where to put himself. Before Nini could greet him, several people came up behind Otis, cut him off and headed directly toward Nini. Nicole Dhroshky was the first, resplendent in a long satin dress with a sable collar and cuffs. Moorehouse Dhroshky and Barry followed.

Barry was smiling. "Surprised, Nini? Don't worry. I told Doreen to set a couple of more places."

Nicole and Moorehouse had barely aged since Geneva. Moorehouse's hair seemed thicker and Nini wondered if he had had a transplant.

"A shocking thing for us to do to you, Nini," Nicole said loudly. "But we didn't know we were coming to Ottawa until a couple of hours ago. We flew in with General Leroy, one of our five-star men, on the Challenger. Moorehouse has just been appointed Secretary of Defense. I'm very pleased. It's nice to have one's own plane." She looked Nini over. "You've lost a few pounds – it suits you. I always said to Moorehouse that you wouldn't miss the extra weight you carried in Geneva." She turned around and said, "Who are these people?"

Barry introduced the Dhroshkys to the company, who stared at the couple without warmth.

Moorehouse gave Nini a gentle squeeze on the arm and a peck on the forehead. "Congratulations," he said. "I can't think of a better man."

Nini didn't know what he was talking about.

Nutt began to serve another round of champagne. Nicole spoke to him directly.

"No more champagne. I had plenty on the aircraft. Moorehouse is starving. We all want to eat now. Don't wait on account of us. Tell the chef we're ready."

Nutt looked at Nini, who confirmed that dinner should start.

"What do you think of my dress, Nini?" Nicole asked. "I knew it was going to be cold here. Everyone said I look like Catherine of Russia. Moira painted me in this dress. I now have two portraits of myself, one bare, one covered up. Like the Duchess of Alba. Moira has become a fantastic success in Washington. Lucky for Stephen."

She peered at Nini's dress. "Don't wear red when she paints you. Red is aging for a woman past forty," she said loudly. Mrs. Gross, standing next to her, was also wearing red. She was at least fifteen years older than Nini.

Nicole must have intimidated Nutt. Instead of telling Nini that dinner was served, they heard him beating a dinner gong from the hall. Nini had bought the gong in Malaysia and now realized the purchase had been a mistake.

Nicole commented favourably on the flower arrangements as they sat at the table, which gave Fowler his cue.

"A murdered man arranged those flowers, Mrs. Dhroshky. What do we know about the gardener, Barry? Is he an agent for the KGB or what?"

Barry looked surprised, as if he had almost forgotten about Janos. He set his fork and knife down on his plate and spoke with little concern.

"The police haven't found any recent connection between Janos Molner and the Hungarian secret service or the KGB. Molner had a million friends. Bank robbers, escaped convicts. His taste was eclectic. He was a friend of Roland Neville's, as well. But as much as I would like to see Neville get his come-uppance, he's only one of a hundred men the gardener used to see. Hardly a reasonable suspect, given the kind of company Janos kept. Neville doesn't go in for physical violence. The man they're looking for is probably on a bus to Mexico. He'll likely never be found."

Nini and Eleanor exchanged relieved glances and simultaneously looked at Nutt, who was inexplicably placing several glasses in front of Moorehouse.

Nutt paused as Barry spoke, stared at Nini and then at Eleanor, scratched his warty nose and then shrugged as if to show his indifference. Chang, in the meantime, had removed the duplicate glasses. This seemed to arouse Nutt, and he raced out of the dining room to give Chang a piece of his mind.

"Too bad we can't nail Neville," Gross said. "He's always had a vendetta with you, Barry. Nothing but bad press ever since you've been prime minister."

"I don't like it," Fowler said. "An unsolved murder at 24 Sussex. I'm not sure the journalists will ever leave it alone."

This, Nini knew, was a preamble to why Barry should quit.

"Nothing but a seven-day wonder," said Barry tranquilly. He picked up his wine and changed the subject. "I want to make a toast to my wife. She's been ill and this is her first dinner downstairs. I'm sure she's looking so well because of the fine care of Dr. Campbell. Let's drink to both of them."

As they lifted their glasses, Chang and Nutt returned and deposited the little blue curled-up trout on the plates.

"Mind the bones," Nutt said to Mrs. Gross. "If one catches in your throat you'll have to stick your finger down and bring it up. Or else you'll be a goner."

"Don't speak to the guests while serving," Nini said to Nutt.

"I don't think Mrs. Gross has to worry," Jack said. "We have a doctor present."

"No fish left for Dr. Campbell, the chef ran out," Nutt proclaimed. "Can't help it, Mrs. Pike, what with all the extras for dinner."

"Yves Marius always has enough. Go to the kitchen and bring Dr. Campbell a plate. And don't ever speak in my presence again," snapped Nini. It was either Nutt or her.

"I don't want any fish," said Eleanor unhelpfully.

"I think he's eaten your portion, Dr. Campbell," Mrs. Gross interjected, pointing at Nutt with her fork. "I see fish bones on the corners of his mouth."

"Take mine," Otis said. "I think he should have served the ladies first."

Nutt lifted Otis's plate, peered at it closely and shook his head. "Don't eat it, Dr. Campbell. See those little black spots? Probably worms."

Everyone looked at his fish for little black spots.

"I can't see anything now," Mrs. Gross said in dismay. "He dumped all that yellow gravy on it." Mrs. Gross put her knife and fork parallel over the plate to show that she would not eat it.

Why was she not able to play this game tonight, Nini asked herself silently. It was just too silly for words. She might as well say what she liked.

"You're a ridiculous woman," Nini said evenly. "There's nothing wrong with the fish. And the 'yellow gravy' is hollandaise sauce. Or don't they serve hollandaise in Alberta?"

"Quite right," Nicole said. "The fish is delicious. You shouldn't listen to foolish servants," she reproached Mrs. Gross. Then, turning to Nini, she warned, "But he does need training."

Nini decided she had lost her taste for Nicole. She hated the woman, she realized. Once Nicole had been her mentor. Now Nini saw her as a rude, boasting woman. In one graceful motion, Nini rose, pointed to the door and stared hard at Nutt. "I will not sit down until you leave. For good."

Nutt looked to the guests for an ally. Although Fowler was smirking, he kept his eyes down. Slowly, swaying a little, Nutt backed out and shut the door behind him.

Everyone turned to eating the fish, even Mrs. Gross.

Fowler turned to Moorehouse and asked, "Have you seen our latest opinion poll?"

"Very bad for Barry," Gross chimed in. Mrs. Gross nodded, in accord with her husband for the first time that evening.

"He's got to change his image," Fowler said.

"Or the country will change prime ministers," said Gross.

"His image is perfect," Nini said.

Fowler and Gross knew it was going to be difficult criticizing Barry in front of his wife. They stopped talking, hoping they'd discover a more subtle but effective approach.

Nicole Dhroshky lifted the spine off her trout onto her salad plate and said, "I agree with Nini, his image is perfect. Just what is needed for Barry's new job."

Nini, Fowler and Gross spoke in unison.

"What new job?"

Barry leaned back.

"I did want to consult with Nini first. But I guess it's too late now. You won't have to worry about my image any more, Jack. I'm resigning. I've been prime minister for ten years and it's time for a new man."

Fowler and Gross looked disconcerted. They had thought they might have to get rid of Barry, but they wanted it to be their decision, not his.

Nini thought Barry was announcing that he didn't want to fight anymore. "I'm not going back to Derby to watch you compare malt whiskies, like my father," she warned. "I couldn't stand it."

Barry was amused by her reaction. "Not Derby, Nini, I wouldn't do that to you. Brussels. You always liked Brussels. Remember that job Hilary-Moulds pined for? I've just been asked to be secretary general of NATO. I want to go. But I won't if you don't agree. It's your decision."

"That's why we flew up, Nini," Moorehouse said. "We wanted to congratulate Barry personally. I think it's a wonderful choice."

"Of course, Moorehouse recommended his name," Nicole said. She quickly drank down all her white wine. "Montrachet '75. A little young. And of course everyone who counts listens to Moorehouse. Don't hesitate, Nini. But bring the chef with you. He's excellent."

"It's Yves Marius," Nini said. "Hilary-Moulds's chef."

"Hilary-Moulds's job, Hilary-Moulds's chef. What could be more fitting?" Nicole asked.

Nini stared at Gross and Fowler. They looked disturbed. It was by no means clear their party would win the next election without Barry. They would have to find a replacement quickly. On the other hand, if Barry accepted their advice about his image, Gross and Fowler would have more power than ever. Their influence would not be as great with a new man, even if they helped him win the election. And if the opposition won, there would be no place at the Sussex dining-room table for Gross or Fowler.

"You can't go," Fowler said, confirming Nini's assessment of their position. "All you need is to make a few more promises to the voters. Concentrate on lowering inflation. Don't tell the bad news all the time."

"Folly, prime minister, folly," Gross said. "Keeley will win if you go. A disaster for the country."

"There's no one of your stature to replace you," Fowler almost pleaded.

Mrs. Gross and Suzy Hatch Fowler watched, suddenly worried about their own positions. Otis was buttering his sawed bun, unconcerned. Eleanor was trying to catch Nini's eye, forming a silent "go" with her mouth.

It's delightful, Nini thought. Barry's called their bluff and Gross and Fowler are afraid.

"It's Nini's decision entirely," Barry said, looking at her intently.

There were distant noises in the hall. A muted quarrel between Nutt and Doreen and then the sound of someone being sick. Nutt had finally succumbed to the whisky and the fish. Nini rang the buzzer under the table and Chang and Doreen rushed in. Doreen's eyes were half out of her head. Nini knew that Nutt must be sprawled out on the hall floor, but she didn't want to hear about it.

"Remove the fish plates," she said, ignoring Doreen's signals of alarm. Then she looked at Barry and said, "I'm ready to go tomorrow. As long as I can take Yves Marius. I think he brings us luck."